T0278644

COME OUT, COME OUT

COME OUT, COME OUT

NATALIE C. PARKER

putnam

G. P. PUTNAM'S SONS

G. P. PUTNAM'S SONS
An imprint of Penguin Random House LLC
1745 Broadway, New York, New York 10019

First published in the United States of America by G. P. Putnam's Sons,
an imprint of Penguin Random House LLC, 2024

G. P. Putnam's Sons is a registered trademark of Penguin Random House LLC.
The Penguin colophon is a registered trademark of Penguin Books Limited.

Visit us online at PenguinRandomHouse.com.

Library of Congress Cataloging-in-Publication Data is available.

ISBN 9780593619391

1 3 5 7 9 10 8 6 4 2

Printed in the United States of America

BVG

Design by Alex Campbell
Text set in Scala Pro

For Tessa,
my wife and husband all in one,
because we keep surviving,
trading the horror for the joy.

LETTER FROM THE AUTHOR

"To see a candle's light, one must take it into a dark place."
—Ursula K. Le Guin

I used to tell people that there were only two things in the world that scared me: zombies and jellyfish. It's true that I am afraid of both, but it's a gentle, controllable fear. Zombies aren't real (I hope), and I've gotten pretty good at avoiding the wrong end of a jellyfish. My fear of these things comes with a kind of delight—the kind of thrill I enjoy when a part of me knows something is extremely unlikely to actually hurt me. It's the thrill I chase when I crack open a new horror novel.

But I didn't write *Come Out, Come Out* for the thrill. In this book are some things that truly scare me because they can hurt me: homophobia, transphobia, gender dysphoria, religious extremism, and conversion therapy. They are terrifying because they are very real, they have sharp edges, and I can't control when I encounter them. If you choose to read on, you will find them here along with depictions of graphic violence, body horror, and self-harm.

You will also find friendship and found family and joy, because horror and hope go hand in hand.

I wrote *Come Out, Come Out* because the very act of coming out can be terrifying. I wrote it because sometimes our fear is a light in the dark; it reveals and uncovers danger, and guides those who follow behind us. Most of all, I wrote this book because I have experienced the everyday horrors of being queer in this world. But as often as I have been afraid, I have been exquisitely joyful, too.

With respect,
ncp

Come out, come out, wherever you are;

The Patron's in the trees.

Find his house, make a wish.

He'll do just as you please.

Come in, come in, whoever you were;

Receive your Patron's gift.

The price is small and with it all,

You'll never be adrift.

Come back, come back, wherever you roam;

Come see his deathly hue.

Ask him nice, don't ask twice.

He'll fix what's wrong with you.

THAT
NIGHT

Three friends went into the woods tonight, but only two are left.

They are running. No longer daunted by the dark. Their eyes wide, their breath sharp and fast, every part of their bodies alight with the electric desire to live. Behind them, looming hemlock trees swallow the path they took inside, obliterating every trace of their presence.

One of them stumbles. Lands hard and gives a small cry. Their knees crush damp moss. The other one whips around, eyes marking the shadows in their wake. Something moves from tree to tree, a darting haunt, a hunter.

"Fern," Jaq says, pulling at her friend's arm. "Get up. We have to keep going."

Fern looks up. Tears drop from their eyes, leaving tracks in the blood that mars their skin.

A cry of anguish rings through the dark. The voice grows louder instead of fading away. In its wake the forest is silent and cold. Not even the rustle of wind or chirp of a frog.

"Jaq—" Fern's breath catches. Their voice is too loud. They reach for Jaq's hand and squeeze, fingers cold and wet.

Jaq makes a move as if to look behind her, but she cannot bring herself to search for whoever—or whatever—made that sound.

"Get up," she whispers, tugging Fern's hand, but Fern still doesn't move.

"We have to go back for Mal," Fern sobs. "She might still be—"

"She's not." Jaq cuts them off. "Look at us!"

Blood-splatter paints across Jaq's pale pink hoodie, smeared along the bottom of her jaw. In the moonlight it's a vivid, horrible brown. But Fern almost finds the contrast lovely, their mind desperate to create something beautiful, even now. Especially now.

In a daze they look down at the blood staining their fingers, thinned to a sticky paste. They raise a hand and trace the edges of blood on their cheek toward their ear. Feel the wetness clinging to their blond curls. Wonder if blood can stain hair.

"But what if—"

"No," Jaq whispers. They've been still for too long. Her mind is reeling. The only girl she's ever kissed is gone. "Not now. Fern, we have to—"

RUN.

The voice is a thunderclap between them.

It jolts through their bodies, forcing Fern onto their feet and Jaq into a sprint. They crash through low ferns and slip against crumbling deadfall. Neither of them knows if the direction they've chosen is the right one, only that it is better than going back, better than returning to that house where their friend is nothing more than blood soaking into the earth.

Hand in hand, they run, their hearts twisted and terrified as they race for safety.

How they could have been so wrong? How could the place they'd trusted so well have betrayed them with such malice?

The edge of the woods appears. The trees thin to reveal the

houses beyond, each one wrapped in a peaceful quiet, with curtains drawn against the cold night.

The relief the two friends feel at the sight is ruined by the knowledge that this is what they were running from in the first place. That peace is only ever a lie. But right now, they have no choice.

"They'll help us." Fern pauses. "Won't they?"

"We can't tell them the truth," Jaq answers, thinking especially of her parents. They would have to lie. Keep lying. Only, what lie could explain why she's covered in her best friend's blood? Or why they went into the woods tonight?

But as the two step through the trees and onto the scrubby grass of their neighborhood, something shifts. The sensation is a little like falling and a little like being tugged by the ocean tide. A current runs through Fern and Jaq, swift and cold. It takes. Fern wobbles on her feet. Jaq frowns and blinks.

And when they look at each other again, the blood on their skin and hair and clothes has vanished.

They stand beneath the thin light of a crescent moon, not entirely sure how they got there.

"Are you, um . . ." Fern begins, but the question has no end point. She only has the faintest memory of deciding to come out tonight with Jaqueline De Luca and Mallory Hammond. Neither of whom she knows very well. But Mal never showed.

"I should probably go," Jaq answers, baffled that she ever thought it was a good idea to sneak out with Fern and Mallory. People she's not even friends with. "My parents will kill me if they find out I'm gone."

"Yeah, me too."

The two walk together in silence before going their separate ways.

By morning, Mallory's parents activate the church phone tree. Jaq's parents get the call, and they ask Jaq if she saw Mallory last night. She answers honestly: she didn't. She hasn't seen Mallory since school on Friday.

Fern doesn't hear about it until Monday morning, when the news is all over Port Promise: Mallory Hammond, the closeted, angry girl, has finally run away. Everyone in town believes it's true.

And though something scratches at the back of their minds, muffled as though trapped beneath layers of ice, Fern and Jaq believe it, too.

CHAPTER ONE

Fern

The hallway was thick with hope, and smelling a lot like honey-lemon throat drops. Fern wasn't sure she'd ever seen this many people audition for a school play before. Nearly half the student body was lined up outside the theater, every one of them with earbuds in, humming quietly to themselves. Or, in some cases, not so quietly.

She didn't have to guess at the reason for the sudden popularity of the Port Promise High drama club. It wasn't like *Grease: The Musical* was any more beloved now than it had been during her mom's generation. The reason was posted in bold letters in the light boxes beside the theater doors: GENDER-NEUTRAL CASTING.

The announcement had come as a shock—to everyone, and to Fern in particular. Not because Port Promise was a conservative-leaning town stitched into the curl of an inlet on the Puget Sound, which it was. But because it was Fern's senior musical, and she had expected the audition process to be a breeze.

"Just a reminder, folks! If you haven't signed up yet, the sheet is by the door." Cambria Collier's voice rose above the clamor. She'd been stage manager in all but name since freshman year, and now she'd morphed into a creature that was part girl, part

Excel spreadsheet. While Ms. Murphy was inside the theater managing the auditions, Cam was out here running the show. "If you want to be considered for multiple roles, you are allowed to perform samples of two songs to demonstrate your vocal range. Not three, not four, not two and a half. Two."

Fern angled her steps for the door, passing beneath framed photos of her three older sisters: Holly, Clover, and Ivy. Each one captured as the leads in their own senior musical. Each effortlessly beautiful and talented. They'd all gone on to be so accomplished that Ms. Murphy now claimed that the drama club turned out more success stories than any other department at the school. Holly, the dancer of the group, had skipped college and gone straight to New York, where she'd already done multiple shows on Broadway. Clover headed in the opposite direction to Hollywood, where she'd won recurring roles on not one but two police procedurals. And Ivy was studying drama at Juilliard on scholarship.

Fern had been walking past the evidence of their success for years, increasingly anxious to see her picture next to theirs. And she was so close now. There had never been a more perfect Sandy Dumbrowski than Fern. Not only did she look the part, from her petite frame to her ivory skin and blond hair, but acting sweet and naive was the oldest trick in the book. Last year she'd been the secondary lead in *Once Upon a Mattress*, the year before that, Liesl von Trapp in *The Sound of Music*. Even as a freshman she'd snagged a role with a solo, because of all her sisters, *she* was the singer. The lead in this musical was destined to be hers.

As long as this gender-neutral casting didn't fuck anything up.

"Hey, Cam," Fern said.

"Friend," Cam said with a sigh, cupping a hand over the microphone of her headset. She was tall and broad across the shoulders, with coppery-brown skin. When she shook her head, her short puff of a ponytail shivered with her. "Can you believe this mess? I swear, if I have to explain what a callback is one more time, I'm going to choose violence. And then I'm going to die." Cam turned her big brown eyes on Fern and batted them. "Say something nice about me at my funeral. Even if you have to make it up."

"You want me to tell everyone you were good at math?" Fern teased.

Cam narrowed her eyes. "Are you here to sign up for something, or are you trying to get yourself cut before you ever get through those doors?"

"I'm here to sign up," Fern confirmed, stepping up to the clip-board posted by the door while Cam called up the next person in line.

The parts were divided into solo and ensemble roles and then again by male and female. The sign-up sheet asked for her name, her grade, a phone number, and then there were four checkboxes. The first for female solo roles, the second for female ensemble roles. A third for male solo roles and a fourth for male ensemble roles.

Fern took the pen, added her information, and checked the first box. She knew better than to indicate she was willing to settle for anything less than a solo role. Especially now. Checking one box was a clear signal to Ms. Murphy. It said that Fern knew her abilities, and she was here to be the next Sandy Dumbrowski.

But her gaze stuck on the third box. On the words "male solo."

What would it be like, she wondered, to stand up on the stage as Danny Zuko? Her hair slicked back, her face contoured into sharp angles instead of soft curves, her breasts bound flat.

She was good at pretending to be other people. At convincing others that she was someone else—a mad queen, a hopeful inge-nue, a stilted lover. But there was something different about the idea of performing as Danny.

Her pen hovered over the box, a quiet scratching at the back of her mind. A strange urge to check the box when she knew she shouldn't.

Still, she hesitated.

"I don't think there are any trick questions on there." A voice broke into her thoughts, and though it was gentle, Fern dropped the pen abruptly, her heart kicking out in a panic, as if she'd been caught doing something wrong.

"Oh, I didn't mean to scare you. I just wanted to add my name. If you're done, I mean. I'm not trying to rush you."

It was Kaitlyn Birch. Fern had a policy of not having enemies that anyone knew about. Just like she had a policy of never show-ing her teeth when she smiled and of never coming to school with-out doing her hair. But Kaitlyn Birch made her want to break her own rules, to let it be known how much she disliked the girl.

For one thing, Kaitlyn Birch was gorgeous, even Fern had to admit that. Her skin was a tawny brown, her eyes a kaleidoscope of sepia and copper. Her spiraling black curls were always in mo-tion, and her stage presence had a weight to it that was impossible to fake. Worst of all, she was every bit as talented as Fern.

And three years in a row, Kaitlyn and Fern had competed for the same roles. Fern had won every time by the skin of her teeth. But last year, after Kaitlyn was cast as the Nightingale in *Once Upon a Mattress*, she had looked Fern dead in the eye, smiled with her teeth, and promised that she would win the lead in the next spring musical.

Fern wasn't about to let that happen.

She slipped into a disarming smile without even trying, the one that her mom said made her look sweet and deserving.

"I was just taking a moment," she said, stepping out of Kaitlyn's way. "You know, last high school musical and all."

"It's wild," Kaitlyn agreed, adding her name to the list. "It might even be our last musical ever."

Fern smiled tightly. She was too accustomed to Kaitlyn's subtle barbs to let one as trite as this get under her skin, but the turnout for the audition already had her rattled, and all she managed in response was "Mm."

"Well, break a leg up there," Kaitlyn said, and without a beat of hesitation, she marked all four boxes. Then she turned and took her place at the end of the line.

"I could forget to call her name," Cam leaned over to whisper. "For a fee, of course."

Fern laughed. "I don't need to cheat to win. I need to focus."

And to focus, she needed to be somewhere else.

With a wave, Fern left the crowded hallway and ducked into the stairwell. Far enough away to escape the frenetic pre-audition energy, but not so far that she wouldn't hear Cam shout her name.

She climbed to the first landing, then slumped down beneath the window and pressed her back into the cool, cinder block wall.

Closing her eyes, Fern pictured herself onstage. The scuffed black surface beneath her feet, the hot lights against her skin, the way her voice would travel through the wide-open space. She pictured herself reciting her monologue—a selection from *A Chorus Line*—and she pictured herself nailing it before singing a few bars of "Summer Nights." Then she pictured the smile on Ms. Murphy's face, knowing she'd found her Sandy.

Her mother always said, *If you want to see success, you have to imagine it first.*

And she could already see herself on opening night.

Her phone buzzed, the text thread she shared with her sisters lighting up with a message from Clover, always the one to track important dates. **Break a leg, Fernling!** she said, adding three drama mask emojis.

Holly followed up instantly with a crossed-fingers emoji and several hearts, probably sent on the sly from some dance rehearsal, and Ivy was after that, asking, **Is it already time for the musical? Eeeeeee! Can't wait to hear more!**

It hadn't always been easy to be the youngest of four, especially when the three older siblings were so much closer in age. By the time Fern was a sophomore, they'd all graduated and moved out. Their lives had become impressive and real in the blink of an eye, and everything Fern was worried about seemed small in comparison. Even her admission to the competitive musical theater program at Baldwin Wallace University in Ohio seemed inconsequential compared to their accomplishments. But her sisters had always made an effort to make her feel included, and at moments like this, that mattered.

Fern responded with a string of hearts and shut off her notifications.

Then she heard Cam call her name. It was her turn.

Inside, the theater was dim and quiet except for the beam of the spotlight pinned to the stage and the whisper of shuffling paper. The stage was modest, but the proscenium arch was draped in red velvet curtains and gold tassels, the elegant frame artfully decorated with leaves painted every shade of cream and taupe and rose gold. To Fern, it felt like the beating heart of the school.

"Is that you, Fern Jensen? Come on down," Ms. Murphy called from her seat in the dead center of the auditorium. Even from this distance, Fern could see her signature cat-eye glasses and the plaid wrap she'd worn nearly every day Fern had known her. She was short and white, with a wave of soft brown hair woven through with silver. She had a classic rockabilly-meets-Scottish-lass sort of look that really worked for her. "The stage awaits."

Fern let the slope of the floor draw her down the aisle. The house lights were low, and the spotlight carved a five-foot circle on the scuffed black stage. There was no one in the lighting booth, though, so it wouldn't track movement. Part of the challenge of the audition was staying inside the circle's sharp boundaries. It was harder than it seemed, but Fern was a professional.

When Fern stepped into her light, it was like walking into another world. One where she transformed into something other than herself—an innocent girl falling in love for the first time or one who'd seen some shit and was ready to tell you about it. She could be good or evil or chaotic, and no one in the world would judge her for it because it was all make-believe.

"Ready when you are," Ms. Murphy prompted, already scratching out a note on her pad of paper.

"So," Fern started, cocking her hip to one side and folding her arms over her chest. Defiant but guarded as she settled into the character of eighteen-year-old Valerie Clarke, dead set on becoming a Rockette.

The words flowed, and she relaxed into the scene. Val wasn't as innocent as Sandy Dumbrowski, but that didn't make them opposites. Both were soft girls toughened by injustice. Who'd been hurt once, then made sure it would never happen again.

The monologue spoke to Fern in a way she couldn't explain.

She'd never been hurt like either of them, but there was something about their determination that resonated with her.

She let her eyes adjust to the bright light, focusing on the one spot at the back of the theater she could always see through the glare. With a small jolt of surprise, she realized that there was someone there.

Ms. Murphy was adamant about having closed-door auditions on the first round. There had never been an exception to the open call.

But there was someone here. The barest imprint of a person surfacing through the shadows. Fern shifted, making the slight hitch in her performance seem intentional as she angled her head for a better view. The figure rose from their seat and began to move toward the aisle, their steps slow and stilted.

A chill moved down Fern's back as the figure paused at the end of the row and stopped, their outline small and inky and unmoving in the shadows. When they stepped into the aisle, Fern could see that it was a girl.

Eyes wide. Hair the brilliant red of maple leaves in fall. Mouth open in a silent scream.

Then, all at once, the figure moved again. This time with lightning speed. Racing down the aisle with one hand outstretched. Rushing past the row where Ms. Murphy sat, toward the stage. Toward Fern.

The girl surged onto the stage, white hands reaching for Fern's throat. Fern stumbled back, tripping over her own feet, desperate to escape the terrifying, feral girl—

"Fern?" Ms. Murphy's voice called out. "Is everything okay?"

Fern gasped. She was alone on the stage, her butt aching from the fall. The words she was supposed to say next flew from her mind. Silence rose around her like the tide.

"I—" She shifted her gaze briefly to Ms. Murphy, who was wearing an expression of confused concern. She had clearly not noticed anything other than Fern's little freak-out. "Sorry, there was a wasp and I'm allergic."

"Do you want to take it from the top?" Ms. Murphy asked.

"Um, yes," Fern managed, sweat beading at her temples as she struggled to slide into one of her practiced smiles. "I'm so sorry. Yes, please."

"Okay, just, whenever you're ready." Ms. Murphy adjusted her glasses as she scratched out another note on her pad. It couldn't be good, but Fern felt certain that it was about to get worse, because her speech was gone. The words she'd spent hours memorizing were just gone.

All that remained was the memory of the girl in the dark, her mouth stretched wide in a silent scream.

CHAPTER
TWO

Jaq

Off-campus lunch hour was Jaq's favorite time of day. It was a privilege afforded to seniors who maintained at least a 3.0 grade point average, which she did with ease, and her boyfriend, John, did with a little help from her. They'd been together so long that she knew before he did which assignments he would struggle with, and he'd given her the spare keys to his car because they both preferred when she was behind the wheel.

Today, like every Friday, they were at the Deep Cut Pizzeria, in their favorite booth on the waterside. The windows were dressed in red gingham curtains and offered views of the marina, where dozens of recreational boats bobbed and steely skies promised more drizzle than sun. The pizza was only okay, but the shop was owned by the Clarks, who gave all the members of Port Promise Baptist a "friends and family" discount. That, and the booths were small enough that it made sense for John to sit so close that Jaq could feel the warmth of his body against her own.

"Are you finished?" he asked, glancing down at the crust of the single slice of pizza she'd eaten.

"Yeah," she said, reaching for the small cross that hung on a gold chain around her neck and sliding it back and forth. He'd given it to her last year on their second anniversary. Their third was coming up, and she was dying to know what he'd planned for this year.

"I thought so," John said, as he plucked the crust from her plate and dunked it into a bowl of ranch dressing. He grinned at her. Boyish and sweet.

When he smiled, it filled an empty space inside her. It made her want to smile back. She almost always did. John had this effect on her. From the very beginning, she was pretty sure. He was dazzlingly handsome, with honey-gold hair that curled loosely around his ears, moss-green eyes that were flecked through with drops of amber, and warm white skin with a spray of freckles across his nose and cheeks.

Jaq was going to spend the rest of her life with John Nichols, and everyone knew it. They'd both been accepted to Baylor University in the fall, and as long as her financial aid package came through, they would soon be moving across the country together. John would get a business degree and then go to law school; she didn't know yet what she was going to do. What she really loved was art, but that was a secret hobby, not a career path.

"Tommy says half the school turned out for those auditions yesterday," Susan Meachem was saying, her face fixed in a deceptively neutral expression. As the daughter of their preacher, Susan very rarely took sides or engaged in anything that could overtly be considered gossip, but she always knew exactly what to say to get other people to talk.

Next to Susan, Tommy Webber crammed a piece of pepperoni pizza into his mouth and shrugged his broad shoulders. Though he looked like the type to play every sport ever named, he always went out for the musical. Except for this year. "It's a fucking joke."

"Language," Susan said in a way that somehow communicated that she meant it and also that she didn't expect him to obey. It was a unique skill, the ability to be both judgmental and somehow not in the same breath.

Jaq could never get away with it herself. Her words were always too one thing or another. Too serious. Too loud. Too much. She had to consider her words before she said them aloud. Except to John. He always understood her.

"Sorry," Tommy said with mock apology. "I should have said it's a fucking *circus*."

"Not as big of a circus as the show itself is going to be," John said. "I'm almost tempted to go just to see."

Jaq's cheeks warmed and her insides did that nauseating squirming thing they did whenever topics like this came up. Like her organs were simultaneously liquifying and freezing into solid chunks of ice. It was the same sensation she had whenever Preacher Meachem decried various sins in church. Like she was perilously close to being judged for something she couldn't even put her finger on.

The bell attached to the front door chimed as Cole Clark pushed through it, wearing an old blue hoodie and a tight expression. Behind the counter, his mom held up a box big enough for two slices of pizza and a paper cup.

"Why do you always wait till the last minute?" she asked, mournful but smiling.

"Sorry," Cole answered without offering an explanation, ducking his head to kiss his mom's cheek. As he turned for the soda fountain, Jaq tried to catch his eye, but he avoided looking at their table.

Cole was a senior like the rest of them, and not so long ago, all five of them had been friends. There had even been a time when he would have been sitting with them, a chair pulled up to the head of the table, making the small space even smaller with his half a Hawaiian pizza. Always with jalapeños.

But recently, he'd been off in his own world. Pulling further and further away each day.

Susan thought it was drugs. So did a lot of people. But that had never been Cole's style.

Jaq reached for her cup. "I'm going to get a refill. Do you want one?"

"Yeah, a loaded ginger ale," John said, pressing his back against the booth so that she could crawl over him. "You guys need anything?"

"We're good, thanks," Susan chirped, answering for Tommy, too.

Cups in hand, Jaq made her way to the soda fountain.

"Hey, Cole," she said, quietly so she wouldn't startle him.

He looked up, eyes bright and maybe a little wary. "Hey, Jaq," he muttered, dropping his eyes to his orange soda, then hurrying away before she could say another word. A door closing in her face.

Jaq looked after him. He seemed angry. With her. Though she had no idea what she'd done to earn it. She hadn't talked to him in weeks. Which, maybe that was why. If he was going through something and she hadn't reached out, he had every right to be angry.

Swallowing hard, she filled John's cup halfway with Coke, then topped it off with Sprite. He swore it tasted like ginger ale with the added benefit of caffeine, but she wasn't convinced.

Just as she was about to fill her own cup with Diet Coke, she caught a flash of red hair in the corner of her eye as someone stepped up beside her.

The color came with an overwhelming scent of softly sweet sunflower perfume, and Jaq's mind sparked with memories. Each more foggy than the one before. Of a girl with hair like a violent sunrise and a temper to match. A girl who wore sunflower perfume every day. A girl Jaq had known only a short time and not very well.

In junior high Mallory Hammond had been a vaguely threatening presence at school and at church. Always ready with a sharp word or scathing comment, delivered softly and precisely so no one would hear but the people she intended to. Jaq had been friendly with her, but not friends. Like everyone else, she'd been equal parts shocked and relieved when Mal had run away.

She hadn't thought of Mallory in years.

"Is it broken?" asked the girl beside her. "Please tell me it's not out of ice or something. I am in desperate need of chilled chemicals."

"Hmm? Sorry, sorry, sorry," Jaq said, hurrying to fill her cup. She remembered the ice halfway through and made the critical error of adding it to an already full cup. "Shoot."

Laughter followed. The sound so soft and sympathetic that Jaq looked up for the first time. And her breath caught in her throat.

Windblown mahogany-red hair contrasted with lightly tanned skin. Eyes a soft brown. A pale pink mouth that parted in something like surprise when Jaq turned to face her. Jaq's fingers itched with a sudden urge to find some pastels and a fresh sheet of paper to capture the perfection of these features.

"Wow," the girl breathed. She was staring wide-eyed at Jaq. "Sorry, I'm . . . rude. And also Devyn."

Jaq's instincts kicked in. She pushed one hand out to shake

Devyn's and ended up flinging Diet Coke at her instead. Sticky soda slicked down the front of Devyn's black jacket and jeans.

"Oh my gosh. I'm so sorry." Jaq set her nearly empty cup down and reached for as many napkins as she could pull from the dispenser at once.

"It's okay, really," Devyn soothed, accepting the napkins as Jaq thrust them toward her. "It's leather. And it's old. It's really hard to hurt. See?" She gave the front of her jacket a little shake to prove the point, droplets of Diet Coke sliding right off.

"I'm just so sorry. I don't know what I was thinking! I swear I'm not usually a klutz."

"Only when you're distracted?" The teasing note in Devyn's tone was unmistakable.

Jaq nearly blushed at the implication, but in the next second, an arm fell across her shoulders and pulled her close.

"Who's this?" John asked. "Other than the reason I didn't get my refill?"

Jaq felt her eyes pulled back to Devyn's. She didn't want to give John her name. Didn't want to open up this moment and let him inside. Jaq wanted it, this, *Devyn* all to herself.

It didn't make any sense.

"I'm Devyn," the new girl said, nodding her head once, a single, sharp movement. "I just moved here. Today's my second day, and I thought I'd take the senior privileges for a test drive."

Her eyes fell on Jaq again, as though she was who Devyn really wanted to be talking to.

"You transferred in as a senior halfway through the year?" Susan asked, circling up on Jaq's other side. "That's rough. Where were you before?"

Devyn shrugged. "East."

"East like Eastside? On Bainbridge? I have some friends over there, maybe you know them? What church did you go to?" Susan probed in her easy way, but Devyn didn't bother to answer.

She filled her cup with Diet Coke, dropped her soaked napkins in the trash, then looked back at Jaq.

"See you around," she said, and then she left.

Jaq watched her go, not sure if she wanted Devyn to turn around one more time. Not sure why those last three words left her feeling so effervescent. Fizzy, like a soda.

"Think she tried out for the play?" Tommy laughed at his own joke.

"We have eleven minutes," Susan announced. "John, it's your turn."

"I've got it," John said, whipping out his wallet to pay.

Outside, the clouds had settled in low, bringing with them a soft, persistent rain. Jaq shivered as she turned on the windshield wipers and headlights and drove back toward campus. Port Promise High sat on the hills overlooking Old Town, and between its Gothic architecture and redbrick exterior, it felt like a place that belonged to another time. And certainly not a place that belonged to Jaq. Shrouded in mist, the old building looked even more menacing than usual. They hurried from the senior lot to the nearest entrance and arrived with just enough time for Jaq to swing by her locker before AP French and grab her books. As she pulled open the door, something fell out, hitting the floor by her foot. She stooped, reaching for it, then hesitated.

A thin gold chain attached to a triangle setting with three stones inside, each a slightly different shade of red, from dark burgundy to pale pink.

It looked familiar somehow. Like something she'd lost a long time ago.

She reached out and pinched the gold chain tentatively between her fingertips.

Jaq!

The voice was a scream. Jaq jerked upright, spinning around for the source, but the hallway was nearly empty. A tremble moved through her chest. She squeezed her eyes shut to steady herself, hands curling into fists, and when she opened her eyes again, the necklace was gone.

CHAPTER
THREE

Fern

Fern started lying before she ever left the house on Friday morning.

First to her mom, when she asked how auditions went and Fern answered, "Great!" It happened so quickly and so confidently that there was no way to take it back.

"I don't even know why I asked." Her mom beamed at her, sweeping one soft hand around Fern's cheek to cup her chin. "You are such a star already, and that voice—you are going to light up every stage you touch."

This was a familiar phrase. One Willow Jensen had been sharing with each of her daughters for as long as Fern could remember. And it wasn't just because she thought her daughters were amazing. She knew theater. She knew acting and what it took to be an actress. She'd had her own brief Broadway career when she was younger. As promising as it had been, it had ended almost as soon as it had begun. In the way of so many before her, she'd fallen in love, gotten pregnant, married, and returned home to Port Promise to build her perfect family.

For a while, it *had* been perfect. She'd become a nurse while Fern's dad took a job on the fishing boats that went out early each morning. When there wasn't work in the Sound, he'd take a job as deck crew on one of the ocean vessels that traveled up the Alaskan coast, sometimes for weeks at a time.

Fern's sisters told her stories of how they'd get all dressed up and go down to the harbor when he was coming home. How he'd always have a cooler full of fish that they would cook in a thousand different ways. How he had a beautiful singing voice, and there was nothing as magical as when he and their mom would reenact "You Are My Lucky Star" from *Singin' in the Rain*.

Fern didn't remember any of it.

Dad had died just after Fern was born, in an accident at sea. Mom had never fully recovered. Fern had no idea what her mother's singing voice was like, outside of grainy old YouTube performances Fern dug up on a library computer one summer. Her mom never took her to the water and sometimes cried late at night when she thought no one could hear. The only thing that seemed to bring her joy was her daughters. Specifically seeing them onstage.

"You do look a little tired, though," her mom added with some concern.

All night, Fern had been plagued by memories of her audition. Not of the vision—that had obviously been a truly terrible combination of nerves and stage light, the bad kind of theater magic she needed to forget immediately. What she couldn't get over was the way she'd blown her monologue. She'd never done that before. Not even close. Ms. Murphy had been kind in the moment, giving her time to recover and start over again, but even then, her performance could only be called lackluster at best.

The big question was: Did that matter? Ms. Murphy knew her. She couldn't deny that Fern was the best possible Sandy on her roster. It wasn't even ego to say that she was better than Kaitlyn. Fern's soprano range was objectively superior.

More importantly, Ms. Murphy knew Fern's family. This was about more than a single play. This was about legacy.

Surely Ms. Murphy would count experience over one flubbed audition.

Then again, she was a teacher, and Fern wouldn't put it past her to use this as an opportunity to impart some painful lesson about the real world and ruin the rest of her senior year.

"I'm fine," she lied again, sliding easily into the version of herself that was always okay. Eyes a little wider than necessary, smile light and friendly.

"Let me take a picture." Her mom tugged her phone from her pocket. "To mark the occasion."

Fern sidestepped around her mom, looking for a quick escape. "There's no occasion, Mom. Not yet. Don't jinx it."

"Okay, okay," her mom agreed. "This weekend, then. I'm sure I have a poodle skirt in the costume closet. Saddle shoes, too. We can go to the salon, then do a quick shoot in the park. Sound good?"

The house was plastered with glossy pictures of Fern and her three sisters. Elaborate photo shoots to mark whatever occasion their mother decided must be marked. When Holly was cast as Ella in *Cinderella,* the three younger sisters had been evil stepsisters, and when Clover was cast as Helena in *A Midsummer Night's Dream*, they'd been fairies. Over the years, they'd been everything from princesses to butterflies, anything that sparked their mother's sense of whimsy.

When Holly left for New York almost six years ago and there were only three of them, their mother's obsession seemed to grow. As though that sense of loss touched on the more painful loss of her husband. She needed more photos. Had them printed and framed and added to the walls until their house resembled a mosaic more than anything else. She seemed to have an almost impulsive need to capture every moment before it passed. Everywhere you looked, blond-haired, hazel-eyed beauties stared back.

For the past three years, Fern had been the only one left to bear the entire brunt of their mother's adoration. There had been photos on the first day of senior year, on the day of each audition, each dance, each holiday no matter how inconsequential, even the Port Promise Patron Festival every summer. There was no point in fighting what was only the next request in an endless stream of them.

"Sure," she said, an unexpected twist of nausea in her belly. "This weekend."

"Great. I'll call the salon and see if they can squeeze us in on Sunday morning." Her mom beamed again, that dreamy look in her eyes. "You are such a lovely girl. I wish I could keep you just like this forever."

Fern laughed, giving her mother a placating smile as she scooped up her backpack and fished her car keys from the zippered pocket of her purse. "You've had four daughters in high school," she said. "I can't believe you actually want to keep one forever."

But as Fern moved past the wall of photos, dozens of eyes following her every step, she couldn't help but wonder if she was wrong.

———

The second time Fern lied was at lunch.

"I hear Karima Jones is having a party tomorrow night." Cambria unwrapped another Starburst and popped it into her mouth, a growing heap of rainbow-colored trash next to her half-eaten avocado-chicken wrap. "Wanna go?"

"Of course!" Fern said. Again, the lie was out of her mouth before she could think twice.

It was only after she'd said the words that she felt the drop in her stomach. A sudden sinking sensation that left her briefly nauseated. Because Karima's house was so close to the woods it was practically inside them, and parties at her house always left Fern vaguely unsettled.

In general, avoiding the woods was difficult in Port Promise. The town was established as a logging operation, and the founders settled here because there was just enough room between the trees and water to make hauling and treating the wood for transport possible. The loggers beat the forest back, hacking down hundreds of trees, turning Port Promise into the blade of a sickle that curled away from the water and sliced into the woods.

Today, the town was stitched together by dozens of pedestrian and bike trails that crisscrossed the woods and connected downtown and the schools just above to the neighborhoods that crept farther up the mountain. And while it was common for houses to have some sort of close relationship to the woods, Karima lived deep inside them, as far from downtown as you could get. It was a perfect spot for parties and a terrible place for Fern. This was partly because there was always a moment, usually after most of the alcohol had been consumed, when someone announced it was time to summon the Patron and see if tonight was the night he would show up and grant a wish. The Patron was supposedly a benevolent ghost who haunted the Promise Wood, which put him a cut above basically every other ghost Fern had ever heard of. But she'd never been able to shake the feeling that there was something wrong with the woods of Port Promise.

That wasn't a good reason to skip the party, though. And if

Karima was hosting, it *would* be fun. So maybe saying she wanted to go wasn't a *lie* lie.

"I was hoping you'd say that. Can you drive? I know, I *know*, it's technically my turn—"

"What do you mean 'technically'?" Fern cut in, the injustice of the moment clearing away her nausea. "It's absolutely your turn. In fact, if I'm counting correctly, you already owe me one for the party at Leo Liu's. It's your turn."

"Don't be dramatic. I was just hoping since you don't really partake at these things that . . ."

Fern cast a helpless glance across the table at Melissa Trang, who was watching the exchange while sipping her bottle of soda through a metal straw. The straight line of her heavy bangs gave her the impression of always being a little bit bored by conversations, which she probably was.

The three of them were the perfect trio. They were all in theater, but they existed in three distinct spheres and were never in competition. Cambria was able to command chaos without breaking a sweat, which made her perfect for a life of stage management duties. Melissa was an artist and had never had a desire to do anything other than crew. She was a marvel with the lights and could create moods with extremely limited resources. And Fern, of course, was a natural star.

"Don't look here," Melissa said, raising her hands in surrender. "I haven't magically convinced my parents that I'm old enough to own a car. I, too, need a ride. But I agree that it's Cambria's turn, and if Fern agrees to drive, some sort of concession should be made to appease her mighty fury."

"Concession?" Cambria asked, then perked up. "Yes, I'll pay for gas!"

"Starbucks for a week," Fern countered.

Cambria gasped, her face falling. "A whole week? You'll ruin me!"

"Now who's being dramatic?" Fern asked, then turned to Melissa. "Impartial judge?"

Melissa pushed her soda away and then frowned like an old man. Thoughtful and patronizing. "One week of Starbucks does seem fair for being DD three times in a row. I rule in favor of the defendant." She banged a fist on the table, punctuating the point.

Fern smiled, but she didn't feel like she'd won anything.

By last period, that feeling had only intensified. She was all but convinced that when Ms. Murphy posted the cast list, her name wouldn't be there. Since she'd stupidly marked a single box on the sign-up sheet, she wouldn't even get a supporting role because she hadn't asked for one. What would her mom and sisters say if she was cast as *Rizzo*?

And now, because the entire school was paying attention to the musical this year, everyone would know that she hadn't made the cut. Even the kids who hadn't cared about the musical two seconds ago cared now. Everyone was talking about who would be cast in what kinds of roles. Would the main pairing end up being two boys? Two girls? A mix of genders? The possibilities seemed endless and exciting to everyone except Fern.

She was in a state of near panic when the final bell rang. The hallway around the theater was packed. At least half the school was waiting for a peek at the cast list. Fern swallowed her anxiety and pulled on a hopeful yet unassuming smile so that if the worst did happen, no one would be able to say she looked like she'd expected anything.

When Ms. Murphy appeared with a single sheet of paper in her hands, the crowd quieted and made room for her to approach the doors. She started to post the sheet, then paused and turned to face everyone.

Her cat-eye glasses winked in the light, and she tugged her plaid wrap more securely over her shoulders.

"I want to say," she started, raising her voice to be heard all the way in the back, "I'm really proud of all of you. Whether this was your first audition or your ninety-first, I'm so glad to see how many of you came out to support a show like this one, and I hope that even if you weren't cast today, you'll keep coming back. We sometimes think that stories that have been told before can't change, but the point of theater is to reflect stories through multiple lenses. That's what we'll be doing with this interpretation of *Grease*, and, if I don't get fired—" She stopped herself with a little snort of a laugh.

"We love you, Murph!" someone shouted in the pause.

"Thank you," Ms. Murphy continued. "And if I don't get fired, I hope we can do this with many more shows in the future. Okay, and without further ado . . ."

Finally, she tacked the list onto the door and backed away.

The crowd surged forward, carrying Fern with it. She kept her face forcefully neutral, her eyes on that single piece of paper, as the people in front of her began to peel away in stages of despair or elation. It was only a matter of seconds before she was close enough to read it.

She held her breath, tracking down the list of female roles to "Sandy Dumbrowski" and then across to the name: Fern Jensen.

"Oh my god." She exhaled hard. Too relieved to be happy just yet.

She moved away from the list, aware that in another few seconds she was going to have to accept a torrent of congratulations.

She was going to need her humble smile for that. The one that was more surprised than joyful. She took a deep breath and—there it was. The burst of noise. The sound of her peers seeing her name and celebrating her well-earned success. But when she turned around, it wasn't Fern that the rest of the cast was congratulating.

It was Kaitlyn.

An entire crowd had formed around her. Everyone was cheering, clapping, chanting her name.

For a single, horrifying second, Fern thought she'd read the list wrong. Had Kaitlyn been cast as Sandy? Had Fern been looking at the understudy?

Before she could make her way back to the list to double-check, Kaitlyn had crossed to her, a beatific smile on her face. "Congratulations, Sandy," she said. "Looks like you and I are going to make Port Promise history together."

Fern's mouth went dry as understanding settled in. She had been cast as Sandy, but Kaitlyn had been cast as Danny.

"Looks like it," she managed in a thin voice.

Kaitlyn's smile softened at the edges. She leaned in closer, speaking so no one else could hear. "Are you good?"

Fern glanced at the sea of glowing faces behind Kaitlyn. Everyone was ecstatic for her. For them. For *this* version of the show. No matter what Fern did now, Kaitlyn was the star because Kaitlyn was the one doing something new.

Something hard formed around Fern's chest. A tightening that made it hard to breathe, but Kaitlyn was waiting and everyone else was watching, and so, for the third time today, Fern lied.

"Yeah," she said, fixing a friendly smile in place. "I'm good."

CHAPTER
FOUR

Jaq

John had a policy of arriving at parties late and drunk so that by the time he was headed home, he'd be sober, and no one would be able to say they'd seen him take a single drink. That meant that ten times out of ten, Jaq was the one behind the wheel. It was a win-win situation. Especially since Jaq's parents thought getting a license was already more than she needed. Much less a car of her own.

Whenever she brought up finding a used car she could pay for herself, her dad asked, "Who needs a car in Port Promise?" and her mom smiled and said, "Honey, I'm sure John will drive you wherever you need to go."

The winding back roads on the way to Karima's house included sharp dives and tight corners, and tonight, Jaq took them at speed. She loved the way the engine rumbled at the press of her foot, the way the incessant scratching in her mind went quiet with focus.

"Shit! Slow down." John laughed nervously, reaching for the roof as the car dove down a sudden hill. "You always drive like something's chasing you."

In the back seat, Susan gave a delighted squeal and crashed into Tommy. They were both several shots of tequila and at least one beer into the night already.

"Sooz can manage, but Tommy's like a bottle of Coke," John said. "Shake him up too much, and he'll explode all over the back seat."

"I'm notta Coke," Tommy protested, slush-mouthed and amused.

"That's right. Why would you call him something so boring?" Jaq answered, giving John a chastising smile. "Tommy is clearly a Mountain Dew."

"I do love Dew," Tommy said very seriously. "I do do the Dew."

"Do you?" Susan asked with a sly smile.

Jaq took another corner a little too fast, and Tommy crashed into Susan with a sound that was dangerously close to vomiting.

Jaq slowed down, and John reached over to set a hand on her thigh with a quiet, "Thank you." He squeezed, the tips of his fingers pressing into the inside of her leg. It was the kind of touch that promised something more and usually left Jaq squirming in her seat, but tonight, it didn't light her up the way it usually did. Instead, the contact felt routine, so comfortable she hardly noticed.

"Here we are," Jaq said, swinging the car into a spot at the end of Karima's already-packed street.

Karima's house was on a sparsely populated cul-de-sac with large lots that sifted into the woods. The night was dark and crisp, and Jaq could smell the cedary smoke of a bonfire before they even saw Karima's house.

"John! T-Dub!" Cries from the other members of the baseball team welcomed them as they entered the backyard.

"Just in time for a round of Edward Fortyhands!" This came from Aaron Werner, who already had a massive beer bottle duct-taped to each hand and was clearly well into both.

The boys were immediately absorbed into a group neither Jaq

COME OUT, COME OUT

nor Susan had any interest in joining, so they wandered into the yard, toward the glowing tower of fire.

"Why do they always make it so big?" Susan asked, squinting at the flames. "This is exactly the kind of thing that gets the cops called."

Susan had a preoccupation with the cops being called. As far as Jaq knew, she'd never been in any real trouble, and the chances of her finding any were laughably small. Her father, Preach Meach, was well known in Port Promise, and while he wasn't technically an authority figure, people treated him like one. It was hard to imagine anyone, cop or not, giving his daughter a hard time.

Jaq didn't think Susan was oblivious to her privilege, but sometimes she seemed to take a strange kind of pleasure in pointing out the rules other people needed to follow more carefully than she did.

"Not out here," Jaq said. "This land is unincorporated. They can do whatever they want."

"Unincorporated? Like a business?" Susan threw up a hand before Jaq could explain. "Wait. Never mind. I forgot I'm tipsy and don't actually care."

Jaq laughed. "Would you care if you were sober?"

Susan screwed up her face and pretended to think hard for a second before dropping the act. "Nope! Let's go check out the fire. I think I see Karima. Karima!"

Susan hurried toward Karima, who was ringed by a sea of faces. Jaq recognized about half of them. The most popular. A few cheerleaders and student council members. She'd say hi to them at some point, but she wasn't ready to step into that much energy just yet.

She headed a little farther into the yard, scanning the crowd, and found Fern Jensen standing with a group of theater kids. They made eye contact, acknowledging each other in the way they always did. Friendly but distant. Nothing of substance. They had never been friends, but five years ago, they'd shared a strange experience that neither could explain.

The night Mallory Hammond ran away from home, Fern and Jaq had been together. They'd snuck out and met up with some vague intention of going into the woods with Mallory for reasons that escaped Jaq to this day. But Mallory hadn't shown up, and she and Fern had spent a few awkward moments standing together in the dark at the edge of the woods until they'd given up and gone home.

It had never made any sense, and Jaq couldn't remember making the decision to go out with them. It was only later, when they'd heard that Mallory had run away that same night, that the incident seemed significant in any way. As far as Jaq knew, Mallory had been an angry, unhappy girl who ran away from home when her parents found out she was gay. It had nothing to do with her. But whenever Jaq thought of that night, she got this uncomfortable scratching feeling in her mind, like she and Fern had missed something important.

Every time she and Fern were in the same space, she felt it again. The sensation of a whispered voice speaking where she couldn't quite hear. Judging by the way Fern avoided her, the feeling was mutual.

Around the fire, the crowd was a flickering band of light and dark. People clumped and spread out into the thick shadows near the woods, the air filled with pops and crackles, and the bell choir of laughter rose and fell in a natural rhythm. The whole thing wrapped around Jaq like a blanket, obscuring her from view.

This was why Jaq liked parties. Here, she could stand in the dark near everyone and still be alone. No one was looking at her with a critical eye. She wasn't a daughter or a girlfriend or the promising young girl who'd gotten into Baylor and had absolutely no idea what to do next. She was one person in a crowd, and something inside of her loosened in moments like this. She felt like she could breathe, really breathe, drawing air all the way into the bottom of her lungs as she drifted past the fire and beyond, where the trees stood in stark contrast to the sky above, their darkness opaque compared to the glittering stars. She ached to sketch the contrast in the notebook she kept hidden under her bed, to create something subtle and surprising in the negative space between trees and sky.

Jaq peered into the woods, curiosity tugging her just a little bit closer than she usually dared to go. She stared into the dark that was somehow both dense and flat, expansive and shallow. Even knowing she was looking at an endless stretch of trees, she couldn't pick out a single one. The forest gave the illusion of being empty. Of being endless and hollow.

But as she gazed into the darkness, Jaq couldn't shake the feeling that something was looking back. The hair at the nape of her neck prickled.

"Hey."

Jaq jumped. She turned, heart knocking against her chest, and looked into gentle brown eyes.

"Hi," Jaq said, a name sweeping through the chaos of her thoughts. "Devyn."

"I didn't get your name before," Devyn said, inclining her head with a lopsided smile that narrowed one eye. "At the pizza place."

"Oh, I'm sorry," Jaq said. Her heart hadn't recovered. It had tripped and was tripping again. *Tip-tip-tap*ping against her sternum.

"Is that what you want me to call you?" Devyn asked, and when Jaq frowned in confusion, she added, "I've never met anyone named Sorry before."

Jaq's cheeks burned. "Oh, no, I'm sorry, that's not my name. It's Jaq."

"Jaq?" A new kind of smile bent Devyn's mouth. "Well, Jaq, I have to tell you something."

"What?" Jaq asked, the anticipation like a live wire. Charged and buzzing.

Devyn's smile deepened, revealing a flash of teeth. "You apologize too much."

"Oh," Jaq answered. "I'm sor—" She stopped herself as Devyn's eyebrows raised in delight. "I do," she said. "It's a habit."

"A bad one." Devyn leaned closer, conspiratorial, until all that was between them was the glint of fire on her mahogany hair, the shadows playing in the dark space between her lips. "Break it," she said, as if it were that easy.

Jaq was surprised to discover that she wanted it to be.

"Okay, I'm not sorry," Jaq said, and then she laughed, simultaneously embarrassed and delighted with herself. "Except that I a—"

Devyn raised a hand. "Don't undo it. That was progress."

Jaq pressed her lips together to keep from apologizing for not apologizing. "But it feels so rude," she admitted.

"I know." Devyn bobbed her head. "My dad keeps an apology jar in the kitchen, and every time one of us apologizes for something that wasn't in our power to control, we have to put a dollar in."

"That's . . . different," Jaq said.

"He's a psychologist," Devyn said with a shrug, as though that explained everything.

"Is that why you moved to Port Promise?"

Devyn shook her head. "My mom's in the navy and was just stationed at the hospital in Bremerton. Dad found a job in Port Townsend, so this was the compromise."

"It must have been hard to move in the middle of your senior year." Jaq couldn't imagine being uprooted so close to graduation, being dropped into a school where she didn't know anyone, where no one knew her, but Devyn merely shrugged again.

"It's not easy, but we've moved a lot. And I kind of like this part."

"Which part?" Jaq asked, eyes drawn to the way the firelight sparked against Devyn's hair. Wondering what combination of yellow and orange and red it would take to capture that luster in a drawing.

"The beginning," Devyn said, lowering her voice so Jaq had to lean in to hear her. "Meeting new people. Finding the ones I'd like to know better. Waiting to see if they feel the same way about me."

Jaq's eyes fell to Devyn's lips as she spoke. Mesmerized by the play of firelight against pale pink. There had been a question in Devyn's words, she was sure. But she didn't know how to answer it, and before she could try, someone shouted, "The Patron's house is going to burn!" The crowd thickened around the bonfire, cheering as Karima approached with a little house crudely made out of a cardboard box.

Karima held it high so everyone could see and called, "Are you ready to summon the Patron?" Everyone cheered, and she tossed the house into the fire.

As it burned, the whole group began to sing, "Come out, come out, wherever you are, the Patron's in the trees. Find his house, make a wish, he'll do just as you please."

Jaq wrapped her arms around herself and squeezed. The song was as familiar to her as it was to every kid who'd grown up in Port Promise, but whenever she heard it, that insistent whisper in her mind hissed and her mouth went dry.

"Is this something you can explain to a poor outsider?" Devyn said.

"It's a game. Like Bloody Mary, except the Patron isn't evil," Jaq answered, doing her best to tune out the song. "They say that he was a kind old man who ran an orphanage in the woods. One day, the orphanage burned down, and everyone inside it died. They say that he feels responsible and terribly guilty, so his spirit still roams the woods, searching for the children he failed so he can make amends. Until he finds them, he'll help whoever is in need. So, if you summon him, he'll grant a wish."

"So why do you burn his house first?" Devyn asked.

Jaq opened her mouth to answer, but there was a crack and a spray of sparks as the bonfire collapsed. The crowd jerked back, forcing Jaq and Devyn toward the woods.

For a brief second, Devyn's hand was on Jaq's arm, holding her steady, but in the next instant, flames caught in the grass, the fire raced out of control and scattered the crowd. Then a body collided with hers and Jaq stumbled out of Devyn's grasp.

She spun, arms splayed out wide as she attempted to regain her footing. Just as she managed to find her balance, someone else knocked into her from behind. The impact sent her flying.

She landed on her hands and knees, and a chill fell over her so suddenly it was as though the fire had been extinguished. The air smelled like moss and ice. It was a second before she realized that she'd fallen into the woods. And another before she realized she wasn't alone.

Fern was beside her. Rising from where she'd fallen, her eyes wide with fear.

"Do you hear that?" Fern asked.

Climbing to her feet, Jaq started to answer, then stopped. She could hear the sounds of the party, but they were muffled, as though someone had pulled a screen down between the woods and Karima's backyard. On the other side, people were scrambling to douse the fires now burning holes in the dry grass. But their panic was far away even though they weren't. As though someone had turned the volume down.

Fern pointed toward the cavernous woods, where even the light couldn't penetrate. Before them, the land sloped at a steep angle, the ground studded with boulders that looked so much like figures crouched down that Jaq wanted to scream. From deep within the dark came a soft, unintelligible whisper.

"What is that?" Jaq asked, willing herself to see whatever it was in the dark. "Fern?"

The whisper grew louder, rushing toward them on the back of a frigid wind. It blew furiously, kicking bits of leaves and pine needles and dust into their eyes, forcing them shut.

Jaq raised her arms to protect her face, but something grabbed her by the wrist. Squeezed with an icy grip. Yanked her back down to her knees so hard pain flared in her shoulder. She cried out. Heard Fern do the same.

Jaq tried to pull away, but the grip on her wrist held tight, kept her on her knees as the whispering grew louder and more violent.

Jaq cried out again. She screamed for *John!Susan!Anyone!* But her voice didn't ring out the way it should. It was dampened, contained, as though she were trapped inside a very small room.

With something that was holding her in place.

"Fern?" she tried again, and this time, a voice called back to her.

It was far away. So, so far away that words were unintelligible. But the pain in Jaq's wrist was close. The pinch getting stronger. Then her arm was yanked again. Jaq opened her eyes and found herself face-to-face with a girl.

A girl with ferocious blue eyes and wild red hair. A girl Jaq hadn't seen in years. A girl who was as furious as a storm. Who was screaming at her to wake up, wake up, *WAKE UP!*

CHAPTER
FIVE

Mallory
THEN

Mallory Hammond was good at hating people. She wasn't supposed to do it. Preach Meach had given a sermon last Sunday all about how hatred was a tool of the devil and letting yourself hate someone else was worse for you than it ever was for them and blah, blah, blah. He'd looked straight at her when he said it, too, like he knew she was sitting there, in the third pew from the front, just hating away. Hating him, for trying to tell her what to do; her parents, for pretending they didn't hate anyone; and especially God, for being the reason she was so miserable in the first place.

But she didn't think she'd ever hated anyone as much as she hated Kaitlyn Birch on the day she came out at school.

Mal had always liked Kaitlyn. As much as she liked anyone. Kaitlyn was confident and smart and nice to everyone, and that made her someone Mal paid attention to. She was on the short list of people Mal considered to be pretty decent. Now, though, Kaitlyn was sitting in the dead center of the cafeteria, telling everyone the story of how she came out to her parents over the weekend like she deserved an award or something, and Mal hated her. Not for being gay. But for having the kind of family and life to be able to say it out loud.

She'd been intolerable all day, starting with her T-shirt, which was pink and in rainbow letters read I'M COMING OUT. In between classes, she'd been in the hallways, handing out Jolly Ranchers like she was campaigning for best gay of the year or something.

And now she was telling the story again, about how she came out to her parents by baking them rainbow-colored cupcakes.

"They were so proud of me," she said, beaming. "They even got me this shirt!"

The chorus of squeals and adoring sighs made Mallory want to eat a rainbow-colored cupcake just so she could vomit it into a cup and offer it to Kaitlyn. "I made it just for you!" she'd say. "All the colors of the rainbow!"

Kaitlyn Birch was talking about coming out like it had been some great hardship. Like she didn't already know that her parents would be accepting. And it seemed like the entire seventh-grade class was falling for it.

"You're so strong!" they said.

"You struggled for so long!" they said.

"If more people were brave like you, the world would be a better place!" they said.

It made Mallory want to scream.

She rubbed at the little bruise on the inside of her middle finger where she could still feel the gentle divot of a pencil held too tightly for too long. Pressed on it until it hurt more than looking at Kaitlyn's adoring crowd.

Mal turned away, scanning the room to see who else wasn't a part of Kaitlyn's new fan club and noticed two girls who seemed almost as unhappy as she felt. Sitting nearly as far as they could get from Kaitlyn were Fern Jensen and Jaqueline De Luca. Two quiet girls Mal only knew because they'd been in the same grade since kindergarten and because Jaqueline went to Port Promise Baptist Church, too.

"You know, I don't really know yet if I'm bi or pan," Kaitlyn was saying in response to a question Mallory hadn't heard. "I think I'm just not ready for labels."

"Except for gay," muttered Tommy Webber. "Glad I never asked you out."

The noise dimmed at the insult as the crowd waited to see how Kaitlyn would react, but she surprised everyone by laughing.

"Tommy, you wouldn't have a shot with me even if I was straight."

Laughter erupted, and Kaitlyn was showered with even more shouts of approval than before. She'd gone from someone people generally liked to the most popular girl in school in the blink of an eye.

Mal gritted her teeth and made a snap decision. She got up, dumped her lunch, then crossed to the other side of the cafeteria and dropped into the seat between Fern and Jaqueline.

"Hey," she said, flashing a smile.

"Hey," Fern answered, seeming surprised but maybe also a little excited by the attention.

Jaqueline's answer came more reluctantly and consisted of a skeptical bobbing of her head.

Across the room, the spectacle continued with other people sharing their own coming-out stories. Mal had to admit it was a bold move. Port Promise was a small town with deeply traditional roots, making it more conservative than most people assumed the Pacific Northwest to be. For some people, coming out at school might not be as unthinkable as it once was, but it still came with a certain amount of risk.

Mal watched as a smaller group of students pulled away from the joyful nucleus around Kaitlyn wearing matching expressions of disdain. Tommy Webber was among them, along with a few others Mallory recognized from her church, including John Nichols, who was the kind of guy who seemed nice until you realized he had no spine of his own, Susan Meachem, who was every bit as righteous as her father, and Cole Clark, who wasn't saying anything outright and actually looked uncomfortable. They were making their opinions on Kaitlyn's story known without saying a single word.

"Looks like people are breaking into camps," Mal said lightly, testing the waters.

"It's almost like they don't realize this has nothing to do with them," Fern said, frowning at Tommy and his friends.

"Maybe they're just jealous," Jaqueline added in a tight voice, eyes pinned to Kaitlyn with an intense kind of envy that Mal recognized.

Emboldened, Mal chose her next words carefully. This was risky, but in the face of so much maddening unbridled freedom, she was feeling a little reckless.

"Must be nice," she said.

"What must be?" Fern asked, turning her hazel eyes on Mallory. Hopeful. Maybe even a little desperate for the answer.

Mal licked her lips, heartbeat hammering in her chest. "To come out," she whispered.

For a second, neither Fern nor Jaqueline said anything, and Mal worried that she'd just made an astronomical mistake. Then, Fern's voice.

"Must be nice," she repeated.

After another second, Jaqueline nodded in agreement. "Must be."

Relief shimmered through Mallory's body. Her head was light, and her muscles quivered as though she'd just sprinted a mile. She was even sweating. But she felt something else, too: elation.

"Fern, right? And Jaqueline?" Mallory continued, swiveling her body slightly to face one, then the other.

Fern nodded, but Jaqueline corrected her quickly. "Jaq," she said. "Everyone calls me Jaqueline, but I really prefer Jaq."

"Jaq," Mallory repeated. "I'm Mal. And I think we're about to become best friends."

She glanced over to Kaitlyn once more, hatred burrowing greedily into her heart like a ravenous worm through an apple. It didn't feel bad. That was the thing about hate. The thing Preach Meach didn't seem to understand. It didn't hurt.

It helped.

CHAPTER
SIX

Fern

In the dark woods, Fern's stomach pitched as though the dank earth had opened beneath her and she was dropping, hurtling down into empty space.

Then suddenly, she hit the ground.

Gravity returned in a slam. And with it something else.

A whole world.

Memories. Feelings.

Parts of herself breaking through, parts she hadn't known were lost, breaking out—snapping into place with such force that it knocked the breath from her lungs. Again. Again.

Jaq sketching two girls kissing during math class. Mal writing curses on tiny slips of paper and burning them after school. Fern demanding that the others cut her hair with a pair of fabric shears.

Their friendship, scattered like tiles on the floor of her memory, was coming together differently. Pieces she'd once known, pieces that had been ripped away from her. An entirely new-old reality that hadn't been there a minute ago.

People didn't just forget things like this.

They didn't forget that moment in the cafeteria when Mal had seen through to Fern's heart and decided to do something about it.

They didn't forget how it felt to meet each other in the hall and know that someone else shared their secret. They didn't forget friendships that were forged in silence and ran deep as an anchor at sea.

Slumber parties at Mal's with face masks and Ring Pops on every finger.

Tarot readings in the woods with Fern's hand-me-down Sailor Moon deck.

The time Fern had asked them to help her bind her chest and take a single picture so she could see it. The way it felt to delete it after, knowing she couldn't risk anyone else finding it. The way her friends had cried with her. Just a little.

The fear. The joy. The trembling certainty that together they were stronger. That together they would survive. Together they were okay. All of it surging through her with such force that all she could do was breathe.

People didn't just forget that they were gay. Or that the gender the world had assigned to them wasn't the one that made them feel at home.

They didn't forget years of struggling inside their own body.

Except Fern *had*.

A part of her heart, her mind, her soul, whatever the hell it was had been made so small she'd forgotten it was there.

In the dark, she sat on the cold ground, stunned, unable to speak around the horrifying realization that this hadn't *just happened* to her. It wasn't possible. So something had caused it. Something had been *done* to her. Long ago. In these very woods. Something had taken a crucial piece of who she was and buried it alive.

That truth scraped through her. A knife flaying the skin from her body and leaving her bleeding and raw, exposed and vulnerable.

The only point of focus was the searing cold clinging to her wrist where something had gripped her.

Her mind stuttered around it all. Circled it and tried again. The whispers on the wind, the way something had surged out of the dark and grabbed her. Dragged her down to her knees in the dirt and refused to let go.

Not something. Someone.

Mallory.

Wake up! Mal had shouted.

Fern was awake now.

And so, it seemed, was Jaq. She was beside Fern on her knees, her long body bowed over, hands clutching her stomach as though wounded.

"What the fuck? What the fuck, what the *fuck*?" Jaq's voice climbed, growing more and more hysterical with each *fuck*. She was breathing too hard and too fast, her teeth clenched against a nameless pain.

Still in a daze, Fern turned to Jaq. More memories rushed back. Of young Jaq in a state of such panic—just like this—she could hardly breathe. The threat of what would happen if her parents ever discovered the truth about her too much to bear.

"Fern." Jaq's voice thin as a blade. Here. Now. In the woods. "Fern, I can't—"

She couldn't finish her sentence, and Fern acted on instinct. She rose to her knees, wrapped her arms around Jaq, and pulled her close. Jaq's head dropped onto Fern's shoulder, and she began to cry, to sob in a way that made no sound but wracked her body.

It was a minute before Fern realized that she was crying, too. Tears driving down her cheeks for too many reasons to name.

Whatever had happened, it had happened to both of them, but that didn't mean they were having the same experience right now.

All Fern could do was hold on tight, cling to Jaq as they cried until, finally, she felt her terror receding, giving just enough ground that she could pull a full breath into her lungs and exhale slowly. She did it again and again, and on her fourth breath, she felt Jaq join her.

For a minute they sat there, breathing slowly and intentionally even as they clung to each other. Fern squeezed Jaq's hands in her own, overwhelmed by the need for physical contact.

Only a few minutes ago, Jaq had been hardly more than an acquaintance. Someone Fern knew in the way she knew most seniors, through a few shared classes over the years and an understanding that their lives were very, very different. The fact that they were both in AP French constituted the extent of anything that could be considered a mutual interest, the only place where the Venn diagrams of their lives overlapped. Beyond that, they were polite strangers who had shared one bizarre moment one night five years ago.

Except that wasn't true.

Fern Jensen and Jaq De Luca were *friends*. With so much more in common than Fern could find words for in this moment.

She and Jaq had gravitated toward each other even before Mal had made them friends. Drawn together by a shared sense of caution that kept them on the outskirts of most friend groups. Fern remembered Jaq as two separate people. The one she'd known before Mal and the one she'd known after.

Before Mal, Jaq had been the girl who never raised her hand but always had the answers. The girl who was always tagged out first in games of dodgeball. Who always wore skirts and kept her hair in a perfect braid.

After Mal, Fern had come to know a different Jaq. A secret Jaq. The one who used pastels to create lush, colorful drawings. Who had blushed five shades of pink when she'd confessed to Fern that she thought Mal was the most beautiful person she'd ever seen. Who had been waiting for the excuse to sneak out of her bedroom window late at night.

It felt like Fern was seeing Jaq for the first time in years.

Except this Jaq, the Jaq she'd known in high school, was the Before-Mal version once again. *Restrained.* Her hair was neatly braided, two perfect wisps curled around her cheekbones, her makeup was neutral, every piece of her outfit precisely coordinated. She was tidy. And she'd come here with John Nichols, of all people.

Fern stood and helped Jaq to her feet.

"Are you okay?" Fern asked, still holding on to Jaq's hand.

Jaq made a sound that was trying to be a laugh but came out as a gasp. "Are you?" she asked, incredulous.

"Fair point."

Fern looked around. They were still in the woods. The air smelled earthy and cold, and the light of the bonfire flickered chaotically through the trees. A few shouts skittered toward them from a short distance away as everyone else struggled to get the fire under control. Between here and there, a seemingly impenetrable chasm of shadow. In here, she knew who she was, but out there—

Would her memories all go away again?

She didn't know. She didn't want them to, but she couldn't stay here forever.

"We have to get out of here."

Jaq's eyes skated toward the edge of the woods, where the party shimmered and spiked. It was another world. One where none of their so-called friends knew who they really were. "I know."

"We don't have to . . . we don't have to go back there," Fern said, gesturing to the party. "We could go somewhere else and talk."

"I want to." Jaq's voice was threadbare. "But I drove my— I drove my friends, and I can't just leave."

"Oh, shit, I did too," Fern said, remembering the Starbucks deal. It seemed unimportant now, but there was no way she'd convince her friends to leave this early.

"We could call in a noise complaint," Jaq suggested helplessly. "See if anyone comes to break up the party."

"I—that's not a terrible idea, actually," Fern said, even though she was relatively sure Jaq was joking. "But maybe we should find an option that doesn't turn us into the pariahs of senior year?"

"Jaq!" The shout cut through the night. Hard on its heels was John Nichols, marching into the woods toward them, his green eyes bright with alarm, golden curls catching firelight like he was born from coils of flame.

He was ridiculously pretty. Fern couldn't deny it, but she also knew too much about him to think he was anything other than a modern-day Ken doll. Right now, though, he was worried about Jaq.

His girlfriend.

"There you are!" he said, taking Jaq's hands in his and pulling her to him. "The fire collapsed, and I couldn't find you and— Hey. What's wrong?"

John cupped Jaq's face in his hands, tenderly peering into her eyes. For all of John's faults, he seemed genuinely concerned for Jaq in this moment.

Still, a part of Fern recoiled to see them together. It was a new reaction, but it was rooted in knowing through to her bones that Jaq only liked girls.

"Nothing, I was just freaked out by the fire," Jaq said, pushing his hands down with a placating smile, but Fern caught the tremor in her voice. "I promise."

"What are you doing out here?" John cast a suspicious glance at Fern, the "with her" part of the question very clear even if he hadn't said it aloud.

"I tripped when the fire exploded and lost my shoe," Fern explained, the lie coming easily. "Jaq helped me find it."

John eyed Fern curiously, obviously surprised to find the two of them together, but he gave a single nod and looped one arm around Jaq's shoulders. "C'mon. Let's go find the others."

Fern felt Jaq's loss as John turned her away. It was like the sun slipping behind a cloud. She hadn't been aware of the warmth until it was gone.

"Wait!" Fern caught Jaq's elbow, then pulled out her phone. "What's your number?"

John looked on as Jaq entered her details with fingers that trembled slightly.

Fern flipped on her sweetest smile and blinked at him, making sure that whatever John saw, it was as far from the truth as possible.

"It's been so long since we were in touch," Fern said, taking her phone back and sending a quick message to Jaq. "Text whenever," she added, hoping that Jaq understood that what Fern actually meant was "Text me as soon as you can."

Jaq responded with a tight smile, then let John draw her back into the party.

Fern watched them go. Everything felt too real and not real at all, like she was still falling and there was nowhere to land. The party was starting to show signs of slowing. A gentle storm with many centers. She would be able to convince Cambria and Melissa to leave soon. She just had to hold it together until then.

With a deep breath, Fern stepped out of the forest and rejoined the world.

CHAPTER
SEVEN

Jaq

Apart from a few patches of singed grass and the addition of a hose now draped across the yard, the party was unchanged. The people, the fire, the ever-present, slightly sour smell of beer, all of it was the same as it had been just a few minutes ago.

All of it, except Jaq.

She was untethered, walking through the yard without feeling any of the steps because her mind was raging. A tornado spinning with inexorable speed, spitting out memories like random junk it collected five miles away.

Of the time she'd caught herself daydreaming about kissing Arwen in the Lord of the Rings movies instead of any of the boys, and realized that she only ever thought of kissing girls.

Of the first time she'd said the word *lesbian* out loud to Mal. Soft and testing, afraid someone would overhear her even though they were in the woods. Of Mal's teasing grin when she'd said, "No hellfire. Must not be evil."

There was one of Fern, winking at her in seventh-grade English when Ms. Mack recited Emily Dickinson's "Tell all the truth but tell it slant." And the delicious joy that had fluttered in her belly at sharing the secrets of that message with someone else.

Of sitting inside a dark closet. Inches away from Mal. So nervous and excited she could hardly breathe.

Mal.

Jaq's breath lodged in her chest.

Mal was gone. She was dead.

Jaq's certainty was a knife to the heart. The only girl she'd ever kissed, the only girl she'd ever loved, was dead. Had been dead for years. And Jaq hadn't remembered any of it.

Sorrow flooded up, up, up her throat, relentless and squeezing. But she couldn't do this here. She had to stay in control. Had to hold on to the tenuous stability she'd found in the woods with Fern.

But with every sip of air, she remembered so much more.

And even though the memories all felt real, she didn't understand how they could be. How they could possibly belong to her. It was too much. Too, too much.

She clung to John, glad that he was there. Sturdy and strong and leading her away from the woods, away from the fire where the crowd was still thickest and toward the patio, but they were moving a little too fast, and Jaq stumbled over an abandoned beer can.

"Whoa!" John caught her before she could fall. "Damn heathens don't know how to pick up after themselves," he muttered with a scowl, in full protector mode now.

"Stop," Jaq gasped. "I mean, sorry, I need to stop."

John paused, swiveling around to look at her. "Are you about to have another panic attack? I can get you out of here. I'm sober enough to drive."

This was the best part of John. The part few people ever bothered to notice because the rest of him was so loud. But John was good at sensing things, little shifts that were the difference between being all right and not being all right at all. He might not always know what to do with that information, but he tried.

"Sober enough doesn't count," she chided. "And I'm fine. Just tired and my stomach is a little upset."

"You never get sick," he said, studying her closely.

"I'm not sick, just . . . queasy." She attempted an encouraging smile and failed.

"Okay, we're leaving." John raised his eyes, scanning the crowd with that same scowl on his face. "You wait here. I'll find Sooz and Tommy." Jaq opened her mouth to protest, but John beat her to it. "I know, I know, you're driving."

Two minutes later, John had found their less-than-sober friends and wrangled them into the car.

"But it's so early," Sooz protested.

"Thisizwhy I should always dribe," Tommy added, as Susan aimed him in the right direction and helped him collapse into the back seat.

"You can 'dribe' next time," she soothed, climbing in after him.

The drive from Karima's to Jaq's was only ten minutes, but the two of them were asleep by the time Jaq pulled up in front of her house at 11:22 p.m.

"Are you okay to dribe?" Jaq asked when she and John climbed the porch steps to her front door.

"Yes," he confirmed. "Sobriety at one hundred percent."

Jaq considered him for a second, but it wasn't like John to lie. About anything, really. If he said he was sober, he was sober. "Okay, thank you for leaving the party early."

"It's just a party," he said, reaching for her hand. "Is there anything else I can do?"

A cold wind kicked up, hissing through the trees. Jaq shivered and shook her head, wanting to be inside her own room more than anything. "I'll be better in the morning."

John nodded, accepting the lie without an ounce of suspicion, then he bent close and pressed a kiss against her mouth. His lips were warm, and he smelled a little like smoke and a little like his favorite mint gum.

Jaq tensed. Clenched her fists. Took a stilted step back. Instincts screaming to get awayawaway*away* from the touch.

Something inside her clawing to get out.

A vital piece of her awake and feral.

A flash of Devyn's face. Smile. Lips.

Mallory.

A flutter of yearning and sorrow she almost couldn't contain.

She saw the confusion in John's eyes a split second before the front door opened and her mother's voice whispered between them, "Hi, John."

"Busted." John hid his confusion beneath a friendly smirk. "Good evening, Mrs. De Luca. I see you had Mr. De Luca oil those squeaky hinges."

Alice De Luca was tall and graceful. Her dark hair was shot through with silver and coiled gently at her shoulders. Like Jaq, she had skin that tanned easily in the sun and wide brown eyes that traveled between sepia and dark coffee depending on what she was wearing that day. Unlike Jaq, she was a striking beauty, with the kind of cheekbones that made her entire face look as though it had been designed by an architect. Standing in the doorway, wrapped in a creamy white shawl, she looked cold and regal.

"I did, in fact. It was long overdue," she answered as though they really were only discussing the maintenance of the house and not her ability to spy on private moments like these. "Thanks for bringing her home on time."

"My pleasure." John beamed, then took Jaq's hand in his and raised it to his lips, kissing her knuckles before backing away. "Always nice to see you, Mrs. De Luca. Good night."

"Good night," Jaq called after him, letting her mother draw her into the quiet of the house. "You didn't have to wait up, Mom."

"I know, but I had some chores, and you know I never sleep well when you're out late. Better to make good use of the time." She leaned in, wrapped her arms around Jaq's shoulders, and drew her close. The sharp scent of cleaning product stung Jaq's eyes.

"Are you bleaching something?" she asked. It was almost midnight.

"Just finishing up in the kitchen," her mother said wearily. "That John is such a good boy. So polite and thoughtful. He's exactly right for you."

This was the kind of thing her mother had said ever since she and John went on their first date. And it wasn't just her mom. The two families were so close that they'd had a standing monthly dinner date for as long as Jaq could remember. She and John had been friends almost from birth. And until now, all of that had seemed so good. So right. The future stretched out ahead of Jaq like a painting with every detail exactly in place.

Until now, she'd liked that feeling.

"Yeah," Jaq half whispered around the nausea tightening in her throat. "I'm going to go to bed."

Her mother released her and patted her cheek fondly. "I'm right behind you. See you in the morning."

"Night," Jaq answered, already halfway up the stairs.

She closed her bedroom door, then pressed her back against it and blew out a sharp breath. Her room was exactly as she'd left it. Tidy and symmetrical. Each wall bisected by a single item: wrought iron bed, window, desk, dresser. A set of floating bookshelves over her desk arranged by genre and alphabetized, walls adorned with evidence of her academic achievements and the driftwood cross she'd made on a summer church trip to Forks. Everything in calming shades of blue and green. Perfect as a picture. Just like her.

Except.

She remembered how these walls had been before: A bright, buttercream yellow, plastered in smeary pastel paintings she'd done herself. Dizzying, galactic swirls and bright red apples and elegant flowers and, her favorite, a jellyfish with tentacles of every color. Art was the place she'd felt free to be vivid and messy, and hanging it on her walls had made this place hers in a way nothing else was.

But she'd taken it all down. It had been at the cusp of her freshman year. Her mother had suggested that it was time to take her life a little more seriously and set aside her childish hobbies and habits. She remembered now with painful clarity how easy it had been to pull each painting off the wall. To stack them together and toss them in the recycling bin. To ask her mother for soft blue paint to cover the yellow.

How proud her mother had been to see her turning into a mature young lady.

She felt like every part of her had been cataloged and organized. If she could peer inside her mind, it would look like this bedroom. Ordered. Picturesque. The unseemly parts of herself packed away into boxes and stored out of sight. So far out of sight that she'd lost them.

She'd lost herself. Lost her art. Lost her mess.

Lost Mal.

But how?

A great sob vaulted up from Jaq's lungs. Surging with such sudden force that she clamped her hands over her mouth. She could feel the next cry trembling deep in her belly. Punching its way up. She tried to hold her breath, to keep it in, but it was no use. All of this had been inside of her for too long, and it wanted out.

Diving into bed, Jaq pressed her face into a pillow and cried.

———

Jaq woke with a headache and eyes so puffy it took her several minutes of blinking to see that it was five thirty in the morning, and she had three missed texts from Fern.

One had been sent last night; the other two had only just come in. They read:

Can we meet somewhere?
Sorry, I know it's early.

Jaq hesitated. It was Sunday and she would be expected for church, but services weren't until ten.

Where?

After a second, Fern answered: **The Dormouse.**

Twenty minutes later, Jaq had slipped out of her house to catch the first crosstown bus and now stood inside the narrow door of the Dormouse Coffeehouse, which was, like its namesake, tiny and adorable and perched right on the rocky shoreline overlooking the Puget Sound.

Most people came here during the week, when they could grab

a coffee and enjoy the view, forever hoping for a peek at Mt. Rainier or Mt. Hood far across the water. Right now, though, the place was barely open, and the single barista behind the counter was visibly not happy about having such early clientele on a Sunday.

They ordered quickly, then tucked themselves into the far corner, where someone had shoved a table and two tiny chairs that were more aesthetic than actual furniture.

Fern perched on the edge of one chair and leaned in. Judging by the rings under her eyes, she hadn't slept any better than Jaq.

"You saw her, too, right?" Fern asked. "Mallory."

Jaq nearly flinched at the memory—still so close—of Mallory's face. Of her icy grip. Of the sound of her voice. She nodded. "Did she speak to you?"

"Wake up," Fern whispered. "She told me to wake up, and . . . I think I did."

Jaq nodded again as a soft buzzing sensation washed over her. That was the best description for what had happened to her in the woods. From one second to the next, she'd awoken into a new— no, not new—an old version of herself. A Before-Jaq.

"Me too," she said. "What do you remember?"

Fern sat back, dipping a stirring stick into her coffee and swirling it around. Jaq raised her own mug and took a careful sip.

"I remember a lot. I remember you and me and Mallory. I remember that I was—am—" She shook her head like the information was still difficult to catalog. The word still difficult to say. "I'm—" she tried again, a slight tremble in her voice. Tears brightened in her eyes, and she shook her head again, unable or unwilling to say the word out loud.

Jaq understood. She didn't know how to say it either.

"It's okay. I remember," Jaq told her.

"How did I forget that?" Fern's explosive whisper won a disapproving look from the barista, who responded by tucking earbuds into her ears and tuning out their conversation. "That's not something people just forget. I mean, clearly it is because we did, but that's not normal. Right?"

"No, it's not," Jaq answered with a slow shake of her head. "And the fact that it happened to both of us is . . . strange."

Fern laughed humorlessly. "That's an understatement."

"Do you . . . " Jaq started and stopped. Everything in her mind was still so unclear. A jumble of thoughts and emotions, flashes of laughter and screams, of hands clasped together and an old house rising up among the trees.

And Mal.

Grief began to roil inside her, but she forced it down.

Last night, it had been too overwhelming to parse, but this morning, she was starting to put things in order. To map them onto the timeline of her life so that they made sense. So that, if there were answers to be found in them, she would know where to look.

But something was missing.

"Do I what?" Fern pressed.

Jaq licked her lips and tried again. "Do you remember that night? In the woods with Mallory?"

"Oh, I—" Fern frowned, eyes moving out of focus for a second. "Maybe—?"

Her frown deepened, as if she were working to find the answer in her own jumble of newly returned memories. Jaq waited, unsure whether or not she hoped the answer was yes or no.

Everything else about that night was there. And even though she didn't like what had led the three of them into the woods, she was more alarmed by the void that followed.

Her last memory was of Mal standing just outside the trees before they went in, head tipped to look at them over her shoulder. "You owe me this," she'd said, each word an accusation.

An accusation Jaq had deserved.

"No," Fern breathed, sounding bewildered. "I only remember before and after."

Jaq nodded, a chaotic wave of emotions churning inside her. "If she's a ghost, does that mean . . . Do you think she's dead?"

The story had been that she'd run away. That was what they'd said at church, at school, in the paper, even. She'd been "troubled," and so it wasn't entirely unexpected. That had been that. And Jaq had believed it. Where Jaq thought there might be answers, there was only a gaping hole in her memory. And inside that hole was Mallory's last night.

Fern drew her bottom lip between her teeth. It was such a familiar gesture, so specifically Fern, that Jaq wanted to cry. Not only had she lost parts of herself, but she'd lost her friend. For the past five years, they'd been little more than strangers. Passing each other in the halls, sitting two rows apart in AP French, nodding without ever saying hello.

"I think she has to be," Fern said at last, tears brimming in her blue eyes. "I don't believe in ghosts, but . . ." She shrugged, two tears slipping down her soft cheeks.

"But we saw her," Jaq finished as answering tears rose in her own eyes.

"We saw her," Fern echoed, a faint smile appearing on her lips. "And she gave us our memories back."

"Not all of them," Jaq said. "Why would she hide what happened that night from us?"

Fern's smile faded at once. "I don't know."

To Jaq, it sounded like a lie. Because Jaq had already started to suspect that the reason they didn't remember that night was because they didn't want to. Or couldn't bear to. Or Mal didn't want them to.

"But it's good, right?" Fern said, hope in her voice.

"What is?" Jaq asked.

"It's good to know the truth about who we are, right?"

Jaq tried to smile. She wanted to believe it. But right now, the truth just hurt.

CHAPTER
EIGHT

Mallory
THEN

Mallory had never really had friends before. Not in the way that other kids seemed to have friends. People who were like them in some way, who understood them without having to say a single word. It had always seemed so much easier for other kids. Who didn't have to worry or keep secrets.

But Fern and Jaq understood. Other kids thought secrets were fun. For the three of them, they were the only thing that kept them safe. And that bond had sparked a near-instant friendship that ran deep.

Within days, they'd gone from hardly knowing each other to being best friends. Passing notes between classes and sharing inside jokes with nothing more than a glance. And every day, they walked home together, choosing the path through the woods so it would take as long as possible to reach Mallory's house, which was always their first stop.

Mallory's parents had a lot of rules. More now than last year, before Mallory had tried, and failed, to run away. That was when she'd learned that no one listens to kids. The person selling tickets at the bus station hadn't listened when she'd said she was going to visit family in Seattle, the cops hadn't listened when she said she didn't want to go home, and of course Preacher Meachem had only listened to her parents when they explained how willful she was. How troubled.

Now she was supposed to come straight home after school so she could finish her homework before dinner. If she didn't, there were consequences. Endless hours of copying Bible verses at the kitchen table until her fingers were bruised and the only words in her head were so hateful she couldn't help but let them spill out, which only earned her more hours at the table.

Sometimes, it was worth it, though.

"Tommy Webber asked me to the spring formal again today," Mallory said as the three of them dashed out of school and made for the trails cutting through the Promise Wood toward their subdivision.

Fern and Jaq groaned in unison.

It was late February, and the earliest rhododendron of the season flashed pink between the craggy, thin trunks of Douglas fir trees. The air was damp and too cold for Mallory's thin coat, but this was her favorite time to be in the woods. The spring was when things you thought had died came back. It was when secrets could be discovered and shared.

"I know." Mallory ducked under the trees ahead of them, vanishing into the dark for a split second. "He said that he would keep asking until I said yes, and I think he thinks he's being romantic."

"Gross," Fern muttered.

"Where are we going?" Jaq asked when Mallory detoured from the trail that would lead them home. "Won't you be late?"

"We won't be late if you hurry up!" Mallory called, racing ahead, taking them deeper into the woods.

She knew it was irresponsible. None of them knew these trails very well, and if she came home late, she'd be copying scripture for years. But she had friends now, *real* friends, and that made consequences worth something. She could endure any punishment with Fern and Jaq by her side.

"Have you guys ever heard the story about the Patron?" Mallory asked when they could hear the rushing water of Whisper Falls nearby.

"Hasn't everyone?" Jaq asked. "We've been singing that song since kindergarten, and my mom always makes us go to the Patron Festival."

Mallory knew about the festival. It wasn't so much a festival as it was a massive community service event. For three days in June, right after school let out for summer, the whole town would come together to clean up the public pier or the waterfront park or start a community vegetable garden—whatever the organizers decided was most needed. It was all in honor of the story of the Patron. There was live music and food trucks and games. The Hammonds had never attended. The story of the Patron might be nice, but it was still a story, and revering him was, according to Mrs. Hammond, essentially a pagan ritual.

"Yes, but there's more to him than a song and a festival. He was real." Mallory's brows arched with delight. She was never allowed to talk about the Patron at home, but she was obsessed with the idea of him.

"My sisters said that, too," Fern added. "That, a long time ago, he was a real person, and the song we sing is based on all the nice things he did for Port Promise. He ran an orphanage, right? There was a big fire in town, and all these kids ended up without homes, but he took them in and cared for them, which is why he's called the Patron and why the festival is all about charitable acts."

"I've heard that version." Mallory shrugged. "But I also heard that it was his orphanage that burned down, and his ghost is still here to make amends."

"That's really sad," Jaq said. "All those kids died."

"Yeah," Mal agreed. "In these very woods, and they say that if you sing his song where he can hear, his house will appear, and he'll grant you a wish."

"Do you think it's true?" Fern asked, eyes wide and hopeful.

Mal had spent hours considering that exact question—usually in church, when she was supposed to be thinking about Jesus, which was sure to have put her on the "going to hell" list if nothing else had. But she didn't think the Patron was all that different from Jesus. The only real difference was that he was here, right here in Port Promise, and if he was doling out wishes to people who needed them, well, she wanted—*needed*—that to be true.

"Maybe we should find out," Mallory answered, and then she began to sing. "Come out, come out, wherever you are, the Patron's in the trees. Find his house, send up a call, he'll do just as you please!"

"Stop," Fern said with a laugh that wasn't convincing. "Maybe we shouldn't. The woods are freaky enough. I always feel lost in here."

"That's funny coming from someone named Fern." Mallory reached out and ran her hands along the fronds of Fern's namesake. The fluffy plants grew all along the path they were on. "But okay, I get it. It's easy to get lost in here, but that's exactly why this place is so special. Here. Look."

Mallory hurried around a bend in the trail, then scrabbled up over a large boulder where the path became steep and they had to concentrate on climbing instead of talking. But once they reached the top, it was all worth it.

The trail ended in a wide, flat rock overlooking Whisper Falls, the waterfall that rushed through the heart of the forest. From here, they could see how the woods tumbled toward the coastline. Downtown was stamped between the inlet and the trees with slashes of pale gray docks jutting out over the rippling blue.

"Whoa," Jaq said. "I was not expecting this."

Mallory dropped her backpack and edged closer to the end of the rock where water rushed by, plummeting down in a torrent of brutal sound. She spun back to face her friends and shouted to be heard over the roar, "Do you want to see why this place is so great?" Then, without waiting for them to answer, she tipped her head back, cupped her hands around her mouth, and shouted, "I'M GAY!"

"Shh!" Jaq rushed forward with one finger raised as Fern spun around with wide eyes, searching for anyone who might have over-heard.

But Mallory was laughing. "No one can hear us! This is the one place we can say it out loud. Say it. Shout it. Scream it. I'M GAY!" She shouted the last words again.

"But—" Fern's eyes were wide, her bottom lip drawn between her teeth, her shoulders hunched forward as though waiting to be struck from behind. It was a pose Mallory was familiar with.

"Try it," Mallory urged. "We're safe here. I promise."

Jaq pressed her lips together, shaking her head. But Fern took a step closer to the falls, drew in a deep breath, and shouted, "I'M GAY!"

"Yes!" Mallory clapped her hands and turned once more to Jaq. "You don't have to," she said. "But it feels really good."

Jaq inched toward the edge of the rock. Her hands were balled into two tight fists, and she looked like she was on the verge of tears. "I'm . . ." Her voice faded beneath the rush of water. She swallowed hard and tried again. "I'M—"

"It's okay," Fern said, taking one of Jaq's fists in hers.

"We've got you," Mallory added, taking Jaq's other fist. "You and I are in the same boat, remember?"

Their lives weren't identical, but they had similar battles to fight. Fern's were different but no less real.

After two more deep breaths, Jaq leaned forward and whispered, "I'm gay." Then she reeled back, gasping and laughing. "Oh my god, I don't think I've ever said that word out loud before!"

"What are you talking about?" Mallory asked. "The only thing talking out here is the falls."

All three of them burst into laughter, a strange mixture of fear and pure joy making them giddy. When they'd finished and climbed down from the heights of Whisper Falls to the main trail once more, Mallory stopped them.

"I have something for you. Well, for us," she amended, digging into her backpack for three satin pouches and distributing them. "To mark the occasion."

"Mal, did you plan this?" Jaq asked, impressed.

"Not exactly. I was just waiting for the right moment," she admitted. "And this is so obviously it. Open them!"

They emptied the contents of the small bags into their hands. Three necklaces with a trio of gemstones at the end of a delicate gold chain. They were identical but for the colors of the stones.

She'd purchased them in secret, and they represented the entire sum of Mallory's meager savings.

"Red, pink, and a diamond for you, Jaq, because you have such a big heart," Mallory explained, feeling a little shy about it now that she was saying it out loud. "And green and gold for you, Fern, because of your name and because you always remind me of the sun."

"And what about you?" Fern asked. "Blue and purple?"

Mallory shrugged. "I like blue."

"Because you're as bold as the ocean," Jaq said, a blush creeping into her cheeks when she looked up at Mal.

"I, um, I do love the ocean," Mal stammered, suddenly very aware of the way Jaq was looking at her and very unsure how to feel about it. She cleared her throat and forced a casual smile. "Anyway, these are like best friend necklaces, but—"

"Secret," Jaq said, always quick to understand. "Just like us."

"Just like us," Fern repeated.

"Just like us," Mallory confirmed.

CHAPTER
NINE

Fern

Fern's celebratory photo shoot was postponed due to the first thunderstorm of the season.

It was a relief. Even though Fern was still excited about the musical and had been fielding her sisters' congratulatory texts for days, it didn't seem very important right now. She wasn't the same Fern she'd been when she'd auditioned. She felt like a bomb had gone off inside of her, and all her parts were in some kind of stasis. Waiting for her to pull them back together one by one, except she didn't know where they all fit anymore. She was fractured. Disoriented.

In the blink of an eye, she'd become someone new and was still adjusting. She was in no condition to pretend to be somebody else.

But after school on Monday, Ms. Murphy sent her into the musty costume basement with Kaitlyn Birch to do exactly that.

"Every character, every person, is more than one thing, but in theater, you have to build your character, and that is easier to do when you have the first building block. Your touchstone. The single thing—whether that's a piece of your costume or something you carry with you in secret—that encompasses the character for you," she said, repeating the same speech she'd been giving them since freshman year. "More than that, it should represent how *you* connect with the character."

"Aren't we supposed to search for it on our own?" Fern asked, pointedly not looking at Kaitlyn. Usually, she really liked this part of the process. She looked forward to the strange magic of uncovering the thing that would connect her to the person she would become. But she already felt like two separate people. How could she pretend to be a third?

For so much of her childhood, she'd pretended every day. With her mom, her sisters, her teachers and classmates. Until Mal. Until she'd forgotten it all. She wondered if forgetting who she was had made her a worse liar but a better performer.

"Normally, yes, I would let you do this on your own," Ms. Murphy said, pursing her lips in that way that meant she was being very patient. "But I know you two have spent your entire high school career competing with each other."

That was an understatement. While it was technically true, it didn't encapsulate the cutthroat nature of their relationship. Nothing would ever compare to the time Kaitlyn had announced she wasn't auditioning for the sophomore showcase only to change her mind at the last minute and snag Juliet's famous act 2, scene 2 monologue right out from under Fern. That wasn't "competition," that was war.

"To some extent that kind of rivalry is good. It's healthy, but now I need you two in perfect sync. So." Ms. Murphy brought her hands together for emphasis. "I want you to work together. To discuss what these characters mean to you and their relationship to one another. Okay? Here are the keys. Come join us in the theater when you're through."

"Sure thing," Kaitlyn said, taking the keys with a bright smile.

It was a grade-A teacher smile. One that said, "You can trust me, I'm here to learn!" Fern had one exactly like it. But it, along with everything else, felt out of place and hard to reach, like even a smile was something she could misplace.

They left the theater and hurried down the hall toward the double doors that stood at the entrance to the school basement. They were greeted by a puff of stale air and the distant whir of machines as they descended the stairs.

"This way," Kaitlyn said, taking them past a wall of massive metal pipes that traveled in all directions.

"I know." Fern couldn't help herself. She didn't like the implication that Kaitlyn was more experienced when Kaitlyn knew that she had been here just as often. Probably more often, since Fern had started visiting the costume room when she was in sixth grade and Holly was a senior. Still, there were so many twisting hallways down here that it was easy to get lost.

Ancient laminated signs posted at each corner pointed the way. Kaitlyn walked ahead, taking turn after turn until they cut down a wide corridor studded with doors. Fern had no idea what was hidden behind them all, probably moldering athletics gear and a million old computers, but walking down this hallway made her feel like she'd entered a shadow world where vestiges of the past had become trapped, and if she wasn't careful, so would she.

The theater room was all the way at the farthest end of the hall, where the light seemed thinner. Kaitlyn unlocked the door and stepped aside so Fern could enter first. She hit the lights, and they filled the room with icy fluorescence, casting grayscale shadows over racks and racks of costumes for every kind of time period imaginable.

Kaitlyn turned her brown eyes on Fern. "Before we get started, do you have any superstitions we need to get out of the way?"

"About the costume basement?" Fern raised her eyebrows.

Kaitlyn laughed. "Everyone has their thing. One of my friends counts the number of letters in their character's name, then goes to each rack and counts to that same number. They almost always end up with a complete costume that way."

"That's . . . wild."

"Wild, but it works!" Kaitlyn shrugged and tossed Fern a mischievous smile. "And who are we to question theater magic?"

In some ways, it was easy to see why people liked Kaitlyn. Easy to miss how calculating she'd been over the years. Arguing for plays with parts that would be perfect for her, making a show of congratulating Fern when Fern got the better role, sucking up to Ms. Murphy at every possible opportunity. It was so transparent, but everyone else ate it up. Even now, all anyone was talking about was the fact that Kaitlyn was going to play a boy onstage. And she was basking in the spotlight.

It was just like when she'd come out in seventh grade. She'd been so loud about it. So bold and sure of herself. Before a few days ago, Fern had forgotten that she'd ever cared about Kaitlyn coming out. But she remembered now. And she cared more than ever.

"No superstitions here," Fern said. Not that she would tell Kaitlyn if she had any. "You?"

"I look until something snags me," Kaitlyn answered, turning to survey the rows of costumes. "Wanna start at that end and work our way toward the door?"

"Oh, or we could take opposite sides of the room." Fern's words were awkward and disjointed. For all the obvious we're-not-friends reasons, she'd assumed that even though they'd come here to-gether, they wouldn't stay that way.

Kaitlyn tipped her head to one side, gently chastising Fern with-out saying a word. Her eyes caught the light, and Fern caught her breath. The fluorescence revealed layers of gold and amber in Kait-lyn's brown irises. Turned her mouth a deep coral, the tone of her skin tawny and warm.

In the space of a second, one small piece of Fern that had been hovering in stasis clicked into place. Oriented around the single point of Kaitlyn's beauty.

Kaitlyn had always been beautiful. That was one of the things that made her dangerous. She was talented enough, skilled enough, and pretty enough to be in constant competition with Fern. She had been beautiful the same way a poisonous flower was beautiful. Or maybe a venomous snake. It was important to recognize the colors and markings that set them apart so you could avoid them.

But that had been Before-Fern.

Now-Fern didn't see Kaitlyn's beauty. She *felt* it.

The sensation was a simultaneous tightening and loosening in her chest. A drumbeat in her veins and a cramp in her stomach.

When Fern didn't say anything for a long minute, Kaitlyn held out her arm like a gentleman. Then she adopted a crooked Danny Zuko smile and asked, "Shall we?"

Fern stiffened, a small flutter rushing from her stomach to her chest. "Um, yeah, I mean," she cleared her throat, reaching for her ingenue smile and forcing it into place. "Let's go, Daddy-o."

Kaitlyn drew her in close, pulling her down the narrow space between two racks. Fern's cheeks flushed at the contact, at the re-alization that she didn't hate it. Not even a little. And she didn't want it to stop. But before long, Kaitlyn let her go and started searching on her own.

"This always takes me forever," she muttered. "Sorry in advance."

"What kind of piece are you looking for?" Fern asked, hoping her voice sounded normal. "Might help if I can be looking, too."

Kaitlyn pursed her lips in thought. "I think something that feels a little flashy and almost femme, you know? Something that's both me and him. Like a belt or something. I'm not sure, but I'll know it when I see it."

Fern swallowed hard, an ugly clawing feeling of jealousy confusing everything else. Before, she'd been jealous of all the attention Kaitlyn was getting for playing Danny. Now, though, it felt much less defined.

"Sure," Fern said, turning to the rack next to her so she wouldn't have to look at Kaitlyn any longer.

"What about you?" Kaitlyn asked.

Fern blinked, trying to clear her head. Sandy. She needed something that connected her to Sandy Dumbrowski. An innocent, idealistic good girl with the wool pulled so firmly over her eyes she was basically a sheep.

Turns out, it was hardly a role at all.

"You already look so much the part," Kaitlyn continued, echoing Fern's own thoughts. "It would be kind of fun to do something unexpected."

"Unexpected?"

"Yeah, like a hat, or something. Or big combat boots. You know, Sandy with a twist." Kaitlyn continued scraping through her own costume rack. "I'm sure Murph would let you get away with it. She's been so cool about the show already. Giving us room to make a statement even though the school board won't let us have a GSA or anything. Fucking dictators."

A memory crashed into Fern. Of Mal raging about how her parents had organized a small committee of concerned parents—most of whom were from her church—to have the Gay-Straight Alliance at their junior high disbanded. It had been a short leap from that to killing the high school branch. Kaitlyn had tried to rally the seventh grade to conduct a walkout, but only a handful of students participated, and they all ended up with a week of in-school suspension.

Fern, Jaq, and Mal had watched them walk out, too afraid of the consequences to join.

Even Fern's mother had added her signature to the petition, parroting what all the other parents were saying: "*It just isn't appropriate to have an organization like that in a junior high. We need to let children be children. Not confuse them with things they can't understand yet.*"

Fern pressed a hand to the wall to steady herself.

"Oh, this is interesting. What do you think?"

Kaitlyn held up a black leather jacket, tastefully accented with buckles and zippers, the elbows worn pale and scratchy. She slipped it on and planted her hands on her fists, striking a very Danny pose.

"Yes? No?" She spun around once, her long curls drifting around her shoulders, eyes open and inviting.

"Looks great. Very Zuko." Fern managed to make her voice light, but even to her ears, the words were wooden.

"Sounds like a 'no' to me." Kaitlyn turned to face the old floor-length mirror propped against the wall. "Yeah, you're right. That's a no."

Kaitlyn peeled the jacket off her shoulders and returned it to the rack. She hesitated, hand still on the jacket, then abruptly turned back to Fern. "Look, I know we've never been friends, but I get the feeling that you think I don't like you or something. And I want to say, for the record, that I don't hate you. I feel like it needs to be said. Because there's been something weird between us for years, and I'm not exactly sure why, but I wanted you to know that I'm cool if you are. And . . . I hope you are."

Four possible responses rushed through Fern's mind at once— *I don't hate you either; It's been weird because everything is so easy for you; I never thought you hated me; I'm so glad you don't.*

A few days ago, she'd known exactly how she felt about Kaitlyn, and she'd been able to trust those feelings. Now? She didn't trust anything. Least of all herself. "I am. Cool."

Kaitlyn smiled, eyes narrowing with amusement. "You're usually a much better actor than that."

Fern drew her bottom lip between her teeth and sucked a breath in through her nose. "You're right. Sorry, this is . . . I'm just adjusting. And I don't hate you either."

It felt more like the truth than she'd expected it to. Enough that she managed a smile.

Kaitlyn cocked her head. "Adjusting? To what, exactly?"

To myself, Fern thought wryly.

"To this," Fern said aloud, gesturing to the space between them. "To playing Sandy to your Danny."

Now Kaitlyn's humor fell away. "Because I'm a girl and so are you?"

The question hit Fern square in the gut, the word *girl* lodging there like a foreign object.

It wasn't right.

It had never been right. But for the past five years, that certainty had been taken from her. The only version of Fern Jensen anyone knew was this one: the pretty girl who dreamed of being a star.

But at Kaitlyn's question, another piece fell into place. Another memory snapped through her mind.

Of confessing to her mother that she wanted a binder instead of a training bra.

Of the way her mother's face had twisted into a grimace when she'd said, "You're *eleven*."

Of the way she'd taken Fern's hands in hers and explained, patiently, "That sort of thing isn't for girls like you, honey. It's for confused children with parents who don't know any better." She'd said, "Your body is changing, and that's a good thing. We don't want to punish it for becoming what it's meant to become."

Fern had swallowed hard, nausea swirling in her guts. "But it doesn't feel like me," she'd protested. "I don't think I'm a girl."

Her mother had dropped her hands as though they'd burned her. "If there is one thing I know for absolute certain, it's that you are my baby *girl*. You were born into this beautiful body for a reason. I know that puberty can be scary, but, remember, it is the most natural thing in the world—the feminine is sacred. Just look at your sisters. You are like them."

"I don't think I am." Fern had always been too bold for her own good when she was young. Speaking without thinking. Right up until that moment.

"You are." Her mother's tone had been as sharp as any blade and just as threatening. "All of *my daughters* are my girls."

The message had been clear. Her mother only had daughters. Fern was either one of them—or not. She'd never brought it up again, keeping the most tumultuous parts of herself secret.

And then they had been taken from her.

"N-no," she stammered now, reeling from the memory. "I'm not— I mean, that's not it. I just have a lot going on right now, and I'm— You know what? It's personal."

"Okay, I get it." Kaitlyn raised her hands and backed away. "We're not friends, and we don't have to be. But we do have to fake it for Murph, or she'll be pissed."

Fern drew a deep breath, pulling herself—the pieces she *knew*—together. "Sounds like a challenge," Fern answered. "I'm game if you are."

It was a performance on top of a performance. One for their teacher, and one for the show.

Kaitlyn stuck out her hand, and Fern took it, shaking once. The touch of Kaitlyn's palm on hers was almost too much to bear right now.

"Great, so let's find our touchstones and get the hell out of here," Kaitlyn said, moving farther down the rack, swiftly dismissing each piece.

Fern lingered where she was, breathing in the stale air. Focusing on the vaguely unpleasant scents of laundry detergent and generations of body odor. Anything but the wordless cacophony raging inside her. It was too much. Too much to think about, especially in a moment like this.

Her fingers landed on the jacket Kaitlyn had rejected a moment ago. The leather was fake and flaking in spots, but it was soft, and before Fern knew what she was doing, she'd slipped it from the hanger and over her own shoulders.

It slid on easily, the sleeves hitting her exactly at the wrists and the fit loose around her middle. She zipped it up, savoring the way it felt a little like armor, the way it hovered a few inches from her body, then she turned to face the mirror and caught her breath.

It was perfect. It lay flat over her chest, landing just above her hips, hiding the curves of her torso behind straight lines. Somehow it changed her face, too. Made her less of an ingenue, more solid somehow, like the shape of the jacket highlighted the planes of her face rather than the angles. Or maybe it was just that she saw them more clearly now. Saw them and saw herself.

"It's me," she murmured.

"Did you find your touchstone?" Kaitlyn called from the next row.

Before Fern could form an answer, the lights flickered once and went out, plunging the room into darkness.

"Shit," Kaitlyn hissed.

A prickle of fear shot up Fern's spine. Darkness pressed in close, an almost physical presence. She had never been so aware that they were underground, that between here and the surface were labyrinthine hallways that would be impossible to navigate in the dark.

Fern was reaching for her phone when she felt a whisper of movement by her cheek.

"Kaitlyn?" she asked.

"Yeah?" Her voice echoed from across the room.

Fern froze. Muscles tense. Breath caught.

Because Kaitlyn was too far away to be the thing moving next to her right now.

Fern bit her bottom lip and tried to take a step forward without making another sound. But just then a hand covered her mouth, clasping tight with icy fingers.

She tried to run, but her feet were stuck to the ground by some cold, invisible force.

Fern screamed against the pressure. The sound came out garbled and frayed. She could hear Kaitlyn cry from across the room, "Fern?! What's going on?" But the hand remained pressed against her mouth.

She was stuck, trapped, and her entire body began to tremble.

Come back, a voice moaned against her ear. Low and menacing.

She tried to scream again, to rip at the hand that held her, but at that moment the lights snapped on, and whoever—or whatever—had held her was gone.

Instead, Kaitlyn was by her side, a look of concern on her face.

"Fern?" she asked. "Are you okay? You look like you've seen a ghost."

Fern swallowed hard, her mind flashing at once to that moment in the woods, wondering if indeed she had.

CHAPTER
TEN

Jaq

The church parking lot was nearly full on Monday night when the De Lucas arrived and claimed a spot at the back.

"I'll see you in there," Jaq called, abandoning her parents as her father stopped to wait while her mother applied a shimmery pink lipstick.

"Why didn't you do that before we left the house?" he asked, a very specific blend of humor and judgment in his tone.

"Sorry," her mother murmured. "I ran out of time."

"What were you doing that—"

Jaq shut the door on their conversation. She'd heard it a million times before. Her father picking away at something that really didn't seem like a big deal. Her mother patiently explaining until he let it go and settled into his usual silence. It was a boring routine, and she was hungry.

In the two days since that moment in the woods, Jaq's appetite had been nonexistent. Her thoughts swirled around the black hole of her missing memories, raged against the knowledge that Mallory was dead. Her stomach had felt like a sheet of muscle wrapped tight around a stone. She'd focused on that. Sank her awareness into the heavy pressure in her chest and gut. Because as long as she was consumed by the physical discomfort of her own body, there wasn't room to think about anything else. To *feel* anything else.

Her mind was a constant swirling, churning storm, and she wanted it all to stop. To go back to normal, and the only way she knew to do that was to keep doing normal things. Keep her routine: exercise, school, church, friends, homework, and sometimes church again.

Once a month, Port Promise Baptist hosted a Monday-night potluck where the congregation could "come together in joy and fellowship," as Preach Meach was fond of saying. They were technically optional, but in all the years the De Lucas had attended Port Promise Baptist, Jaq could only remember missing two: once when her Granny De Luca had died and they'd been in Oregon for the service, and then when Grandpa Maggio passed. Usually, it was kind of fun to be in the church with her friends when Preach Meach wasn't going on about the Holy Spirit and its role in her life. It was exactly the kind of normal she needed to ground her.

But as she stepped through the side doors that opened into the community room, her thoughts spun away from her, teasing out a memory of standing in this very spot.

She was thirteen years old, Mal standing a few feet away with a secret smile on her lips. The newness of their friendship a giddy, tremulous feeling, like holding laughter in her hands.

She had followed Mal out of the community room where everyone was eating and into one of the prayer rooms, where a simple wooden cross hung on the wall.

"I hate these things," Mal said, dropping into one of the four chairs. "My parents never actually let me eat any of the food."

"Why?" Jaq had asked, sinking into the seat next to her new friend.

"My mom says processed foods are as evil as the devil himself." Mal grinned and pulled a bag of Skittles out of her pocket. "But rainbows are a symbol of God's love. Wanna get holy with me?"

Jaq laughed, scandalized and delighted. "What are friends for?"

Mal poured out half the candy into Jaq's open hand. "We're more than friends, you know."

The flush in Jaq's cheeks was as sudden as the flutter in her stomach. She'd looked up at Mal, Skittles bleeding sweetly on her tongue, daring to hope that the new feelings stirring inside her were also stirring inside Mal.

"What do you mean 'more than'?"

Mal leaned in, a daring smile on her lips. "What do you think it means?"

Candy still in her mouth. Sugar in her throat. And the desire to kiss Mal too terrifying to comprehend. Jaq had swallowed hard. Their parents were so close. They could be discovered at any second, and if that happened, she honestly didn't know what they would do.

She sat back with a sharp exhale. "We're in church," she'd said, shifting her eyes to the cross looming above.

Following her gaze, Mal narrowed her eyes. She considered the cross without an ounce of respect, as though its presence offended her. "You know," she started after a long minute, "I think I'm probably a lot like Jesus."

"What?" Jaq gasped in surprise. She would never dare compare herself to him.

"Yeah, he was wronged, then killed, and then he came back, and he got revenge on everyone. He made everyone believe they weren't good enough. Even us," Mal said as though it were the most rational thing in the world. "That's exactly what I'd do."

The memory had been lost to Jaq for so long, but standing here, now, it was uncomfortably present. Pointed. Accompanied by the pervasive fear that had been erased for the past five years, when she'd lived every day a little bit terrified of being discovered.

But now that fear was back. A sprawl of insidious mold covering the walls of her heart. Threatening to break them down little by little.

"Jaqueline, it is always such a pleasure to see you. Is that your mother's Texas caviar?" Preacher Meachem was standing in his usual spot by the door, welcoming everyone as they came inside. He was dressed casually tonight, a button-down plaid shirt tucked into dark blue jeans ending in a pair of soft brown loafers. His round face was a distant echo of Susan's, with the addition of smile lines around his mouth and eyes.

Jaq had spent enough time at his house hanging out with Susan that he was almost like an uncle to her, but tonight, she felt uneasy in his presence, as if he could see right through to the truth of her.

"Yes, sir," she answered, lifting the red bowl in her hands as proof. "Is there still room?"

"We can always make room for more." He beamed at her, warm and approving. Then his expression softened, tipping toward worry, and he asked, "How are you, dear?"

Jaq resisted the urge to fidget. She wasn't supposed to lie to her preacher, but what choice did she have?

"I'll take that. Hey, Preach," John said, appearing by her side at the perfect moment. He raised the bowl chivalrously from Jaq's hands. "Mind if I cut in?"

"By all means." Preach Meach's approving smile was back, his concerns erased by the sight of the two of them together. "Don't let an old man get in the way of young love."

Jaq nearly wilted with relief, turning to follow John.

"Toward the front, I assume?" John asked. He smelled like the spice of his favorite aftershave, and with his hair still a little wet from a shower, he looked more boyish than usual.

"Like always," Jaq answered, and she let herself relax just a little. "How was practice?"

John was a three-season athlete, but baseball was his true love. He was the top-ranked high school pitcher in the Puget Sound.

"Pretty good," he said, the evidence in his smile.

They made their way to a long buffet table covered in food. John deposited the bowl exactly where Alice De Luca would have wanted it—between a bowl of Mrs. Knudson's homemade salsa and Mrs. Nichols's cheese dip—and then looped an arm around Jaq's waist and steered her toward a table where Susan and Tommy were already seated.

"Hey." Jaq gave a little wave as John pulled out a chair for her.

"Hey," Susan said, waggling her pastel manicure. Her gaze shifted to a spot over Jaq's shoulder, eyes widening. "They're here. I can't believe they came."

"Who?" Jaq turned in her seat.

Just inside the doors stood Cole Clark's parents, the couple who ran the Deep Cut and gave them all discounts on pizza. The last time Jaq had seen them was on Friday during lunch, and everything had seemed fine. They were never overly effusive, but they were nice enough. The only time Jaq ever saw them out of their aprons and signature red-and-white gingham shirts was here at church. Tonight, they looked smaller than usual, and even from this distance, Jaq could see the hint of red in Mrs. Clark's eyes. And there was no sign of Cole.

Everyone turned to look, pausing their conversations in a way that made it obvious they either knew what had happened or sensed that they soon would. She saw her own parents drawing away as though worried that whatever ill fate had fallen on the Clarks might be contagious, and a small shiver of dread slid down her own spine.

"Mr. and Mrs. Clark, so good to see you both." The warmth in Preacher Meachem's greeting was as much a command as it was genuine. "We are so glad that you came tonight. Please, know that we are all here for you in your time of need."

He swept a welcoming arm around Mrs. Clark's shoulders and drew her into the room while Mr. Clark trailed solemnly behind, a Stetson held in front of his chest like he was attending a funeral.

"What happened?" Jaq asked, swiveling back to the table.

"You didn't hear?" Susan leaned forward, excited to be the one to share the terrible news. "It's Cole."

The stone in Jaq's stomach dropped back into place. She'd known something was wrong with Cole, but she hadn't made an effort to find out what.

"Susan," John warned, gesturing for her to keep her voice down.

"Fine." Susan scooted her chair around so that she was right next to Jaq. Even then, she raised a hand to her mouth when she leaned in to whisper, "He's gay."

A fizzing sound bubbled in Jaq's ears, cold sweat at her temples.

"And he *told* them!" Tommy whispered, not too softly. Gleeful and not afraid to show it. "Came home from school on Friday and decided to come out then and there. No shame, no nothing."

"His parents were totally shocked. Horrified, really," Susan picked up. "I overheard my dad saying that they tried to talk some sense into him, but he was already lost."

"And then what?" Jaq asked, though she had a pretty good idea. She didn't remember seeing him at the party on Saturday or church on Sunday. Both bad signs.

Susan shrugged. "Cole left. Abandoned his parents even though all they wanted was to help him. It's totally selfish."

It wasn't that simple. Jaq knew that for a fact. Cole had always been thoughtful and quiet. The kind of person who didn't speak until he was sure he had something meaningful to say. He'd never once ordered anything but a Hawaiian pizza because he knew himself well enough to know anything else would leave him disappointed. He was the sort of person who wouldn't leave without cause. He hadn't *just* done anything.

"I heard he's been hanging out at Frank's," Tommy volunteered. "So, like, is anyone really surprised? I always had a feeling about him."

"What does Frank's have to do with anything?" Jaq asked, not tracking the shift in conversation. Frank's was the one and only all-night diner in Port Promise and, as far as she knew, not otherwise noteworthy.

"Oh, c'mon. You know," Tommy said, raising his eyebrows suggestively.

"You know why Frank left the army, don't you?" John asked. Then, at Jaq's look of confusion, he answered his own question. "Someone asked, he told."

"Dishonorable discharge, baby!" Tommy said a little too loudly.

"It wasn't, though," John corrected him. "Probably because they were just about to repeal that rule."

"Can you imagine what it's like to be his parents?" Susan asked, drawing their attention back to the Clarks.

Jaq turned, searching not for Cole's parents, but for hers. She found them headed right toward her, expressions under lock and key.

"What a fine-looking table," Mrs. De Luca said, beaming at the group. "Everyone okay over here?"

Jaq's insides had liquified. There were no more bones or muscles to make her move.

"We're all just thinking about Cole and his family," John said with a sympathetic smile.

"It is tragic, a good reminder of just how lucky we are." Mr. De Luca's hand landed on Jaq's shoulder. Solid and heavy. "We've never had to worry about you."

"Never," her mother echoed.

Though they were speaking to Jaq, their eyes were on the Clarks. Maybe people who didn't know them as well as she did wouldn't be able to read anything into their stoic faces, but Jaq could see it all.

Pity.

Relief.

Disgust.

It had been the same after Mallory's disappearance, except Jaq hadn't cared as much—hadn't remembered that she should. It wasn't long before the Hammonds moved away and Jaq stopped thinking about Mal altogether.

"It must be terrible for them," John said, sounding genuine. "I wish there was something we could do."

"Like what?" Susan asked.

"The only thing we can do is be here if and when he's ready to return," Jaq's mom said. "Now, eat. All of you."

Her father gave her shoulder one last squeeze, and her mother flashed her an approving smile as they turned to leave.

Jaq didn't know what to do. The muscles in her throat were pulled taut, constricting painfully until she wasn't sure she could draw a single breath. Her fingers curled into fists, fingernails spearing her palms.

"Sorry, I—" She stood abruptly, unable to finish her sentence, and left the room.

She had no idea where she was going. Just out. Away. Not there.

She pushed through a set of doors, not really seeing them, and found herself in the reception area. On instinct, she turned right, into a small room, and shut the door behind her.

It was too much. She was sure that if she opened her mouth, she would tell her secret, and she would be the one everyone was talking about. Her existence the one everyone was mourning. Her parents the ones everyone pitied.

She needed to breathe. But she couldn't. Not with the walls closing in around her. Not with her throat so tight.

Jaq squeezed her eyes shut. Pressed one hand flat against her chest, over her heart where the mold was seeping and creeping, chewing lightly through walls of muscle. Forcing her heart to beat too fast. Blood rushed and raged, rising like the tide, threatening to burst through her skin.

They were going to find out.

Her parents, her friends, her entire church was going to discover the truth about her, and they were going to push her away. She was incompatible with the teachings of the church. Her job was to bear fruit for the glory of God, but she was the blemish on its skin, the speck of decay that would destroy the entire crop.

She tried to count her breaths. In, one-two-three-four. Out, five-six-seven—

The walls pressed closer, tightening like her veins. Forcing her into a box that would be neatly labeled and stored on the shelf. Hardly worth saving. Hardly worth anything at all. Tainted and corrupted and wrongwrong*wrong*.

She sucked in a breath, cold air knifing down to her stomach, and coughed. Fell to her knees in the center of the room. When she looked up, she found a cross. The same one she'd sat beneath with Mallory over five years ago.

It couldn't be a coincidence.

Not here. Here it was a sign. A message from God that he was still here for her. This was the symbol that had brought her such comfort for so many years. Promising unconditional love and redemption for trespasses.

Except it *was* conditional. She'd just seen it in the community room. In the eyes of her parents. She'd heard it in the voices of her friends. The conditions may not exist in heaven, but here they were violent and biting. They were pitying and gleeful and they would toss her out and leave her to the wolves.

"Please," she said, her voice a whimper. But she didn't know what she was asking for. Help or forgiveness? A way out or a way back in?

Her eyes caught on a speck of cloudy gray nestled at the joint of the cross. A pinprick of a blemish on the otherwise-seamless wood. Before her eyes, it began to spread, spidering out in all directions. Jaq stood and stepped cautiously forward, blinking hard to clear her vision, but it continued. Creeping across, up, and down, covering every inch of wood in lacework mold. When she inhaled, earthy rot stuck in the back of her throat.

Jaq took another mincing step forward, and another, until she was close enough to reach out and touch the cross. She pressed shaking fingers to the center of the wood, and when she pulled them away, they were smeared in red.

She sucked in a breath, taking a step back as the red stain began to spread, liquid and viscous as blood, staining the pale mold crimson.

Jaq stared in horror as the beams of the cross expanded. Stretching and contracting.

Ba-dump.

The sound reverberated through the small room. *Ba-dump.* Pumping like a heart. *Ba-dump.* Growing louder as blood splashed against the carpet at Jaq's feet, spattering her taupe ballet flats.

Jaq reached for the cross at her neck. Mind locked in a state of panic even as she told herself this wasn't real, couldn't be real.

Come back, a voice rumbled, vibrating in the floor beneath her feet.

Jaq squeezed her eyes shut. Willing it all to just go away.

A hand on her shoulder spurred a half-realized scream from her throat. She spun too fast, feet twisting beneath her and sending her to the floor in a tangled heap, too tangled to get away from whoever had touched her.

John.

Eyes wide with alarm, hands raised in surrender. "Hey, it's me. Just me."

She spun around, looking for the beating cross, the blood and mold and rot, but there was nothing wrong with the cross. Nothing at all.

"John," she gasped. Voice stilted.

John knelt beside her in a soothing puff of spicy aftershave. He took her hand and stroked his thumb over the ridge of her knuckles, as he always did when she fell into spirals like this. He didn't speak, but he inhaled so she could hear it and match her breathing to his.

She didn't know how long it took—it felt like hours—but eventually Jaq threaded her fingers through his and squeezed.

"You're okay," John assured her, gently helping her to her feet. "I've got you."

"Yeah," Jaq answered, doing her best to brighten her voice.

John watched her for a second before he nodded. "Then let's go. Preach said the blessing, and I made you a plate before all the good stuff was gone."

"Cheesy potatoes and all?" Jaq asked, squeezing his hand, grateful.

"I even got you a scoop of that weird pink stuff you like." John tugged her toward the door.

Jaq smiled weakly as she followed him. Before she left, she took one last look at the cross, searching for any evidence of the mold and blood that had marred its surface. But there was none.

The only rot here was inside of her.

CHAPTER ELEVEN

Fern

Fern started texting Jaq at 6:37 p.m.

> Can you talk?
> I need to talk.
> I just remembered you sometimes had that church thing Monday nights. Does that still happen? Let me know when you get this.
> Please.

It was still strange to be texting someone she hadn't spoken to in five years, but Jaq was the only person Fern could imagine talking to right now. A ghost had strangled her in the middle of the costume basement, and that wasn't something she could say to just anyone.

It was after nine when Jaq finally answered: **Can you come get me? Park at the end of the street.**

The De Lucas were just as strict as they'd always been, so even though nine p.m. wasn't considered late for most eighteen-year-olds Fern knew, Jaq wasn't allowed out on a school night. Following Jaq's instructions, Fern parked down the street and waited while Jaq snuck through her bedroom window, then shimmied down the maple tree. She did it so quickly that Fern suspected this was an established routine. That, at least, felt familiar. Like the Jaq she'd known was still in there. Beneath the good Christian veneer and muted color palette was the girl who preferred vivid jewel tones and whose fingers were always smeared with chalky pastels.

Then again, it was weird to feel like she knew Jaq at all. There were multiple Ferns living in her head: The one who'd known Jaq as a best friend. The one who didn't know her at all. And the one who felt a surreal kind of connection to her now.

"Thanks for picking me up," Jaq said, slightly out of breath from jogging down the street. She closed the door gently behind her and reached for her seat belt. "Where are we going?"

"I don't know," Fern admitted, pulling away from the curb. "Somewhere we can talk. In private. But the Dormouse just closed. Any ideas?"

Jaq thought for a moment. "What about Whisper Falls?"

She turned to Fern, their eyes locking. It was too dark to climb to the top and technically illegal after sundown, but they could park at the bottom and sit by the water. The chances of anyone else being there this late on a Monday were slim.

Without a word, Fern turned the car around and drove them there.

As expected, the parking lot was empty when they arrived. Fern picked a spot at the far end, and they walked in silence down the dark path, the falls roaring in the near distance. Fern hadn't been here in years, and it felt strange to return but also right to be doing so with Jaq.

The last time she'd come to the falls, it had been the three of them. Standing at the top and shouting their secrets into the vortex of water and sound. When things were still good and their friendship made Fern feel safe. Bold, even.

"Oh, wow," Jaq breathed as the path opened wide and the falls appeared before them. "I forgot how pretty it was."

The falls vaulted over the cliff above and streamed with moonlight into the glittering pool below. A puff of spray churned at the base, covering the rocks in dew like starlight that glimmered and winked.

They continued around the pool until they came to a picnic table and sat next to each other facing the water. Fern slouched back against the table while Jaq tucked one leg up to her chest, curling in on herself.

"I haven't been back either. I kind of keep my distance from the woods," Fern said.

The forest tucked in close around the falls, reaching with shadowy fingers toward the place where they sat. They were just out of reach, but close enough to stir a memory in Fern. A wall of dark trees driving into the night sky. She remembered passing between them, taking that first step into the woods and then . . . nothing. When Jaq shuddered, she wondered if she was having the same memory.

"Me too." Jaq reached for the small golden cross at her throat. She and Mal had been raised in the same church, and maybe because of that they were good at believing in things they couldn't see. Fern had always needed more than that.

"Did anything weird happen to you today?" she asked.

Jaq didn't speak, but the answer was written clearly in the widening of her eyes.

"Oh, good." Fern breathed out a sigh of relief.

"Good?" Jaq's voice was sharp. "Why is that good?"

"Because it means I'm not alone."

A mix of relief and trepidation moved across Jaq's face. "I—yeah," she stammered. "Not alone."

The way she said it made Fern feel a little more alone than she had a minute ago, and she realized that she'd been making assumptions about Jaq's feelings. That just because she felt like a missing piece had been returned to her didn't mean Jaq felt the same way.

"Do you want to know what happened to me?" Fern asked.

Jaq pursed her lips and nodded, still clutching the cross. "If you don't mind."

Fern dove into the story before she could stop herself. She told it quickly, not wanting to linger too long on any single moment. The memory of those icy fingers was still too close for comfort.

"And you're sure it wasn't Kaitlyn?" Jaq asked when she'd come to the end.

"Positive. She was halfway across the room when the lights came on. There's no way it was her."

Jaq gave a thoughtful nod and turned her eyes to the water, absently dragging the cross charm back and forth on her chain.

"What happened to you?" Fern asked, trying to mask the irritation in her voice with concern. "You said something happened to you today."

"I—I don't really want to talk about it," she said after a long minute.

"But you think it's connected, right?" Fern pressed.

"To what?"

"To . . . this!" Fern gestured at the air between them, disbelief making her louder than she'd intended to be. "To whatever happened to us on Friday night. Whatever it was, it's obviously still happening, and I want to know why."

The muscles in Jaq's jaw flinched once, and Fern saw the first shimmer of tears building in her eyes. "But I don't."

Fern stared at her in shock. "Why?"

Jaq took a shuddering breath, hugging her knee against her chest with one arm. For a second, Fern thought she wasn't going to answer. "Because maybe it will go back to the way things were," she said.

"The way things were," Fern repeated. "You mean, you want to forget? Again?"

"I think it would be better," Jaq answered, voice tight and small. Maybe even a little sad. "Safer."

That word. It sat so firmly between them that Fern couldn't argue. She remembered what Jaq's parents were like. What Mallory's parents had been like. *Safe* hadn't existed for them the way it did for other people. It was something they'd had to create together, something they found in each other and in the woods.

That sense of safety was one more piece of the past that had been taken from them. Before, Fern had never felt the odd fear she did now whenever she was near the woods. In fact, she and Jaq and Mal had spent every minute they could inside the woods all because they believed that the Patron would keep them safe.

Mal had been the instigator, because she always was, but the two of them had been more than willing to follow. Another memory clicked into place, a scene unfolding in Fern's mind.

"If the Patron grants you a wish, what will you wish for?"

Mal had asked it one day as they'd walked through the woods. She turned her eyes on Jaq, whose cheeks had flushed as crimson as the darkest jewel in her necklace.

Fern was starting to sense the growing attraction between her two friends. Jaq had been terrible at hiding it, but even Mallory had her tells. The way she had always looked to Jaq first when she had a question, or the way she always put herself in the middle when the three of them were together. As though she didn't want anyone else to be close to Jaq.

It hadn't bothered Fern, but by then it was starting to make her anxious that soon there wouldn't be room in their friendship for three.

"Oh, um, I don't know," Jaq had stammered.

"C'mon," Mal teased. "Isn't there someplace you'd like to be? Someone you'd like to kill? Or kiss?"

"Mallory!" Jaq sputtered. "Oh my god, okay. I guess I would wish for enough money that I never had to rely on my parents for anything again."

"Riches. That's a solid and very traditional wish," Mal said, nodding sagely. "What about you, Fern?"

Fern had known it was coming, but it wasn't an easy question, and she hadn't had a ready answer. There were a lot of things she would have changed if she could, but not about herself.

"You know," Fern started, intending to tell Mallory that the Patron wasn't real. He wasn't going to grant them any wishes. But she'd stopped herself. Arrested by the vulnerable desperation she'd seen in Mal's eyes in that moment. Mal had needed it. She had needed to believe that someone out there—even a fake someone— wanted to help her when no other adult in her life did. And Fern hadn't been able to be the one to take that away. She'd cleared her throat and said, "I would wish for my mom to accept me the way I am."

"You would change her?" Mal asked. "Against her will? That's dark."

"No! That's not what I meant!" Fern protested.

But Mal had flashed that wicked grin of hers and said, "I would."

"Would what?" Fern asked.

"I would change my parents if I could. But I don't want their love. I used to. Now I just want them to feel the way they've made me feel." Mal's expression went dark, her voice so low that Fern had shivered when she'd said, "If the Patron gave me one wish, I would wish for the power to hurt all the people who ever hurt me."

Now Fern bit down on her bottom lip. Jaq was right—they'd been safer before their memories had been returned. But had they really been themselves? Was it better to be a fraction of their true selves? A version that fit neatly into the part of the world they'd been born into? Fern didn't think so. Even knowing that it would upset her mother, she knew this was better.

What she didn't understand was why Jaq didn't feel the same way.

"I don't think it's going to go back to the way it was," Fern said, trying to be gentle.

Jaq sniffled and pressed the heels of her hands into her eyes for a minute. "Do you think that was Mallory today? The hands that grabbed you."

"She told us herself that she would get revenge on the people who hurt her." Fern thought for a minute, then shrugged. "I don't know what else it could be. Do you?"

"No," Jaq said, but she sounded less sure than Fern.

Fern desperately wanted to know what it was Jaq had seen today. She wanted to lay their experiences side by side and find the similarities. The differences. But Jaq was clamming up. Shutting down. Fern wasn't going to get anything out of her by making demands. A distant part of Fern's mind reminded her that Jaq had always been less sure of herself.

If Fern was good at faking confidence, and Mal had been a simmering pot of rage, then Jaq was the timid one. She'd always required a lighter touch.

"I feel like I've been split in two," Fern said, changing tactics. "I know who I was before Friday and who I was before we forgot everything, but who I am now feels . . . amorphous. Not exactly a blend of the two."

Fern paused, giving Jaq room to enter the conversation. When she didn't, Fern continued.

"I can't tell if the things I feel are real or if they're left over from when I forgot." An image of Kaitlyn appeared in her mind, bringing with it a conflicted maelstrom of emotion that was impossible to untangle. There was jealousy, sure, but Fern could no longer tell where it came from. Was it because Kaitlyn had always had an easier time of being gay? Because they'd been in competition for so many years? Because she had the role Fern wanted now?

"I don't want to dismiss who I've been for the past five years, but I feel like . . . like—"

"Something was taken from us," Jaq finished.

"And I don't want to give it back, but I also want to know why. And I think maybe the only place we'll find any answers is in the woods. Maybe if we went back—"

"No." Jaq's voice was a hammer.

She didn't elaborate, and a soft silence settled between them, buoyed on the whooshing of the falls and the occasional call of an owl from somewhere deep inside the woods.

"What I saw scared me," Jaq said after a long while. "I think you're right. It must have been Mal. I may not remember what happened that night in the woods, but I know whatever it was, it was my—our—fault. We made a mistake when we went into the woods last week. Mal's been waiting for us. And the night of Karima's party, she got to us, and I don't think she's done."

"What are you saying?" Fern asked, afraid she already knew the answer.

"I'm saying that Mal died that night, Fern. We may not remember, but we both know it's true. It's probably our fault, and she's pissed and wants us to suffer." Jaq turned to her, eyes filled with dreadful certainty. "If we go into the woods, she'll kill us."

CHAPTER
TWELVE

Mallory
THEN

"I'm going to kill him," Mal said, leading the others into the woods at a brisk pace.

"Who?" Jaq asked, hurrying close behind.

"That fucker Tommy Webber," Mal spat, taking pleasure in the way it felt to say a cuss word like *fuck* out loud. "Do you know what he did? After I turned him down for the dance the third time?"

It was the Monday before seventh-grade prom, and the mood at school was irritatingly frothy. People were so excited, it almost felt like the days before winter break. There had been several dramatic promposals, including one from Kaitlyn Birch to Karima Jones in the middle of lunch, and people weren't shy about asking anyone who they were going with. It seemed like everyone in the entire school was looking forward to the dance. Except for the three of them.

It was hard to be excited when they couldn't ask who they wanted to ask or wear what they wanted to wear.

"He asked my parents!" Mal slapped at a low-hanging branch as she charged ahead of the other two.

"To the dance?" Fern asked, calling from her position at the rear.

"For permission to take me! He told them that he'd asked me but that he wanted their permission, too. And they gave it!" Mal had been seething all day. Quiet and tight-lipped, even when Jaq had asked her what was wrong. She was too mad to explain anything at school, so she'd waited until after, when she could explode more safely in the woods.

"I can't believe he lied like that," Jaq said. "In church!"

"Oh, I can. Boys get away with stuff like that all the time. My parents don't even consider it lying. I tell my mom that he's bullying me. She says he's just being persistent. I tell her that I think he's gross. She says I'm being bullheaded. I tell her I don't want to go to the dance at all. She asks me what color dress I want!" Mal gave a vicious growl of a scream. "Sometimes, I want to tell them that I like girls and only girls. Just to see what would happen."

"Me too," Fern echoed. "Except, I'm pretty sure my mom would put me in the bad kind of therapy. I mean, she put Ivy in therapy because she was failing math."

"My parents would disown me," Jaq added sadly.

"Mine would kill me. One way or another," Mallory said with finality. "I wish we had somewhere safe to go."

"One day we will," Fern said. "We just have to survive until then."

"I hate surviving," Mal muttered as they came around a bend in the trail and abruptly stopped.

On one side of the path stood a large black stone. Its surface was shiny and scalloped all over, with edges sharp enough to cut.

"What is this?" Mallory asked, momentarily distracted.

"Basalt," Jaq answered. "It's volcanic rock. You find it around here sometimes. But that is huge."

"I don't remember passing it before," Mallory said, turning to look back down the trail. "Did we take a wrong turn?"

"No." Jaq pointed ahead to where a splash of blue paint marked a tree trunk several yards ahead. "We're still on the Whisper Falls trail."

"Then where—"

"Is this a new path?" Fern asked as she stepped past the stone to where a narrow trail slipped between the trees.

The thing was, they knew it wasn't. They knew that to carve a trail like that took time, and cutting down trees, even small ones, took equipment. There would be sawdust and fresh stumps poking out of the foliage like little mushrooms. The air would smell like resin.

But this path was worn smooth, as though it had been created years ago and walked by hundreds of feet. This path was the opposite of new. It was very, very old.

And it should not have been there.

Even knowing all of that, the girls paused for only a moment to consider. Then, without a word spoken between them, they stepped onto the trail and followed it past the black rock.

They walked in silence, each aware that they were doing something they shouldn't, yet somehow convinced that the trail had appeared for them.

They walked and walked, eventually climbing a steep incline that made them sweaty and breathless from the effort. At what appeared to be the top, the land leveled out in a wide clearing. On one side, the mountains continued their steep climb; on the other, the land fell away sharply, the cliffs sheer and treacherous, and in the center, facing the open air above the cliffs, stood the bones of an old house.

The wooden walls stretched tall despite being scarred by holes and blackened by some long-ago fire. It looked almost castle-like, with its collection of turrets tucked beneath pointed roofs. The windows were long and narrow, the glass panes mostly broken or missing altogether. And at the top of a set of stone steps, marbled with lichen and moss, stood a heavy wooden door. It was the only part of the house that wasn't marred by decay or rot.

"Isn't this a national park or something? I didn't know people were allowed to build out here," Fern said softly, as though afraid of being overheard.

"I don't think they are," Jaq said. "At least, not anymore."

"It's an endowment," Mallory added. "Which means that these woods used to be privately owned, so this could have been built by whoever owned it back then, but at some point it was gifted to the town. That's why the trails are maintained and why they lead to the school and the park and the falls."

A soft wind sifted through the trees, and even though it wasn't cold, all three of the girls shivered. They stared up at the house, unnerved by its presence and even more by how they'd found it.

"Do you think . . ." Mallory started, then paused, her eyes settling on a point high on the house before turning to her friends. "Do you think we should go inside?"

The question hung between them, unanswered, for a long minute as each of them wrestled with a sudden discomfort.

Then, before any of them could say another word, they heard a long, slow creak. Mallory could have sworn she heard a whisper on the wind: *Come in, come in.*

And when they turned to look at the house once more, the door was open.

CHAPTER
THIRTEEN

Jaq

Three days later, Jaq was at the baseball field alone because Susan had to go into Seattle with her family for what she'd described as "obligatory religious networking." Usually, she was glad to have Sooz with her for the games, but right now, it was best that she was alone. She was having a hard enough time keeping herself together in school when there were dozens of distractions. She didn't think she could manage prolonged one-on-one time.

Everywhere she turned there was a new memory to uncover, each one blossoming like a bruise on her skin. Fern might be glad that their missing past had returned, but Jaq was drowning in it. In the knowledge that Mallory was gone.

She'd endured three nights of nightmares. They were all the same. Shattered scenes that played in her mind out of order. Half memories that she couldn't make any sense of. Slashes of dark trees, of broken walls, of blood that arced across her vision and a scream that speared her heart.

And Mallory's face. Pale and angry. Her hard eyes shimmering with tears. All her fury directed at Jaq.

"Kiss for luck?" John leaned over the chain-link fence separating the baseball field from the bleachers. He always looked so sharp in his uniform, the dark blue and gold of their school colors setting off his golden curls and moss-green eyes. With the sun setting behind him, he was gilded in copper and bronze.

"When have you ever needed luck?" Jaq asked, forcing her full attention onto John. She leaned in for a kiss, pressing her lips briefly to his, trying to ignore the part of her that felt like she was kissing her cousin.

"True, I don't need luck," John said, grinning as he locked his arms around her ribs and pulled her as close as she could get with the fence between them. "But I do need kisses. Do you have any more to spare? I feel like my kiss tank is running low."

"Your 'kiss tank'?" Jaq couldn't help but smile at this.

"It's like a gas tank, but way more important."

"What does it do, exactly?" Jaq asked.

"What doesn't it do, that's the question you should be asking." John's arms tightened around her. "It heightens cognitive function, increases reflexes, improves physical stamina. I think one study even linked it to something about being a potential cure for cancer."

"I'm skeptical," Jaq said, raising an eyebrow. This part—talking and teasing with John—felt easy. Their patterns were well-worn and friendly, the way things should be. "What sort of controls were present in this study? And who were the participants?"

"Men, of course," John answered. "Don't they always start the important stuff with men?"

Jaq snorted.

"Nichols! Line up!" the coach shouted.

"See you after?" John asked. "Pizza?"

Jaq shrugged. "Maybe. If you don't perish from a low kiss tank."

"You'd never let that happen," he said, voice gentle and sincere.

Before last week, hearing him say something like that would have sent a small thrill down her spine, an easy warmth coiling in her belly. Nothing overwhelming, but familiar. The promise of so many good days to come.

Today, it felt off. Like he was offering his trust to a different Jaq. This Jaq wasn't worthy of it. And this Jaq didn't want to kiss him back.

She wanted to be the old Jaq again, the one John deserved and who deserved John.

Forcing a smile, Jaq turned to the bleachers and spotted two kids hiding beneath them. They peered out between the rows of benches, their eyes alight with mischief.

And just like that, there was another memory of Mallory. Of the time they'd stolen away beneath these same bleachers during a Little League game neither of them cared about.

"I hate baseball," Mallory had said, offering Jaq Starbursts in rapid succession.

"Is there anything you like?" Jaq asked. "Don't say candy."

Mallory had glared at that. "Fine. While I think candy should have been an acceptable answer, I guess . . . gray whales."

"Whales? Why?"

"Not 'whales' generally. Although lots of them are very cool. But gray whales are special for three reasons." Mallory held up a finger. "They are friendly across species, so they are genuine." She paused and lifted a second finger. "They suck sludge off the bottom of the ocean to feed, so they are shameless. And"—she raised a third finger—"they're gay."

Jaq had jumped at the word, turning around to see if anyone was near enough to hear them. "I don't think that's possible," she'd said.

"It's more than possible. It's true," Mal answered. "Gray whales are known to travel in same-sex groups of two or three. They even swim fin in fin like they're holding hands. It's romantic and awesome, and one day, I want to see one for myself."

Mal reached out to offer another Starburst, and this time Jaq grabbed too quickly, her fingers tangling with Mallory's. She stopped, startled by the touch, by the way it sent a bolt of something delicious into her stomach. And when she raised her eyes, she found all the humor had vanished from Mal's expression.

She watched Jaq like she knew what Jaq was feeling.

Like she was feeling it, too.

The memory surfaced with all the same anxiety and wonder Jaq had felt when it happened, fresh as if she were still a thirteen-year-old kid hiding beneath the bleachers.

Now the crowd cheered as the team took the field, and Jaq found a spot just in time to see John taking the mound, his golden curls shining beneath the stadium lights. She watched until the game was underway, then she pulled out her phone.

She had a series of tabs open in her web browser. The first three were archived articles from the Port Promise Ledger about Mallory Hammond's disappearance. They covered a span of about six months and after that, the news had dropped it. Mallory's family had told the police that she'd run away, and it turned out that when even the parents didn't seem to care about the whereabouts of their daughter, no one else did either. Not that looking for her any longer would have helped. Jaq wasn't sure of much, but she was sure Mal was dead.

Next, she'd done a useless search into the paranormal. She'd known it was going to be a waste of time, but she tried it anyway.

She got as far as "are ghosts" when Google offered a series of popular searches:

   . . . *undead*

   . . . *real*

   . . . *evil*

Jaq closed the tab. She knew they were real. What she didn't know was why Mallory would want to hurt them. All her memories were tangled up and sticky. Bound together with the ever-present desire to touch Mallory and be touched by her. To kiss her again. With the bottomless sorrow of knowing she never would.

With the agonizing confusion of wanting to forget all over again.

She had thought that John was her first, true love. But thinking of him, being with him had never lit her up like these memories of Mal. And that wasn't fair. Not to him. Not to her. She wished she could shove these new memories back in a drawer. Beneath her bed with all the pastels she kept hidden there. The brightest, truest parts of herself were too much to be let out.

But thinking of Mal made her heart beat faster, made her ache for having lost her, and made her wonder how things could have gone so terribly wrong in the space of those few hours she couldn't remember. So wrong that Mallory's ghost was still here. Still angry and hateful and ready to hurt Jaq.

The crowd surged again, celebrating something Jaq had missed, and she looked up to see one team jog off the field while the others climbed out of the dugout. Her vision blurred over the colors. Blue smearing into green into an endless black that shifted like trees in the wind. The shrill sound of a whistle fracturing into jagged screams.

The sharp smell of blood.

The sound of Mal's voice crying out for help.

The murmurings of the crowd softening into a voice that whispered, *Hushhh*.

"Hey, Jaq."

Jaq's phone clattered to the bleachers. She looked up as Devyn took a seat on the bench at her feet. In one fluid movement, she dipped down to retrieve Jaq's phone and handed it back to her. Then she stretched her long body across the space between them and planted one elbow on the bench, inches from Jaq's thigh.

"Good game?" she asked, peering up at Jaq through gently curled lashes.

The way Jaq's entire body paused at the sight of her. A moment of perfect stillness, followed by a buzzing that started in her head and dripped slowly, languidly down to her stomach. She didn't know what to do with that feeling. But she liked it.

Devyn was waiting for her to answer a question Jaq couldn't remember hearing.

"I—sorry, what?"

Devyn's lips tipped into a smile. "I said, 'Good game?'"

"Oh, um, yeah, I think so," Jaq answered, searching for the scoreboard. "We're winning."

"Mm-hmm," Devyn said, tilting her head so that the light sank into her pale brown eyes, revealing those endless subtle rings. "You looked like you were reading something upsetting."

"A little," Jaq admitted, surprising herself with the truth. Or, at least as much of the truth as she was willing to admit.

"Wanna talk about it?" Devyn was watching her intently. "Alternately, do you want to get out of here?"

Jaq looked at the faces surrounding them, searching for anyone who might notice her leaving with someone who wasn't John. Not sure she cared what anyone except John thought.

The crowd was on its feet again. This time Jaq stood with them. "Yes," she said, almost urgently. "But I don't have a car."

Devyn held up a key. Then, without another word, she caught Jaq's hand in hers and guided her down the bleachers, past the concession stands, and through the side gates into the parking lot.

"Wait. *This* is yours?" Jaq didn't know what kind of car she'd been expecting, but she'd been expecting a car. Not a motorcycle, its sleek body a shimmering ruby red with black leather seats and accents. This was a death trap. A safety hazard. To herself and others.

And yet, it was so enticing.

She felt an indecipherable swirl of wants inside her, belonging to two separate Jaqs, just as Fern had described. One that wanted to return to the game and cheer for her boyfriend, and one that wanted this and so much more. And she didn't know which was most real. Which was the one that *deserved* to be real.

"Is that a problem?" Devyn asked, as she released one helmet and then another from the back of the bike.

The Jaq from last week would say yes. She'd turn down the ride and go back to the game. But the Jaq from this week was rattled. Unpredictable, even to herself.

And desperate to get out of here.

"Not a problem," she said, pulling out her phone and sending a text to John saying she'd gone home early and would meet him for pizza after the game. Then she accepted the helmet, fastened the chin strap in place, and swung one leg over the massive bike and balanced there.

Devyn considered her for a second, eyes crinkling with some-thing like amusement, then she nodded, pulled her own helmet on, and climbed on in front of Jaq. "Hold on," she said over one shoulder.

"Am I going to fall off?" Jaq asked, alarmed.

"I won't let you," Devyn promised. "But hold on." With that, she stepped down hard.

The engine roared to life, rumbling between Jaq's legs like a tamed beast. Then they were moving, slowly, as Devyn meandered between rows of parked cars. Jaq allowed her hands to rest lightly against Devyn's waist, maintaining some distance between them, but the second they pulled out of the parking lot, Devyn hit the gas, and Jaq's careful distance collapsed.

She slid forward until her chest was pressed against Devyn's back and her fingers fisted tight in the soft leather jacket.

Jaq felt like the wind had been knocked from her lungs as they shot forward with an exhilarating burst of speed. They zipped past a yellow light and careened up the steep incline of the foothills.

The wind was a constant crush against her body, the darkness an endless strip of road, the glitter of streetlights drawing them forward.

Devyn sped up, shooting past the turnoff for Jaq's house and diving down the other side of that first rise. This was where civ-ilization ended and the edges of the national park began. Where houses vanished and the roads grew narrow and winding.

Devyn accelerated again, leaning down low as they hugged the sharp turns. Jaq's entire body felt electric and alive, curling against Devyn and the wind.

"Faster!" she cried into Devyn's ear.

They sped up, the road rising and falling beneath them at tantalizing speeds. Jaq held on even though part of her wanted to let go. Just to see if it would feel more like flying or falling.

Eventually, Devyn turned them back toward town, the lights of downtown winking against the dark water beyond. She steered them into the parking lot by the docks, nearly empty this late in the evening, and they parked facing the water.

"That was amazing," Jaq said, still perched on the back of the motorcycle, helmet clutched to her lap. "My whole body is vibrating."

"You look better." Devyn had swung one leg over the bike and turned to face Jaq.

"Did I look that bad before?"

"Not bad." Devyn tipped her head to one side, appraising. Jaq's cheeks flushed warmly at the attention. "Just . . . unhappy. Like you needed to be somewhere else for a minute so you could process whatever that was." Devyn waved one hand in a circle to emphasize the point, as if "that" were too amorphous to pin down. Which it was.

"Are you going to be a psychiatrist like your dad?" Jaq asked.

"Absolutely not," Devyn answered with an amused laugh. "I'm not sure what I want to do, but becoming my father is definitely not it. What about you?"

"I've always wanted to be an artist," Jaq answered, then stopped abruptly. That was wrong. That wasn't what she wanted at all. She knew what she wanted: Baylor, John, a degree that would help her get a decent job back here in Port Promise.

"Really?" Devyn sounded surprised, though not as surprised as Jaq felt. "Do you have a portfolio? Anything you'd be willing to share?"

"No." Jaq's answer was sharp, and she saw the way it set Devyn back. "I'm sorry. I didn't mean to snap."

"It's okay," Devyn answered with a little shrug. "I didn't mean to pry."

Jaq shifted her gaze away, searching for a new topic, something that wasn't about her, when her eyes landed on the bike. "I can't believe your parents let you drive a motorcycle. Mine would never."

"Believe me, it was not easy. I started campaigning early, though. I've known I wanted to drive a bike since I was little. My aunt had one, and I loved the way it looked. Like she was riding a dragon or something."

"That's kind of how it feels." Jaq could still feel the echo of a vibration in her thighs. Warm and alive.

"I'm glad you liked it." Devyn's voice was low and soft, a bit like the purr of an engine itself, drawing Jaq closer. "I had a feeling you might."

For a second, Jaq felt as though the world had dropped away beneath her feet, her stomach tightening with the thrill. There was something almost magnetic about Devyn. Being with her was like standing at the edge of a tall cliff. Wind whipping at her cheeks. The entire world unspooling before her feet.

Jaq wanted to leap into the sky.

"They are dangerous, though," Devyn continued, and it took Jaq a second to realize she was still talking about bikes. "My parents found every statistic you can imagine to make that aggressively, viscerally clear. So, it took a lot of convincing, plus a motorcycle training course on my own dime." She leaned back, grinning at some private joke. "But when it comes right down to it, who doesn't love a dyke on a bike?"

Jaq's face reacted before she could stop it. The shock making her mouth fall open, the discomfort widening her eyes, the imme-

118

diate instinct to distance herself from that word in the way her body drew away.

"What?" Devyn asked, her own smile transforming into one of bemused disappointment. "Is it the word itself or me?"

"I—I just wasn't expecting—I mean, I don't—" Jaq stammered, a riot of emotions erupting inside of her.

She knew this feeling. She hadn't felt it in five years, but it was surfacing now, breaking through sedimentary layers, seeking the surface, and there was nothing she could do to stop it.

Tears sprang to her eyes as she realized that even without meaning to, she'd created room for this previous version of herself. In spite of wanting to go back to the way things were, she might not be able to because, Lord, Devyn was beautiful and there was no denying that Jaq wanted nothing more than to slip her arms around her waist again. To rest her cheek against Devyn's shoulder as they flew through the darkening streets of Port Promise.

But she couldn't.

She had been down that road before. She knew where it ended.

"I'm sorry," she said, gasping, wrapping her arms around her stomach and squeezing, doing her best to keep that slippery panic contained. She was too close to the edge. Any closer and she might tumble over. And John wasn't here to catch her. "I should go. Home, I mean. Would you mind?"

"Sure." There was only kindness in Devyn's voice, so much that Jaq had to bite back the full force of her tears.

Devyn turned the key and waited for Jaq to get her helmet in place before she revved the engine. This time, Jaq made sure to keep a measurable distance between their bodies as they moved through town at a more moderate pace. The drive was soothing, and in spite of everything, Jaq found that she could breathe again. Every breath was full and deep, and the panic that had threatened to overtake her was quiet.

When Jaq's street appeared, she asked Devyn to pull over. Well away from any curious eyes that might be searching for her.

"Thank you," she said, guilt and something even worse worming its way through her gut as she avoided looking directly into Devyn's eyes.

As she swung her leg over the bike, her ankle caught on the seat, throwing her off-balance. Just as she was sure she would careen face-first into the street, an arm encircled her waist, catching her in a solid grip.

Straightening, Jaq found herself in Devyn's arms, their bodies pressed flush, their noses only an inch apart.

"Got you," Devyn said, eyes darting down to Jaq's mouth.

Jaq swallowed hard, at war with herself. Demanding that her feet take her away and at the same time not sure her legs would support the movement.

"I'm fine," she managed, stepping back so suddenly that her heel caught on the curb, and she nearly toppled again and would have if not for Devyn's quick reflexes.

This time, though, Devyn caught her hands, steadying her with a devastatingly lopsided grin. "Got you again," she said.

"Yeah." Jaq's cheeks were flushed beyond reason when she finally excavated herself from Devyn's grip. She couldn't think of anything else to say, so she blurted, "Good night," before hurrying down the street.

She was halfway home before she realized that she was smiling.

CHAPTER
FOURTEEN

Fern

By the time the weekend rolled around, Fern had almost relaxed. No ghosts had tried to strangle her since Monday, and she was starting to entertain the idea that what she was experiencing wasn't supernatural at all, but a really intense trauma response.

That it was a really intense, *shared* trauma response was where it got weird, but things seemed to be improving, and she had more immediate concerns. Like the show and her feelings for Kaitlyn and the fact that she was currently standing at the top of Whisper Falls, preparing to jump over the edge with a portion of the senior class.

Jumping off Whisper Falls was one of those senior-year traditions that no one knew the origins of and did anyway. It wasn't safe, exactly. The cliff everyone jumped from was at least twenty feet up and the water below just deep enough to provide a layer of protection from the rocks beneath. History was littered with stories of kids who'd broken toes or even legs on their own senior jumps, but apart from one story that Fern was pretty sure had been exaggerated for effect, no one had ever died here. Every one of her sisters had taken the leap. Even Clover, who was not only afraid of heights, but pulled the Five of Coins from Fern's Sailor Moon tarot deck the night before—the card that symbolized hardship and loss—and screamed bloody murder all the way down.

Even she had told Fern it wasn't that bad.

Still, it had seemed like a better idea before she'd made the hike with Cam and Melissa and remembered just how steep the drop was.

"I'm only doing this once," Melissa informed them, stripping her top off to reveal a solid blue one-piece beneath. "And only because I don't want people saying that I chickened out."

There were at least a dozen other seniors here already, with more on the way up. The air was tense with a palpable mix of anticipation and dread as people came face-to-undeniable-face with what this tradition entailed.

The event was always held on the last Saturday in February, before the snowpack higher up in the mountains melted and the falls went from an almost gentle drop to something more torrential and dangerous. There was no alert on social, no announcement at school, but people always showed up. In Fern's case, Cam had reminded every senior in drama club to make sure to get their jumps in *before* rehearsal in the afternoon.

"I left towels at the bottom. There's two for each of us: hair and body. And also a thermos of proper Irish coffee to warm us up," Cambria said, as though either of her friends had asked. Her eyes shifted back to the edge. "OMG, are we really doing this? Are you ready? Do you want to—"

Melissa didn't give Cam time to finish. She strode forward and flung herself over the edge, making her body stick-straight so that she knifed through the spray.

"Why is she like this?" Cambria asked, peering over the cliff.

It seemed to take longer than it should to spot Melissa's head when she surfaced. Pale arms flashing against the bright blue water as she swam toward shore.

"You know Melissa. She doesn't like to give herself time to overthink anything," Fern explained. It made perfect sense to her. Especially right now.

Cambria shrugged, then pulled her shirt over her head, revealing the top of the pink-and-white-pinstripe swimsuit they'd picked out together at the end of last summer. It perfectly accentuated the curve of Cambria's breasts and complemented her brown skin. Fern had the matching suit in green to draw out her eyes. She was wearing it right now. Beneath a baggy T-shirt and jeans.

The problem was, she didn't want to take them off. And at the same time, she did. She didn't love the feeling of the shirt draped over the modest lift of her own breasts. The way the suit sculpted her into a specific form. A form her body could not, would not achieve on its own but was only possible through the combination of fabric and wire.

It all combined to create a nausea she could only partly describe. She wasn't going to vomit. But she didn't have another word to describe the sickening sensation that permeated every cell in her body when she focused on that one feeling of fabric against breast.

Cambria glanced back at her. "You ready?"

"Not yet," Fern said, hoping the struggle didn't come through in her voice. "But you should go."

"Without you?" Cambria narrowed her eyes. "Why would I do that?"

This wasn't a big deal. Fern knew that. She could tell Cambria that she didn't want to take her clothes off, and even if Cam thought it was weird, she'd hardly give it a second thought. But this was about more than her clothes. This small moment had blossomed into something much bigger. Something she wasn't prepared to share with Cam.

"Because I might not jump," Fern said.

"Why? Nothing bad is going to happen. The Patron protects us all," she said, with a grand sweep of her arms as though she knew it was ridiculous. Then the humor fell from her face, and she tipped her chin down to give Fern a disbelieving look. "Up to you, pretty bird, but this is the full measure of my disappointment."

She stuck out her tongue, then tossed her clothes in the pile that would be retrieved later and took center stage at the top of the cliff. The waiting crowd erupted in whistles and applause, and Cam gave a confident, coy little bow before assuming a running stance.

"Three!" shouted the crowd. "Two, one!"

Cam shot forward and jumped, opening her arms like wings before vanishing below the cliff.

It continued just like this. The next person stripping down to various kinds of applause and encouragement before the countdown.

Fern pulled her knees up to her chest and watched the slow but steady progression of seniors take the plunge. There were whoops and screams and laughter as one after another they dove over. Some more than once.

Fern wanted to join them. She wanted to feel that same reckless joy, but she felt stuck. Uneasy and off-balance in her own skin. And she didn't know how to explain why. Not even to her best friends. She didn't know how to say to someone that she felt right in her mind and wrong in her skin. But only sometimes. They were nonsense words to anyone except herself.

"Are you going to jump?"

"I haven't decided," Fern answered before she'd fully registered that the speaker was Kaitlyn.

All week, the two of them had been playing at being friends. They ignored each other all day, but the second rehearsals started, they played two roles at once: friends for Ms. Murphy, stilted lovers for the musical.

But even that felt off. Like something the previous version of Fern would have wanted but didn't fit anymore. This Fern looked forward to the moment she and Kaitlyn bent their heads together and read from the same script and pretended to be friends. But Fern was losing patience for all the fake things in her life.

Which was why she was wary when Kaitlyn took a seat on the ground next to her.

"I haven't decided either," she said, wincing as John Nichols did a picture-perfect jackknife in the air.

Fern looked around, but there was no sign of Jaq. Not a surprise, except that it was.

The Jaq she'd known had been straining at the limits her parents placed on her, eager for any and every opportunity to push the boundaries, especially where her parents wouldn't see. That Jaq didn't exist anymore. Not in the way Fern remembered. And judging by the way Jaq had reacted the last time they'd talked, she was going to do everything in her power to make sure it stayed that way.

But Fern wanted this new version of herself. She'd been robbed of so many years of finding the right words and ways of being. She was never going to get that time back. All she had was now.

"I swear half of these people are only here for the excuse to take their clothes off," Kaitlyn murmured fondly. "But then, who am I to throw stones at someone's need for an audience?"

Kaitlyn gave Fern a natural smile. The kind it was impossible to fake. Effortless and unassuming. Arresting in a way Fern wasn't prepared for, one that made her want to lean forward and press her lips to Kaitlyn's.

Which wasn't what she wanted at all.

"Is that why you're in theater? You need an audience to feel good about yourself?" The words came out more viciously than Fern intended, the discomfort she felt inside spilling out of her mouth like sludge.

Kaitlyn blinked, taken aback. "I don't think that's what I was saying, but I guess it's not entirely wrong. I really love feeling a connection between me and an audience. You know those moments when you can just feel that you've carried them with you on whatever journey you're on? When you've convinced them that what they're seeing is at least a little bit real. I love that. What about you? Why are you in theater?" She narrowed her eyes at Fern, volleying the challenge right back.

"Because—" Fern started and stopped, her usual answer failing her.

Whenever one of her mother's friends asked this question, she offered some version of, *Because I love being a part of something that's bigger than myself.* But right now, all she could think was, *I'm tired of pretending.*

"Why do you want to know?" she asked.

"First of all, you started this, and . . ." Kaitlyn paused, leaning back to study Fern for a moment. "Second, there's something different about you this past week. I'm not sure what it is, but you seem, I don't know, a little withdrawn. Less sure of Sandy at rehearsals than I expected you to be. I thought it had to do with me, but even in the scenes I'm not in, you're different."

"I'm not different," Fern protested, trying to find an answer that wasn't too personal. "I'm, well, honestly, when I auditioned for Sandy, I thought she was a different sort of character. Now that we're in it, though, I'm not sure how to relate to her."

"Because she's so sweet?" Kaitlyn asked. "Or because everyone is in her business all day, every day?"

The suggestion landed a little too close to home for comfort.

"I thought we'd agreed we weren't friends," Fern said, changing the subject. "You don't have to fake it here. Ms. Murphy will never know."

"I'm not doing this for Ms. Murphy, Fern." Kaitlyn shifted so she could look into Fern's face. "I'm doing this because I genuinely like you. For reasons that continue to elude me because, for fuck's sake, you are prickly. But you know what? I'm not fooled. I know you like me, too. You want to know how I know?"

Fern gaped. Mouth dropping open like a fish. "Uh, yeah."

Kaitlyn grinned, already triumphant. "You don't smile at me." She leaned closer, conspiratorial. "You smile at everyone. But they aren't just smiles. They're specific and targeted. Super fake. But you don't do that to me."

Fern didn't know what to say. She couldn't even call her a liar, though she wanted to. "Maybe I don't smile at you because I don't think it's worth the effort."

Again, Kaitlyn smiled, the insult sliding off her as easily as rain. "Tell me, then. Say that you don't like me even a little bit. If you can say it, I'll jump off that ledge and leave you here to hate me in peace."

Fern opened her mouth to give Kaitlyn exactly what she'd asked for, but there were no words ready. It took her only a second to realize that she couldn't say it because she didn't want Kaitlyn to leave.

"Did you just bully me into friendship?" Fern asked.

Kaitlyn's laugh was warm and husky. "Maybe I did."

Fern smiled, laughing a little.

"So that's what that looks like?" Kaitlyn said.

"What what looks like?"

"Your real smile."

For a second, Fern stared at Kaitlyn in something like disbelief. She didn't know what was happening between them, but she knew that whatever it was, she liked it. She liked *her*, and now she knew that some imprisoned part of her had always liked Kaitlyn. That part of herself had come back. She felt whole. She *was* whole even if she didn't know how all the pieces fit together yet. There was no part of her that doubted this was the best, truest version of herself.

She felt her smile spreading, deepening, the simple movement sending waves of warmth through her entire body.

"Fern! Why haven't you jumped yet, and why are your clothes still on?!" Cam called, emerging from the woods at the trailhead, her hair still dripping.

"I still haven't decided," Fern answered, pulling her knees more tightly to her chest.

"C'mon," Cam begged, catching Fern's hand and tugging her to her feet. "Let me see that beautiful suit. You're going to love the jump. Even Melissa said it was, quote, 'an experience.'"

Cam reached for the hem of Fern's T-shirt, playful and tugging. It sent a sudden bolt of fear through Fern's chest, and she danced away as though she'd been burned. She could see the hurt in Cam's face immediately, and she regretted her actions. Cam was her best friend. That hadn't changed, and she wasn't doing anything wrong. They had spent years sharing dressing rooms and changing in front of each other. Hell, Cam had helped Fern through at least a dozen quick costume changes and had seen way more than a bikini top.

"It's just so cold," Fern said, trying to play off the moment. She rubbed her arms for emphasis. "And that water was literally ice a few days ago. I can't believe you're back for seconds."

"That's the fun part," Cam said, letting the strange tension ease just a bit. Her gaze slid to Kaitlyn, then back to Fern. "See you at the bottom?"

"Yeah." Fern gave a confident nod. "Don't judge me if it's on foot."

"Oh, I won't be the only one judging," Cam promised. Then she turned and vaulted over the edge once more.

"You know you can jump in your clothes," Kaitlyn said softly, coming to stand next to Fern. "There's no rule that says you can't."

It was true. There weren't any rules. But there were expectations, most of which were fairly based on the person she'd been for the past five years. And if she jumped fully clothed, Cam was going to ask some questions.

"I should just get it over with." Fern grabbed the hem of her shirt, but then Kaitlyn's hand was on hers, preventing her from taking it off.

"I'll do it with you," she offered.

"Do what?"

"Leave my clothes on. We'll make a statement together." Kaitlyn pulled her hand away and raised her eyebrows in a question.

Fern smiled again. This time, she knew it was a real one.

A swell of emotion made Fern bold enough to hold out her hand. Kaitlyn took it, her thumb skimming lightly over Fern's. Then together they raced toward the cliff and jumped.

For a split second, Fern was weightless, a piece of the sky and nothing else. Then she plummeted toward the pool below. Her head filled with the roar of the falls and the roar of the wind and the roar of her own blood. Her thoughts were a scream and her stomach ballooned with panic. At the last second, she remembered to close her eyes and make her body stiff, then she hit the water with a concussive smack.

Cold and pain were twin punches to her entire body. Water drove up her nose and down her throat, and Kaitlyn was ripped away as Fern shot toward the rocky bottom of the pool.

She was disoriented, but alive and whole. The cold a welcome embrace to her quivering nerves. She opened her eyes and tipped her head toward the surface of the water, which was gilded in sunset and still full of chop from the impact.

A laugh bubbled between her lips. She felt electric. Like her skin would forever hum with this frantic feeling of being alive. She closed her eyes again and let the water cradle her until her lungs protested, then pushed toward the surface.

A hand latched on to her ankle.

The grip tightened, fingers pressing firmly against her skin, and then it pulled.

Fern gasped against the water, choking, and tried to kick free, but the grip squeezed painfully tight and dragged her downdown-down. She flailed, arms scratching uselessly for the surface. Lungs burning, desperate for air.

Bright spots appeared in her vision, bursting like stars as her brain ran out of oxygen.

A voice whispered into her mind, *Come back.*

She felt her muscles going cold and weak. No matter how much she wanted to keep moving, to keep fighting, her body could not.

Then another hand gripped her wrist and pulled.

The pressure at her ankle vanished, and she was moving up. Breaking the surface. She sucked in a ragged breath and then another, disoriented but aware that it was Kaitlyn who had pulled her up. Was still pulling her toward shore.

"What was that? Are you okay?" Kaitlyn asked when they were close enough to stand on the rocks.

The entire crowd of seniors was watching them. Staring at her as she hacked up cold water. Cam and Melissa looked like they'd been on the verge of diving into the water themselves, clearly convinced that Fern was drowning. They were worried and confused, as invested in Fern's answer as Kaitlyn was.

"I'm okay," Fern managed, adopting a reassuring smile. "My foot got caught on something, maybe a root, that's all."

"Roots?" Kaitlyn frowned at the pool. "I didn't think there was anything under there except rocks."

Fern clung to her smile and shrugged. "I'm glad you were there."

"Me too. You sure you're okay?"

"Mm-hmm," Fern hummed, still smiling.

It was a relief when Kaitlyn finally relented, not accepting the lie but letting it go, and turned to lead them the rest of the way to shore.

Because the truth was, Fern wasn't okay.

Jaq was right: something was trying to kill them.

And if they didn't do anything about it, she was afraid something would.

CHAPTER
FIFTEEN

Mallory
THEN

Every time they went looking for the house, they found it. Mallory wasn't sure how, exactly, because the black stone seemed to appear in a different place every time, but that part didn't matter to her.

Inside, it was just as run-down as out. Maybe more so, with holes opening in the floors and the coil of a once-elegant stairwell now protruding from the wall like ribs. Cracked sconces lined the hallways, blackened by fire and age, and ancient wiring dangled from what remained of the ceiling like veins. And it felt more like home than any other place in Mallory's life.

"It's like I don't even exist!" Mallory ranted as she yanked the dress her mother had picked for her to wear at the dance out of her backpack. "I'm just a thing to them. An object to be dressed up and moved around, even kissed without anyone ever bothering to ask if I want any of that. Which I don't."

Seventh-grade prom had been just as awful as Mallory expected it to be. Tommy Webber's mom and dad drove him to her house, and she had to endure both sets of parents fawning over how adorable they looked together while he stuck a boxy corsage on her wrist. It took every bit of willpower she had not to smack him in the face when he leaned in and kissed her cheek and her own mother—*her own mother*—declared him such a decent young man.

Once they'd arrived at the dance, Mallory had ditched him, and the most infuriating part of the whole thing was that she was pretty sure he didn't notice.

"They could have dressed up a dog and been just as happy," she spit, flinging the dress over what remained of the banister at the base of the stairway.

"I'm sorry," Jaq said.

"What are you sorry for? You didn't do it! You didn't do anything! And neither did I!" Mallory shouted without thinking. She saw the way Jaq flinched, and part of her softened. She didn't want to hurt Jaq. Especially Jaq. There was something exciting and fragile and new between them, and Mal didn't want to destroy it without meaning to. "Sorry," she said.

"It really is pretty," Jaq mused, letting the fabric of the dress slip through her fingers.

"Yep." Mallory studied it for another minute, thinking about how happy her mother had been when she'd presented it to Mal. The way her father had mentioned more than once how much it had cost. How the dress seemed more important to both of them than the person wearing it. Thinking of that, she retrieved a pair of steel fabric scissors from her bag and cut the long skirt off at the knees.

"Oh my god, Mallory. Your mom is going to kill you!" Fern gasped.

"If she notices," Mal answered without concern. She scooped up the extra fabric and shook it in front of her, little bits of wood and whatever else was on the ground in there falling away. "On the plus side, we have a curtain now. Where should we put it?"

"The drawing room window," Jaq suggested. "I think it even has a curtain rod."

None of them knew exactly what a drawing room was, but it sounded fancy, and even in ruins, the house felt like the kind of place that would have had a drawing room.

They picked their way from the parlor to the little room that bore the charred remnants of an old sofa and a fireplace on the far wall, and Fern stood back while Jaq and Mal worked to arrange their new window dressing.

"It needs a little more drape in the middle," Fern said, taking her job very seriously.

"Like this?" Jaq asked. In the same second, another voice called from outside, "It's this way. Hurry up!"

"Who was that?" Fern hissed.

Jaq shook her head, but Mal knew. "Tommy. Webber."

"You think they're coming here?" Fern was hiding now, back pressed to the wall next to the window. Across from her, Jaq was doing the same.

"No, this is our house." Mal ground out the words.

The sound of someone crashing through the woods was getting louder. Closer.

"Did we really have to come all the way out here?" A second voice.

"Where else are we going to do this without getting caught?" Tommy asked. "C'mon. We're almost there."

"Hide," Jaq whispered to Mal, tangling their fingers together and pulling her away from the window.

In the next second, they heard the sounds of two boys emerging from the woods. Mal listened as they trudged across the clearing toward the house, then plopped down on the front steps. A second later, there was the telltale crack and hiss of a can opening.

"Your dad isn't going to notice you took two?" the second boy asked.

Tommy snorted. "That guy can't count."

There was a brief pause while they each took a drink, then smacked their lips and laughed.

"Don't they see the house?" Fern whispered. "Why aren't they coming in?"

Jaq only shrugged, but Mallory crept toward the broken window and peered around the edge.

Tommy Webber and John Nichols sat on opposite sides of the stoop, sucking down cans of beer, burping and laughing and telling bad jokes. But they weren't looking at the house. Mal was sure that if two thirteen-year-old boys saw an old, abandoned house in the middle of the woods, they'd go inside.

Curious now, Mallory stepped more fully into the gap of the window frame. She was only a few feet away from the two boys. So close she could see the individual freckles splashed across John's nose. But in spite of this, neither of them noticed her. They didn't even tip their heads in her direction.

"Leave," she said.

Jaq gasped. Fern held her breath. But still, neither boy moved.

Encouraged, Mal spoke again. This time with her full chest. She said, "Tommy Webber, you're a real dick."

Again, neither of the boys gave any indication that they'd heard anything. Then, without warning, there was a crack overhead, and a tree branch crashed down on the steps, narrowly missing the two boys.

"Shit!" John cried, leaping away.

"What the fuck was that?" Tommy added, a hair slower than his friend. "Jesus, where did that even come from?"

"We are in the woods, Tommy," John answered. He sounded stone-cold sober now. "We should go."

"Yeah, okay," Tommy agreed, tossing his empty can into the yard and following John back into the forest. They left without a backward glance.

"What just happened?" Jaq asked.

"They didn't see us. They didn't even see the house," Fern answered. "And they littered."

Mallory placed a hand flat on the blackened wall, gentle and loving. "It protected us," she said as though it were a normal thing for an old house to do. "*He* protected us."

"Who?" Jaq asked.

"Find his house, make a wish, he'll do just as you please," Mal sang in answer. At her words, a shiver of silver light shot through the wood panel beneath her fingers. Racing up and vanishing so quickly she almost missed it. When she looked at the others, it was clear that they hadn't seen anything. But it *was* real. She'd always known it, and now here was the proof.

"The Patron?" Fern shook her head. "I buy that maybe—*maybe*—this was his house, but magic isn't real. There's not actually a kindly old ghost in here who grants wishes." She paused and looked uncertain. "Right?"

"Well, we didn't make a wish," Jaq pointed out.

"Not out loud." Mallory shrugged, unbothered. She had been making wishes her whole life. Praying to God and Jesus for help. But no one had answered her until now. "The point is, this house really is here for us. Just us. We're *safe* here."

It took a minute for that realization to sink in, but when it did, it was like a rock dropping deep into the ocean.

It didn't occur to Mallory until much later that there was a danger in hiding—that when you hid yourself away from the world, there was a possibility you might never be found.

CHAPTER
SIXTEEN

Jaq

"We'll use the nice china tonight, I think. Will you please go get it from the hutch in the living room and set the table, Jaqueline?" Mrs. De Luca was lifting a steaming beef tenderloin from the oven.

Her hair hung in long, soft curls that draped perfectly over each shoulder. Her makeup was crisp, and she wore a skirt and blouse, feet in modest heels that clicked against the tile floor as she moved from one side of the kitchen to the next. She had cooked the entire meal in yoga clothes and, while the beef cooked, had showered, dressed, makeup-ed, and done her hair. Jaq had seen her transform from Weekday Mom to Sunday Mom in less than twenty minutes before. It was both impressive and enviable.

"Why the china? The Nicholses have been over for dinner a million times." Apart from Christmas dinner, Jaq could count the number of times they'd pulled out the good china on one hand. Because it was zero. No occasion was ever good enough to risk the delicate set that had been passed down for generations.

A secretive smile appeared on Mrs. De Luca's pink lips. "It's not every day a young couple has their three-year anniversary. And Mrs. Nichols says John has something special planned for tonight."

Jaq swallowed hard. She'd forgotten. All morning at church,

John had been reminding her about dinner tonight. Saying how her mom had let it slip she was making beef tenderloin because it was his favorite. How sweet it was that she remembered those things. How it was the little things that made nights together special. Jaq had been so preoccupied wondering if her mom had any idea what *Jaq's* favorite food was, she'd completely missed that John was being coy because today was their anniversary.

It wasn't like her to forget. She intentionally tracked important dates because they were important. They mattered to her. But she'd let herself be distracted. By things that shouldn't have mattered as much as John. By a confusing past that had no business interrupting her future. By Fern making it all just a little bit worse by refusing to let it go.

By Devyn.

She thought about Devyn constantly. Always without meaning to. She thought of what it felt like to fly on the back of a motorcycle, and of Devyn's smile, and of Devyn's arm around her waist, catching Jaq before she could fall.

The way her cheeks burned and her stomach squeezed and her skin tingled pleasantly as that moment looped over and over again in her mind.

"Do you have something nice for him?" her mom asked, bringing her back to the moment. "I'm pretty sure he has something a little extra special for you."

Shit.

"Mm-hmm," Jaq answered, spinning on her heel and leaving the room as fast as she could, hoping her mom hadn't picked up on her urgency.

She headed straight for the stairs, remembering at the last second that her mother had asked her to set the table. Cutting left into the sitting room, she forced herself to take her time removing the plates and bowls from the hutch and setting the table exactly as her mother liked before she darted up the stairs to her bedroom and shut the door behind her.

There had to be something. Jaq scanned the room, searching for anything that felt like John, hoping that she was more prepared than she felt in this moment. Maybe Past-Jaq had found something she thought he would like and bought it, stashing it away for a rainy day. But even as she hoped for a miracle, she knew that Past-Jaq had been saving up for a bottle of Polo Blue cologne. Maybe it was uninspired as far as anniversary gifts went, but John liked to smell nice, and she knew he would love it.

Now, she had the money, no cologne, and less than thirty minutes before the Nicholses arrived on her doorstep, expecting to bear witness to a thoughtful, endearing exchange of gifts.

Jaq moved to her bedside table and threw open the top drawer. Lip balm, notebook, and a half dozen fidget spinners. She opened the second. Noise-canceling headphones, college brochures, random candy.

Fuck.

Maybe Susan had something she could bring over. But calling Susan would mean letting her in on the secret, and right now Jaq didn't know what was worse, admitting that she didn't have anything to give to John, who would forgive her, or to Susan, who would interrogate her until she discovered that Jaq wasn't sure who she was anymore and spent more time thinking about a girl she'd just met than she did about the boy she'd known for years, and didn't that mean she didn't like John anymore?

That maybe she'd never really liked him at all?

She ripped open the third drawer. An old pink hoodie, a planner three years out of date, and a box of pastels. Jaq nearly slammed the drawer shut again but paused, the pastels catching her eye. She didn't have time to draw anything right now, but she didn't need to.

Jaq crouched down to peer beneath her bed, dragged out a slim plastic container, and popped the lid. She didn't draw often because her mother said it made too much of a mess, and the dust irritated her father's allergies. When she did draw, she did it with her door firmly shut, her windows open to account for the supposed dust her pastels generated. Then she tucked each drawing away beneath her bed, where it was contained and hidden. It was her own private rebellion, and for the past five years, it hadn't seemed as important as it did now.

She paged through the drawings until she found the one she was looking for. It was a portrait of John. He was turned toward the viewer, staring out at them—at Jaq—with an almost smile on his face. His eyes were narrowed the slightest bit, his lips hitching up at each corner, his golden curls flopping over his temples.

When Jaq pictured John, this was how he looked. Open and kind and focused on her. He knew more about her than anyone ever had because he was always looking. Always watching. Always *seeing* her.

Maybe things were confusing right now, but looking at him, even a drawing of him, made everything feel clear again. She loved John. He was her best friend. That hadn't changed.

Grateful that Past-Jaq hadn't let her down, she rolled the drawing into a loose tube, then pulled a satin ribbon from her collection of hair ties and secured it with a bow. She had just opened her bedroom door again when her mother called up the stairs to say that the Nicholses had arrived, and it was time for dinner.

After that, the evening was a breeze. The two families had been sharing Sunday dinners for so long that Jaq knew exactly what to expect from one moment to the next. She and John would be seated across from one another, next to his parents, while her mom and dad sat at either end. Their fathers would split a bottle of red wine between the two of them while their mothers nursed a single glass of white over the course of the evening. Jaq and John would tap their toes together beneath the table whenever one of their parents said something ridiculous, and when the conversation inevitably turned to something only their fathers cared about, John would stand and offer to help Alice with dessert.

Tonight, though, when John stood up, he tapped a knife against his glass to get everyone's attention.

"Before we enjoy what I'm sure will be another outstanding dessert"—John paused to offer Mrs. De Luca an utterly charming smile—"there's something I'd like to say." He paused again, clearing his throat and turning his eyes on Jaq, his focus pristine. "Jaqueline Marie De Luca, three years ago, you said yes to me for the very first time. I'm still not sure why, but when I asked you if you wanted to go with me to see the next Trolls movie—an underrated gem of modern storytelling—you said yes. I think I knew right then and there that we had something special. You are kind and smart, you drive a car better than anyone I know, and over the past three years, I've realized that I don't just like you. I love you."

Jaq couldn't look away from John, so she couldn't say if the small gasp came from her or one of their mothers, but she felt it in every cell of her body.

"Some people say that eighteen is too young to make decisions that will impact the rest of your life. Everyone here knows I'm not anything close to the smartest kid in class, and who am I to doubt them?"

This time, Jaq felt the gasp lodge in her throat, pinning her voice in place like it was a bug in a curio.

John suddenly winked. "Jaq, I can see the panic in your eyes, and I want you to know that this isn't a proposal."

Laughter erupted from either side of Jaq, but she was stock-still as John moved around the table and took her hands. Pulled her to standing. His eyes the sweetest, softest green when he captured her gaze.

"It's okay," he whispered, just for her.

Then he pulled a slender velvet box from his pocket and stepped back, cracking it open. Inside was a ring. The band glinted rose gold, as slender and delicate as a spider's web. In the center was a pale green stone, buttressed on either side by smaller stones. It was lovely. Understated and something she might have picked out herself.

"Three years ago, you said yes to me," he said again. "And I'm so glad that you did. To honor that moment and to show you that one day in the future I would like to ask you another question, I would like to give you this ring. To promise you that for as long as you will be mine, I will also be yours."

"John," she said, her voice barely able to unstick itself from her throat. But she could feel her mother vibrating at her back, could see the pride on the faces of John's parents and her father.

She could see all of that as clearly as she could feel how much she didn't want this.

"Don't you have something for him, Jaqueline?" Jaq's mother prompted.

"I—yes." Jaq swallowed hard, already anticipating her mother's disappointment. Her gift was nothing by comparison, but she had no options. It would be worse to have nothing to offer in return.

She collected her hastily beribboned gift from the sideboard and returned to John. With every step, she wracked her brain for something to say. Something that sounded sincere enough to match his presentation. But she was sweating and panicked, and for some reason all her thoughts were coming in French.

She took a deep breath and held the scroll out to John, who took it with a curious smile. "What's this?" he asked.

"It's you," she said. "How I see you."

With care, John untied the ribbon and unrolled the portrait. He studied it in silence, eyes tracing the lines on the page as though they held some secret he couldn't decipher.

"Did you do this?" he asked after a long minute. Jaq nodded, and he shook his head, saying, "I had no idea."

He said it with wonder, curious that there were things he didn't know about Jaq. Impressed that she had such secrets, but not upset. Because John was good. Not perfect, but good.

"You're so talented," Mrs. Nichols said, peering over John's shoulder. "Alice, she's really good. I'm no artist, but this looks professional."

"We don't like to brag," Mrs. De Luca answered, darting a nervous glance at her daughter while her husband frowned and said nothing.

"I love it," John said, rolling it back up with care. Then he pried the ring from its velvet nest and set the box on the table. "May I?" he asked.

Jaq's heart thudded painfully against her sternum. With every ounce of attention focused on her, there was no answer she could give other than "Yes."

But as her mother sighed and John slid the ring onto her right ring finger, Jaq had to shut her eyes against the sudden press of tears.

They didn't belong to her. They belonged to another Jaq. One with secrets that would tear this family apart. Jaq swallowed them down. Because this was the life she wanted, the one with John. The one with her family. This was where she belonged.

CHAPTER
SEVENTEEN

Fern

Fern sat on a bench, her back stick-straight, her hands clasped together in her lap, eyes pinned to a single spot on the far wall. Next to her, Kaitlyn lounged like a king, legs spread so one knee knocked against Fern's, hands planted behind her so she could lean back.

It had been two weeks since Whisper Falls, weeks since anything had tried to kill Fern. Two weeks since she'd spoken with Jaq. She still didn't know what had pulled her under the water. Jaq would tell her that it had been Mal, but Fern didn't think so. She might not have a memory of that last night in the woods, but she couldn't believe that they would have hurt Mal—or that Mal would have hurt them. There had to be something else in the woods.

Mal had always said there was something in that house. But something that wanted to hurt them? Kill them?

"Hey," Kaitlyn said, pulling Fern's attention back to the present. "You're not seeing anyone else, are you?"

"Why?" Fern answered, sitting up even straighter than before.

"Just curious."

From the corner of her eye, Fern could sense more than see Kaitlyn moving. A single jerking movement, then a little hopping action. A smattering of laughter echoed around them.

"I have something for you." Kaitlyn held out a bright blue Ring Pop, the candy jewel winking in the lights.

"Oh," Fern said, feigning innocence. Batting her eyes. Turning her face demurely toward Kaitlyn. "I'm speechless."

Fern knew she was stiff. She knew she was holding back, but she also knew that this scene was swiftly trundling toward a kiss, and she hadn't been able to stop thinking about it all day. She'd known this scene was coming, of course. And she was a professional. Stage kisses weren't real kisses. They were simulations. Lips touching with a little pressure. The kiss wasn't nearly as important as the acting that went along with it. That was where acting was partly physical. Maybe even mostly physical. The kiss was nothing without her ability to convince an audience what kind of kiss it was. Whether it was passionate or chaste or full of longing. She knew how to fake a kiss.

Then Whisper Falls had happened. There had been Kaitlyn's hand in hers and, more than that, her understanding. Even still, Fern hadn't realized the depth of what had happened until she saw "Starlight Drive-In Scene" on the schedule this morning and thought about kissing Kaitlyn.

She wanted to kiss Kaitlyn.

And she wanted it to be real.

"Nothing wrong with that." Kaitlyn's voice was soft as her eyes flicked up to Fern's and held them. "Want me to put it on for you?"

Fern clamped her teeth together and nodded. "Uh-huh." It came out strangled, but that was fine for someone like Sandy.

Kaitlyn scooted forward, reaching for Fern's hand. The contact between them sent Fern's heart slamming into her ribs, a flush burning in her cheeks, every nerve in her body screaming because in the next second they were going to—

"Okay, I'm just going to stop you right there," Ms. Murphy called from the audience. "I know you both know the scene; you've got your lines down and we're getting there, but you're both still playing this a little too straight."

Kaitlyn snorted. So did several of the others. There were four other couples spread out across the stage, each seated together on a bench and facing the audience to mimic parked cars. Behind all the cars, three others stood at the top of a set of bleachers. They were the actors in the movie the couples were all supposed to be watching.

"Ha ha," Ms. Murphy answered. "You know what I mean. This is supposed to be the thing they both want, but they're playing the roles they think they *should* play rather than letting themselves become the people they want to be."

"Ms. Murphy, that may be true for Danny, but Sandy isn't playing a role right now, is she?" Fern asked.

"It's more subtle, maybe, but she's definitely playing a role." Ms. Murphy paused in a way that signaled she was giving Fern room to find the answer herself.

Heat seeped up Fern's neck, reaching toward her cheeks, but she forced herself to consider what she knew about Sandy. Which, honestly, wasn't much. Danny was the one who started off charming, then as soon as he was around his friends pretended to be a player. Sandy was only ever one thing.

"The good girl," Fern said.

"I think so, too," Ms. Murphy said, nodding. "I think she's been putting on a show most of her life. Performing the kind of 'good girl' she thinks people like. Does that make sense?" When Fern nodded, Ms. Murphy clapped her hands, the sharp sound reverberating through the theater. "Right, let's take it from the top."

"Places!" Cam shouted from her preferred spot in the wings. She gave Fern a quick thumbs-up, then tapped a finger to her headset and gave instructions to Melissa in the lighting booth.

The cast shifted, the couples in the cars settling into a variety of cuddly poses, and the three actors at the top of the bleachers created a still life of a scene in a movie. The girl hunched over, covering her face as though crying while the other two reached toward her in concern. Everyone froze, giving the tableau a second to create the impression of cars at a drive-in theater, then Ms. Murphy called, "Action!"

The girl gave a shriek and looked up, eyes fixed on the middle distance as she tearfully began to tell her story of an animal attack.

The scene rolled forward with the movie scene playing out with melodramatic flair and the couples in the other cars doing everything from sweetly leaning their heads together to having a fake make-out session.

Kaitlyn moved toward Fern again, awkwardly attempting to stretch one arm around Fern's shoulders, as the hero had just done in the movie, and Fern inched away primly.

Once more, their conversation began with Danny wondering why Sandy wouldn't come a little closer and ended when Danny slid the ring onto her finger, leaning toward her. Fern's stomach flipped. She held her breath, her entire body rigid with something like anticipation and something like dread.

She didn't want to kiss Kaitlyn like this. Like Sandy. She didn't want to keep pasting on smiles like masks. Every day a performance of the only Fern Jensen she'd ever been allowed to be. Except she most definitely did want to kiss Kaitlyn, and it was about to happen—

"Okay, cut!" Ms. Murphy called.

Fern gritted her teeth and swallowed hard as Kaitlyn gave a little sigh and sat up straight.

"Okay," Ms. Murphy repeated, pursing her lips in thought. "I want to try something. Just to see if we can shake the two of you up a little bit. Get you to loosen up. Let's take it from the top, but we're going to swap roles."

"Swap?" Fern asked, frowning. "You mean you want me to be Danny?"

"Just as an exercise. I assume two professionals like you know both parts?"

When they nodded, Ms. Murphy clapped once. "Fantastic. Let's go again!"

"Top of the scene, everyone!" Cam called. "Places!"

Fern and Kaitlyn swapped sides and assumed each other's positions.

"Wait." Ms. Murphy waved one hand in the air, then leveled a gaze at Fern. "Remember that you're not a girl anymore. You're not Sandy, you're Danny. Do you need a second to find a touchstone for that?"

"I—"

Fern gripped the bench, her fingernails driving into the metal. The very idea that she wasn't a girl wrapped around her like a comfortable blanket. The rightness of it drove deep into her stomach, down her legs and rooted into her toes.

Every eye in the theater was on her. Waiting and watching. Every person here had heard Ms. Murphy tell her that she wasn't a girl anymore.

But none of them knew how true those words felt. And she didn't want them to know. Not yet. Not when this feeling was so new.

"No," Fern said. "I'm good."

"Great, then . . . action!"

This time, Fern told her body to relax, to let her legs flare wide and her torso bow casually. The change was easy. Natural. The shedding of an outfit that she'd been wearing for too long and didn't fit right anymore. It was like bringing the way she always felt inside into alignment with the outside. She settled into her body, into the idea of Danny Zuko with surprising ease. Just like that, Sandy was gone, but so was the Fern that had reigned for the last five years. The one who had a smile for everyone except Kaitlyn.

And then it was her line.

"Would you like to come a little closer?" she asked, mouth twisting in a half smile that was equal parts smarmy and innocent.

There was a flash of excitement in Kaitlyn's eyes. Recognition and joy. Then she fluttered a hand between them. "I'm good."

The next line flowed, the two of them slipping seamlessly into their new roles, the air between them electric. The stiffness that had existed before was gone, replaced by a sinuous energy that snaked between and around them, drawing them together. This was how the scene was supposed to feel. Alive with anticipation.

Fern slid the bright blue Ring Pop onto Kaitlyn's finger and said, "I've wanted to give this to you for a long time." She cupped one hand behind Kaitlyn's head, leaning in, breath hitching in her throat as her eyes landed on Kaitlyn's mouth. Her lips gently coral and full, glittering in the stage light. Drawing her closer and closer until their lips touched.

For a perfect second of stillness Fern forgot that they were onstage. Forgot that they were surrounded by people and, maybe more importantly, their drama teacher. Forgot that she was supposed to pantomime wanting so much more while physically restraining herself.

Because she did want more. And she wasn't restraining herself. And neither was Kaitlyn.

Fern tangled her fingers in Kaitlyn's curls, and Kaitlyn leaned forward, her own hands sliding around Fern's neck, her thumbs brushing Fern's jaw.

"I said cut!" Ms. Murphy's voice was a shout, bright with amusement.

Fern jerked away from Kaitlyn. Heart pounding. Cheeks hot. Lips tingling.

Kaitlyn did the same, covering her mouth with one hand.

"That!" Ms. Murphy cried. "That's where we need to be. You nailed it! We're going to stop there for the day, but I want you to hold on to this feeling, and we'll pick it up again tomorrow. If you've forgotten your next assignment, check in with Cam before you leave. Otherwise, a big round of applause for your work today, everyone! Remember, we are on a compressed rehearsal timeline, and there's only a week and a half left till we open."

All around, the rest of the cast and crew broke into applause, dragging their hands in the customary circle before leaving the stage in search of wherever they dropped their bags.

Fern climbed to her feet, unsure of basically everything. Had anyone else noticed that that kiss was one hundred percent off script? That she hadn't been acting, maybe for the first time in her life?

Fern felt like she was expanding. Like rightness was a feeling that could fill her lungs and veins and make her as light as air.

Ms. Murphy climbed up onstage and approached Fern, stopping so she stood close enough to lower her voice. "Fern, that was excellent, but I need you to bring that same energy and focus to Sandy tomorrow or we're going to have to find another approach. I know you have it in you, but if you can't find it, then we may need to talk about finding a new Sandy."

Shame crashed through Fern, her body flashing from hot to cold in a split second. A choking frustration hard on its heels.

"You don't need to do that," she said.

"I hope not," Ms. Murphy answered with a blend of concern and sympathy. "Just remember, if the role is causing you harm, it's okay to put it down."

"It's not!" Fern struggled to keep from shouting. "I promise. I can do it. I'll be back on my game on Monday."

"Okay," Ms. Murphy gave Fern's shoulder a reassuring pat. "See you Monday."

It took Fern a second to realize that Kaitlyn was still onstage with her. Seated on Sandy's side of the bench, watching her with curious intensity.

Fern flushed again, unsure what to say, so she didn't say anything. She just turned on her heel and fled.

CHAPTER
EIGHTEEN

Jaq

Saturday morning, Jaq and her mother drove to Port Townsend and took the ferry across the Sound to Seattle. The day was overcast and misty, which fit Jaq's mood just fine, and they spent the trip listening to the radio instead of speaking, which was a relief. Two weeks had passed since John's pre-proposal, and her mom still hadn't let it go. She was fixated on the ring.

She commented on how it complemented Jaq's slender fingers. Instructed her on how to care for it properly. Told her again and again what a fine young man John was turning out to be. How lucky Jaq was to be with him.

She never once asked Jaq how she felt about any of it. As if Jaq's feelings were so inconsequential they might as well not be a part of the equation at all.

It reminded her of Mallory before seventh-grade prom, and she did *not* want to think about Mallory anymore. Except she'd spent the past two weeks listening to her mom paint a picture of a future that left her cold, trying to shove her heart into a box that was the wrong shape, and she was exhausted. She wished she could tap into a fraction of Mal's eloquent anger right now.

By the time they reached Pacific Place, the mall was in full swing. Crowds surged up and down the five floors, each level built like the cones in a beehive. The air smelled like fried food and overly sweet cookies, and the halls echoed with a cacophonous blend of chatter and Top 40 music.

Jaq usually loved these trips. She and her mom would spend a few hours shopping, then stop at the Clinique counter for a new lip gloss or sugar scrub, then they'd treat themselves to sushi and a fancy tea before heading home. But the whole way there, all Jaq's mom could talk about was John.

"I assume John is waiting to pick his tux until you've gotten your dress for prom, yes?" Jaq's mom asked, as she held out the skirt of a sage-green gown, then dropped it again.

"Yeah," Jaq answered. They always coordinated for dances, and he'd already told her to pick her favorite dress and he'd match.

"Is his favorite color still blue?"

"Yep," Jaq confirmed. Actually, he liked a very specific kind of blue, the darker shades like navy and cobalt and indigo. He liked it because last summer he'd read a book called *Moon Dark Smile*, and blue was an important part of it. They'd spent an entire afternoon driving through the summer-green foothills, discussing nothing but the color and the meaning of words and how the sky was blue but also every shade of blue. Blue was so much more than his favorite color. It was his favorite *idea*, and that was the sort of thing that made him so incredible.

But her mom didn't want to know all that.

"It's a shame. He looks so striking in blue, but it really isn't your best color," her mother murmured. She held a blue dress up to Jaq, a delicate frown pinching her brow. "I think you should try this one anyway."

"You just said blue isn't my color," Jaq said, taking the dress out of habit.

"It isn't, but something in this shade will flatter John's coloring perfectly."

Her mother turned away again, studying a second blue dress. One she knew wouldn't suit her daughter but was considering anyway because blue looked good on her boyfriend.

"We could try pink," Jaq suggested.

"Why would we do that? Pink is an awful color for boys," her mother said, without even looking at her.

"Because it's my favorite color," Jaq answered, daring her mother to take the request seriously.

Her mother laughed, waving a hand dismissively in the air. "That hasn't been true for a long time."

Jaq didn't know how to respond. Didn't know which part was more offensive to her: the fact that her mother seemed to be shopping more for John than she was for her own daughter, or the fact that her mom didn't know that pink—every shade from the faintest blush of a seashell to the brightest, most violent Barbie pink—was still her favorite color.

Before she could decide, her mother had moved off, carried away on a current of chiffon and satin.

Jaq turned her attention to a rack of dresses with long sweeping trains and skirts that fanned out like mermaids' tails, with sweetheart necklines and elegant Queen Anne collars. She paused on one in a luscious salmon pink, the bodice off-shoulder and studded with little pink pearls, the high-low skirt layered with tulle. She imagined how it would open around her legs like the petals of a flower and wanted nothing more than to try it on and spin. To feel the skirt flying up around her thighs and Devyn's hands catching her around the waist.

Jaq stopped herself and pushed the vision away. She hadn't meant to think of Devyn. But now that she had, the images were stuck in her mind. Stubborn and tantalizing.

Devyn dressed in a sleek suit, a bodice hugging her curves beneath a loose jacket, her mahogany hair styled in big curls around her pale cheeks. Devyn tipping that lopsided smile at her and holding out one hand in invitation. Devyn drawing her close to dance, her breath ghosting against the exposed skin of Jaq's jaw.

For two weeks, she'd been passing Devyn in the halls at school. They never spoke. But whenever Devyn was near, Jaq's gaze drifted toward her, as though pulled inside a gravitational orbit. When their eyes met, Jaq's entire body responded. In a way that left her tense and breathless and dreaming about Devyn's hands and where they might touch her next.

It was different from how she'd ever felt about John's touch. She hadn't known it before, but she couldn't help but make the comparison now. Things had always been more comfortable with John. Their pace considerate and slow. She'd always assumed that was because they were being careful, but now . . . Now she thought that her body had remembered more than her mind. Her memories had been taken, but there was something inside her that sparked for Devyn in a way she had never sparked for John.

In a way she had only ever sparked for Mallory.

In a way she had only ever desired other girls.

She squeezed her eyes shut and tried to replace Devyn with John. Imagine him touching her instead. The way things should be. The way things were.

If only she could talk to him about all of this.

"Don't tell me you like that."

Jaq jumped and turned to find her mother standing perilously close, long nose wrinkled in distaste.

"I do." Jaq sifted through and found one in her size, taking it down and holding it against her body. Layers of tulle puffed in all directions.

"Mm, it's not you," her mother said, squinting as though even looking at it was causing her pain. Once more making decisions and determinations about Jaq without bothering to take Jaq into consideration. "Too revealing."

"You haven't even seen it on me. How can you know it's not me?"

"I'm your mother. Trust me, I know. I know who you are and where you're going and with whom." She tapped Jaq's ring and smiled.

Suddenly, it was all too much. The ring. The dress. The future unfurling before her, every choice made by committee and never by herself alone. The value of each choice tethered to how it related to John and John's choices.

It wasn't his fault, but that didn't matter right now. What mattered was that her mother treated her like an accessory, an object in someone else's life.

"Mom, what would you do if John and I broke up?"

Some of her mother's pleasant demeanor fell away, her attention crystalizing around the comment. "Why would you break up?"

"I don't know." Jaq tried to keep her tone conversational, exploratory. "Maybe because we're still in high school, and who knows what will happen next year. Or tomorrow, for that matter."

"You know, a lot of people will tell you that young love is fickle, but I don't believe that. I think God brought the two of you to-gether for a reason, the same way He brought your father and I together. Love doesn't have to feel perfect to be perfect, and I can't imagine a better person for you." Her mother graced her with a smile that felt equal parts adoring and menacing. "Can you?"

Another image of Devyn flashed through her mind. Wind mak-ing rivers of her hair, dragging a laugh from her lips.

Jaq blinked it away and swallowed hard. Instead of answering, she returned the dress to the rack.

"Oh, here we are!" her mother declared. "Just look at this. *This* is you."

Her mother held up a powder-blue dress with a full skirt and a long-sleeved bodice in an even paler blue, the whole thing glitter-ing with iridescent sequins.

"This looks like something a Disney princess would wear."

"Doesn't it?!" her mom trilled, pushing the dress into Jaq's hands. "Try it on."

"I don't like it." Jaq stared at her mom, willing her to hear her words and believe them.

"You're only saying that because you haven't seen it on you yet. Trust me. This is going to be the one. And just imagine how in-credible John will look in a dark blue suit. It will make his eyes look like emeralds."

Jaq waited for her mother to imagine how the colors would work with Jaq's complexion. Whether it would make her hair shine or her skin radiant. Whether it would accentuate some part of her, flatter some piece of her. Waited to hear what space Jaq occupied in her mother's imagination.

And she thought again of Mallory. How she'd found her way

into rebellion so young. How she had struggled to stand up to her parents, but did it anyway because at the end of the day the most important thing was being true to herself. She had been so brave.

"Come on," her mother said, oblivious. "I can't wait to see it."

Numb, Jaq followed her mom to the dressing rooms, where an attendant wrote her name on a little chalkboard, then hung it on a hook by door number three. Luckily, her mom didn't ask to go inside with her, so Jaq had a minute to herself, which she used to cover her face with the wretched blue skirt and scream silently.

"Take your time," her mom called over the gap between the door and the ceiling. "And just remember how dashing John will look standing beside you. The dress is only one piece of the ensemble."

Jaq wondered if other parents used words like *dashing* to talk about their daughter's boyfriends, but she didn't say anything.

The dress hung from a hook high on the wall, the hanger designed to hold the shoulders out and prevent the whole thing from drooping. Still, it looked less like a prom dress and more like something a cartoon-obsessed six-year-old would wear on Halloween. Or as pajamas.

Slowly, she slipped out of her clothes and unzipped the dress. She let the skirt pool on the floor, then stepped inside and pulled the whole thing up. She had to hand it to her mom, the fit was exquisite. The sleeves and bodice cinched against her body as she dragged the zipper up, and the skirt flared out from the perfect point of her hips. For a second, the dress felt good. But when she turned to face the mirror, she was surprised it didn't crack.

Against the olive undertones of her skin, the combination of powdery-blue fabric and iridescent pastel sequins made her look gray. Half-dead. The wide scoop of the bodice accentuated her already broad shoulders, and the bodice somehow made her torso look stubby and truncated. The blue lace at the collar feathering against her skin like mold.

It was truly awful.

She felt the panic swirling in her chest, spurring her heart to beat faster and faster, and she pressed the heels of her hands into her eyes. When she opened them again, her reflection in the mirror had changed.

The princess dress was gone, and in its place was a wedding dress.

White lace over white satin, every layer sculpted to her body, the skirt reaching gracefully for the floor. Behind her, the dressing room had been replaced by the inside of her church. Pews garlanded in green and yellow flowers. Dozens of happy, approving faces looking up at her. The aisle strewn with rose petals like a spray of blood.

And next to her, grinning that golden grin, his green eyes locked on hers, was John.

Come back.

The voice was a torrent of cold water in her mind. Bracing and violent.

"No," Jaq whispered, hand flying to her belly, grasping at a line of satin buttons. "No, no, no."

She reached for the collar of the dress and tugged, but it didn't budge. She tried again, harder this time, and still the dress stayed exactly where it was. Panic knifed from her lungs to the back of her throat, making it harder to breathe as she tried again.

But when she tried to slide her fingers between her skin and the fabric, they wouldn't go. The dress was too tight. Tighter than it had been a second ago. The fabric was glued to her body, constricting with such force her skin was turning red where the seams dug in.

Jaq gasped, bending at the waist, and reached behind her for the string hanging from the zipper. Catching it, she tugged. Pulled. Ripped with all her strength.

The dress squeezed again, the fabric cinching in around her hips and stomach, forcing the air from her lungs so it could cinch even more.

She gasped for breath, but there was no room left. No space inside her for air.

Her vision began to swim. She clawed at the neck of the dress, driving her fingernails into her own flesh, desperate to get *outoutout*.

And then the door behind her flew open, and there stood her mother.

Jaq gasped, filling her lungs with as much air as they would hold.

"I'm sorry, I didn't mean to scare you, but I just couldn't wait anymore and, oh—"

Mrs. De Luca covered her mouth with one hand. Her eyes shimmered with instant tears as she took in her daughter. "Oh, Jaqueline."

Jaq found herself standing upright in the princess dress once more. The wedding dress was gone, and she could breathe again.

"It's perfect," her mother declared. "We're buying it. Get dressed and let's go get some sushi. I've been craving a California roll for I don't know how long, and your father never wants sushi at home."

She was still talking about her sushi order as she left the dressing room.

Jaq was too stunned to protest, the terror of the vision still too close.

But as she got out of the dress and stood in the little room in only her bra and panties, she knew it had been real. She could see the evidence in the marks on her chest. Eight crescent moon gouges where she'd clawed her own nails into her skin.

Thin streams of blood running from each.

CHAPTER
NINETEEN

Fern

In the eighteen years of Fern's life, the Jensen house had never been a quiet place.

Her sisters had been loud, confident, and demanding, always competing for something—the bathroom, piano time, even roles when Holly and Clover were both in high school at the same time, overlapping their senior and sophomore years respectively. The house was constantly buzzing with songs, conversation, or fights, and Fern, the smallest baby bird in the nest, had learned to be loud in order to get what she wanted. The decibel level of the house slowly declined as one by one the sisters graduated and left home, but even without them, Fern and her mom always had the radio or TV on in the background, something to make the house feel full.

On Sunday afternoon, though, the house was silent. Fern's mom had taken a swing shift at the hospital, and the maelstrom of Fern's thoughts was too loud to add anything else to the mix. She'd been lying face down on her bed for she didn't know how long while her thoughts cannibalized her brain.

She was blowing it. None of her sisters had ever blown a role before. All three of them had sailed into their senior years with the same self-assuredness she'd had only a few weeks ago. They'd made everything look so easy.

Their group text was still active, and they'd been checking in on her—or, in Ivy's case, offering plenty of unsolicited advice on how to approach a role like Sandy—but Fern couldn't talk to them about this. As far as Fern knew, none of the three of them had ever had a piece of their heart ripped away. They'd never felt like they were trapped inside their own bodies. Or spent five years believing in a false version of themselves. Like they'd spent so long living a lie they didn't even know where to look for the truth.

The worst part was that Fern didn't know what—*who*—she wanted to be. It wasn't like there was a Platonic Ideal of Fern in her head, and everything would suddenly feel good if she could just be that version of herself. All she knew was that right now, being this Fern was making her physically uncomfortable—and it was getting in the way of her ability to play Sandy.

Five years ago, she'd only just started untangling these feelings for herself. She hadn't had any answers then either, but that had been okay because Jaq and Mal were there to make it okay. They'd made the nebulous space of not knowing feel normal.

Fern vividly remembered the relief she'd felt whenever she was with them. How one afternoon, when they were hanging out in the house in the woods, Mal had asked, "Fern, do you want us to try different pronouns? Like, we can have a conversation about you using he/him or they/them and you can see how it feels?"

Fern had agreed, and Mal had turned to Jaq, pretending Fern wasn't there when she said, "Did you see Fern's outfit today? I thought he looked amazing in that green skirt."

"Yeah, it really brought out his eyes," Jaq added without missing a beat.

Fern's body had reacted as much as her mind. Squeezing and relaxing, warming and sighing as her friends traded he/him for they/them for she/her, letting their conversation be as easy as a summer breeze. She had liked it. All of it. And they hadn't made any demands of her. She'd had the freedom to explore and feel and exist.

Maybe if she'd been able to keep doing that, she wouldn't be fucking up so royally.

Or maybe if she'd hadn't gone into the woods the night of Karima's party, she'd be happier right now. Less confused and distracted. Maybe this was exactly what Mallory's ghost had wanted to happen. To see her struggle and fail.

Fern screamed into her pillow.

Mal had hated as viciously as she'd loved, but Fern still couldn't believe that she would torment her like this. Maybe cut off her hair or slip laxative into her coffee, but not attack her identity. No, there had been something else in the woods all those years ago; she knew it with the kind of certainty she wished she had about literally anything else right now. There had been someone else there that night. They'd gone to the house and—

Fern sat up. Remembering what Mal had always said about the house. That it had belonged to the Patron, and he was the one keeping them safe. It had been a nice story. So nice that Fern hadn't really cared if it was true or not, but now it made her wonder. The old nursery rhyme whispered through Fern's memory.

Come out, come out, wherever you are. The Patron's in the trees. Find his house, make a wish, he'll do just as you please.

There had been more to it, but she couldn't pull it all together. She grabbed her phone and searched the words. A single hit popped up. When Fern clicked the link, the song was there, at the top of the page, beneath the words "The Patron of Port Promise."

Fern's eyes slid over the second stanza.

Come in, come in, whoever you are, receive your Patron's gift. The price is small and with it all, you'll never be adrift.

Come back, come back, wherever you roam, come see his deathly hue. Ask him nice, don't ask twice—

He'll fix what's wrong with you.

The final words echoed in her head, as though someone had spoken them aloud. Here. In her room.

Fern dropped her phone, whipping around. Certain that whoever had said those words would be standing there. Next to her bed. Right behind her. Their breath still cold on her ear.

But there was no one.

The house was empty. And except for the distant hum of the furnace, it was silent.

Fern sat as still as she could. Convinced that if she tried to move, someone—something—would grab her. Smother her the way it had done in the costume basement, only this time there was no one around to hear her. No one to—

Fern almost screamed when the doorbell rang, reverberating too loudly through the quiet house.

She blew out a breath and vaulted out of bed, using the momentum to propel her out of the feeling of someone standing at her back. She hurried downstairs and flung the door open, ready to keep on running if she heard anything behind her.

Instantly, she wished she'd taken even twenty more seconds to check that her hair was presentable or maybe that she didn't have a smear of toothpaste on her chin or something equally embarrassing. Because standing right there on her doorstep was Kaitlyn Birch.

Her summer-brown skin was radiant in the diffused light of spring. Curls piled on top of her head like a crown, those kaleidoscope eyes a shock of copper and gold. Her coral lips parted slightly in a smile as her eyes skimmed up and down Fern's body.

Even though Fern was wearing a pair of old sweats and a T-shirt, she had never felt more naked in her life.

"What are you doing here?" she blurted, and immediately wished she could take it back.

But Kaitlyn laughed, eyes sparkling with humor. "You really do know how to sweep a girl off her feet," she teased, then held up a box Fern only recognized as a Blu-ray because her mom refused to make the switch from analog to digital. The cover was unmistakably the 1978 original film *Grease*. "I thought we might return to the source for a little inspiration. If you have time?"

"Um," Fern said, aware that her mind had gone blank and unable to do anything about it.

"It's okay if you don't," Kaitlyn continued when Fern didn't say anything else. "I know I should have texted. I just . . . I heard what Murph was saying to you after rehearsal on Friday, and I thought maybe this would help. Maybe I could help." She shrugged. "And I didn't know how to say any of that over text, but now I think that it was the wrong choice coming here."

Kaitlyn took a small step back, and Fern threw up a hand to stop her.

"No, it's okay. I was just . . ." Fern paused, weighing her options, and before she knew what was happening, she was telling the truth. "Having an existential crisis about how royally I'm fucking up this role, so I'm a little out of it."

Kaitlyn's eyes widened, clearly as surprised as Fern was by the confession. She stepped inside and closed the door behind her. "Then I've come just in time. I know we're talking ancient technology here, but do you have a Blu-ray player?"

Ten minutes later, they were sitting side by side on the sofa in the living room with two cans of Fern's mom's fancy carbonated cherry limeades, a bag of popcorn, and the movie rolling. Fern was doing her best to focus on the screen and not on the way Kaitlyn smelled both earthy and sweet, like rose hips and almonds. Or on the way Kaitlyn's shirt hugged her body just a little too tightly when she sat down. Definitely not on the way she could feel Kaitlyn's arm so close to her own.

"It's so different from the musical, even though it's the same story," Kaitlyn said when they'd paused to get another drink. "I also kind of hate it," she added with a laugh. "I think we can do better."

"No offense to John Travolta or anything, but he's no Kaitlyn Birch," Fern said. "I know we can do better."

"Wanna try?" Kaitlyn asked.

"Now?" Fern asked, a spike of nerves driving her voice higher.

"Why not? We can run the lines as many times as you want. Until they feel right." Kaitlyn caught Fern's hand and tugged her back onto the sofa. "Let's stick with the same scene from Friday. The drive-in, okay?"

"Oh . . . kay," Fern said, dragging the word out to hide her discomfort. Because that was the kiss scene. She checked the time, confirming that her mom wouldn't be home for hours, then followed Kaitlyn's lead and assumed her position. Back straight. Knees pressed together. Eyes locked on an invisible movie screen somewhere ahead of them.

Kaitlyn started the scene, teasing Fern and inching closer as she gave Fern a ring and then angled for a kiss. But every word from Fern was stilted, late, uneven. Like this was her first time running lines and she wasn't ready to be off book.

"I'm sorry!" She broke the scene before the kiss, getting abruptly to her feet and pacing toward the sliding glass door. "I don't know why this is so hard for me. Sandy is the most basic character in the entire play, but I can't connect with her!"

"Did you ever find your touchstone?" Kaitlyn asked.

Fern shook her head. "Nothing felt right. It's just such a ridiculous role. I don't get why Sandy is so willing to change herself for someone else! You were so right to sign up for Danny. At least he's interesting. It was so easy to find a connection to him in rehearsal the other day."

"Then let's switch again." Kaitlyn stood and crossed to where Fern was standing. "On our feet. So every piece of the scene is a little different. Maybe if you can connect to the scene, you can find your way to Sandy's role in it. Maybe Danny can be your touchstone."

"That doesn't make any sense at all," Fern said, but she could feel the edge of her frustration falling away anyway. "But okay."

Kaitlyn nodded and closed her eyes the way she did before every scene. When she opened them again, she had transformed. Kaitlyn's natural gravitas and humor gave way to an effervescent sweetness and light. Even her eyes seemed to shine with a kind of hopeful naivete that Fern had never seen in Kaitlyn herself. God, she was good.

It took Fern a second to find her own bearing. To relax her grip on the girl she was supposed to be and slip into Danny. Someone who knew what he wanted, even if he didn't know how to go after it. Someone who was afraid of what others would think if they saw who he really was.

Fern swallowed hard and started the scene. "You're not seeing anyone else, are you?"

"Why are you asking?" The look of surprise on Kaitlyn's face was elegant and glorious, even a touch suspicious.

"Only curious," Fern murmured, reaching out to take Kaitlyn's hand in hers. Running her thumb over Kaitlyn's knuckles—Danny's thumb over Sandy's knuckles.

The scene continued, every moment perfection as they traded lines back and forth. Fern's heart thudded as she settled into Danny, into the parts of herself that were also a boy, that were also neither. That were flexible and fluid and welcoming and wonderful.

Fern moved in for the kiss. Unsure if Kaitlyn would stop the scene here. Unsure if she should stop herself. Then Kaitlyn tipped her head up, Sandy tipped her head up, her eyes on Danny's. On Fern's.

Fern slid one hand along Kaitlyn's cheek, let Danny's fingers curl at the back of Sandy's neck as they came together for the kiss. At first it was only warm pressure. Then something shifted between them, some indecipherable spark of recognition, and Fern leaned in, pressed her lips more firmly to Kaitlyn's.

Kaitlyn made a sound low in her throat, surprised, then her hands were on Fern's waist, and the space between them was gone.

One kiss tumbled into another, cherries and lime on their tongues, each one deeper than the last, panting and hungry for the next until finally they slowed down. Let their kisses become soft and languid. Parted while they could still breathe.

"That was. . . . good," Kaitlyn said, a smile pressing into the corners of her mouth.

Good was an understatement. Fern didn't think she'd ever felt this good in her entire life.

"Yeah," Fern agreed, clearing her throat. "Really good scene."

Kaitlyn narrowed her eyes at that. "I wasn't—" She paused, reconsidering. "Fern, I'm going to ask you a question, and I would appreciate an honest answer." Fern nodded, and Kaitlyn continued. "Was that Danny kissing me just now? Or was it you?"

Fern felt her mouth fall open and her muscles tense. The pleasant warmth that had spread through her body just a moment ago was washed away, cleared out by the sudden terror of having been caught doing something she shouldn't.

Except that wasn't right. She had done nothing wrong even if her brain was trained to think the opposite was true.

"I—"

She took a deep breath and did her best to calm the rapid-fire beating of her heart. She wanted to tell Kaitlyn the truth. And, she realized with a sense of sudden euphoria, she could. She wasn't thirteen years old anymore, worried her mother would freak out and send her to a million biased doctors. She was eighteen. On the brink of her own adulthood and college. She might still be figuring her shit out, but that was okay. She was okay, and she had time to be a little messy as long as she was honest about it.

Starting with Kaitlyn.

"It was—" she started, and stopped. "It was—"

She stopped again, the words dying on her tongue as a flush burned its way through her pale cheeks.

"I mean, it was—" When she stopped this time, it was abrupt. As though someone had taken a pair of scissors to her vocal cords and snipped them in half.

"It was—"

Come back.

The voice ripped through her mind, taking her words with it. Stealing them so thoroughly that she couldn't even remember what she'd been trying to say.

Except she did remember. She was trying to tell Kaitlyn that it had been her. Not Danny. Maybe it had started out that way, but that's not how it had ended. And she wanted to do it again. Wanted to kiss Kaitlyn again, but as she cleared her throat and tried to dredge the words up from inside her, something stopped her.

An invisible hand around her throat.

She looked up at Kaitlyn, a new kind of panic lancing through her now, but instead of anger or irritation on Kaitlyn's face, she found only patience.

"It's okay," Kaitlyn said with a smile. "I get it. You don't have to answer right now. Just, when you're ready."

Stepping around Fern, Kaitlyn retrieved her movie from the player and her purse from where she'd tossed it on the couch.

"I'm gonna go, but I think this was good. I think we're getting a lot closer to where we need to be."

"Yeah," Fern said, voice thin and hoarse as she followed Kaitlyn past the wall of family photos to the front door. Dozens of versions of herself watching her. "A lot closer."

"Just one more thing about Danny and Sandy." Kaitlyn spun around, so close Fern could see the crushed pink of her lips, could still taste the cherry and limes on her tongue. "Maybe you shouldn't think of it as Sandy changing for him. Think of it as them changing for each other."

When the door shut behind her, the house was silent once more. Fern was left alone with the echo of that voice in her mind and the ghostly press of a hand around her neck.

CHAPTER TWENTY

Mallory
THEN

Mal had a good feeling. About everything. Ever since that tree branch had nearly crushed Tommy Webber, she'd felt like her life was about to get a lot better.

The house in the woods was protecting them, which meant the Patron was real and looking out for them. Maybe it was strange to believe it as easily as Mal did, but she'd spent her whole life learning about a man who'd risen from the dead, so a friendly forest spirit didn't seem that far-fetched.

Even Fern seemed to sense the change. They'd asked Mal and Jaq to start using they/them pronouns to refer to them. Not in public, but when they were safely tucked away in the house. When it was just the three of them.

And then there was Jaq.

Sweet, gentle, creative Jaq. She was a world of surprises and secrets, each one carefully guarded and hard to see until you knew where to look. She was playful, making faces and quiet jokes that could move Mal to stitches. She was always doodling in the margins of her notebook, turning blank spaces into landscapes of flowers and suns and spirals. And she was so deliriously lovely.

Sometimes Mal found herself staring at the long line of her nose or the perfect pout of her bottom lip. Found herself wondering what it would feel like to kiss that lip.

Every day her feelings for Jaq got sharper. More distinct and urgent. And something about having the house, and the Patron's protection, made her want to do something about it.

When her birthday came around, she asked her parents for a sleepover. She was shocked when they agreed, and she quickly picked a date for the event. A Saturday because that would give her a few, precious hours alone with her friends while her parents attended adult Bible study with the other miserably devout members of the congregation.

When the day arrived, Mal's mother left a plate of ants on a log on the kitchen table along with a pitcher of too-tart lemonade, as though they were three and not thirteen.

"We have to make sure the candy is gone—even the smell of it—before they get back, or I'll spend the next week eating nothing but oatmeal, hard-boiled eggs, and spinach, and trust me when I say I would rather die," Mallory said, cracking the window in spite of the pounding rain.

Jaq eased open a full-size bag of M&M's and set it on the floor between them, while Fern contributed a pack of tropical-flavored jelly beans and a bag of green tea Hello Kitty marshmallows they'd stolen from Ivy's secret stash.

Then, propping Fern's hand-me-down tablet against the bookshelf, they started *Crimson Peak*, which Mal's parents would never in a million years let her watch, and snuggled down into a nest of blankets and pillows.

As the movie played, Mal leaned close to Jaq, vibrantly aware of the way their fingers brushed beneath the blanket where Fern couldn't see. At first, it was just their pinkies, lightly skipping past each other, then Mal took a chance and skimmed her thumb down the inside of Jaq's palm, all the way to the tender skin of her wrist. She heard the breath catch in Jaq's throat, and she paused, waiting for some sign that this was okay.

Then Jaq shifted, her hand slipping over Mal's knee, fingertips grazing along the inside of her thigh, and Mal's entire body ignited.

She lost track of the movie as their fingers quietly, secretly explored the little bits of skin inside their wrists, around their knees, and higher, to the edges of their shorts. It was torturous and delightful, and Mallory had never wanted *more* than she wanted it in this moment.

When the movie ended too soon, neither one of them moved. Not even when Fern turned on the lamp and came to sit in front of them.

"I would kiss Mia Wasikowska in an instant," Fern said, voice barely above a whisper even though they knew no one else was home.

"Same," Mallory confirmed, surreptitiously pulling her hand away from where it rested against Jaq's thigh and trying to appear like she wasn't dreaming of lowering Jaq to the floor and pressing their lips together.

"It's the other one for me," Jaq offered shyly, a faint flush sitting high in her cheeks. Like maybe she was thinking of the same thing. "Jessica Chastain. She's so regal and commanding. I know she's older now, but in that movie? I can't look away from that dimple."

"What dimple?" Mal asked.

"The one in her chin," Fern said, agreeing. "Yeah, she's definitely hot, and so is the main guy. I forget his name."

"I don't feel that way for boys," Jaq said, casting another glance at Mal. "Only girls."

"Have you ever . . . ?" Mal started to ask. Her eyes fluttered, uncharacteristically embarrassed by her own question.

"No," Jaq admitted. "Have you?"

Mal shook her head, then, peeking through her lashes at Jaq, she asked, "Do you want to?"

Fern looked between the two of them, a blush creeping over their cheeks as understanding dawned.

Jaq caught her breath and held it for so long Mal was sure the answer would be no. Then Jaq nodded. "Yes."

Thunder rumbled overhead as Mal disentangled herself from the blankets and made an awkward gesture at her closet. She wanted this moment to be special. Just for the two of them.

"Guys," Fern said in protest. "Why don't you wait until we're at the Patron's house?"

"It's okay," Mal promised. "My parents won't be home for hours."

"You keep watch," Jaq said, eyes alight with excitement. She turned and followed Mal into the narrow closet and shut the door behind them.

Inside the closet, the world was muffled. They pushed the hangers of Mallory's clothes to either side, leaving them space to stand. Warm light spilled down from above, casting their faces in shadow.

Mallory reached for Jaq's hands. "I, um, I'm not really sure how to do this," she said.

Jaq bit her bottom lip and shook her head. "Me either."

"Okay. Then we'll just . . ." Mallory stepped forward and pressed her mouth to Jaq's.

The kiss was light and wet, and at first, it was odd and confusing.

Mallory had puckered her lips as she'd seen others do, and so had Jaq. The result was something stiff and a little disappointing.

She pulled away, saw her own disappointment reflected on Jaq's face, and made a decision.

"Let's try again," she said. "But this time let's make our lips, I don't know, softer?"

"Like this?" Jaq leaned in and pressed her mouth to Mal's once more, but this time, her lips were soft and slightly parted.

Mal mirrored Jaq's approach, letting her lower lip slide between Jaq's in a way that made her head spin and her stomach pitch.

They parted again. Smiling, sure they'd done it right this time and too overwhelmed by the feeling to do anything but crash together once more. Kissing and smiling and even laughing a little.

It was unlike anything she'd ever experienced. Perfect and devastating and precious.

Mal wanted to live inside this moment forever. For a second, she dared to believe that she could. That her life didn't have to be what her parents dictated. That she could make decisions for herself.

But then the door opened, sucking all the warmth from the enclosed space. And several things happened at once. So quickly that afterward, Mallory would be unable to say which had come first.

Her mother stood there, staring down at them in horror. "Mallory! Oh my god, what are you doing?!"

From somewhere behind, Fern's voice whimpered, "I'm sorry."

Jaq drew back, pulling away, making herself smaller. Invisible.

A rush of defiance was the only thing that kept Mallory on her feet. All the anger she'd kept inside, the fury she'd pushed down and down and down, had hardened into something stronger than she'd ever expected herself to be. A foundation that could support her even while her mother stared down with crushing detachment.

"What were you doing just now?" her mother asked.

Mallory met her mother's hard gaze with one of her own and answered, "I was kissing Jaq."

"Why?" Mrs. Hammond asked in a dangerously low voice.

"Because I wanted to," Mallory said, buoyed by her defiance. She'd been caught, and she saw no reason not to be up-front about it. The punishment was coming either way, and at least this way, she could feel good about herself.

"What's going on in here?" Mallory's dad's voice boomed around them, an echo of the thunder outside.

Mrs. Hammond stepped back, her posture shifting the way it always did when Mr. Hammond entered the room. Shoulders rounding forward, head bowing ever so slightly, eyes angled down. It made Mallory angry every time.

"Our daughter and her friends have been . . ." She hesitated. "Experimenting."

"What do you mean 'experimenting'?" Mallory's dad strode into the middle of the room and stopped at the sight of his daughter in the closet with another girl. With Jaq.

All at once, he seemed to understand his wife's code. A shadow settled over his face, and the muscles in his jaw clenched and unclenched.

"Sarah," he growled.

Mallory had so seldom heard her mother's first name that at first she didn't understand that it was a command. He was telling his wife to act so that he wouldn't. If he had any paternal instincts toward his daughter, they were used up in that one word.

"Fern," Mrs. Hammond said, turning away from Mallory. "I think it's time you and—you and your friend go home, don't you? Mr. Hammond will drive you."

Fern hesitated only briefly before nodding. "Yes, ma'am."

"Mom—" Mallory started, fear blossoming in her chest at the thought of being left alone with her mother.

But Mrs. Hammond held up a hand. "Not yet."

Mr. Hammond didn't speak again as Jaq and Fern gathered up their things. Neither of them even looked back at Mal as they left her in the room. Alone with her mother.

The front door slammed, and the car engine rumbled outside. The whole time, Mallory stayed in the closet. Something about it felt safe and secure, warm and almost comforting.

When the sound of the car engine had faded into the distance, Mrs. Hammond turned back to her daughter, stepping into the doorway of the closet so Mallory had no choice but to remain.

"You are my daughter," Mallory's mother said. "Your character is a reflection of your parents, and I will *not* overlook your flaws. It is my responsibility to help you overcome them, and that is exactly what I'm going to do."

Mallory resisted the urge to wrap her arms around her stomach, to make herself smaller.

"For now, I want you to sit with this. I want you to consider what you've done tonight."

"I know what I've done," Mallory protested. "And I'm not sorry."

"Not sorry?" her mother repeated. "All right. Then let's start there. If you enjoy the closet so much, Mallory, then stay there."

With that, Mallory's mom shut the closet door, turned the lock, and switched off the light.

And in the darkness, Mallory burned.

CHAPTER
TWENTY-ONE

Jaq

Jaq had never felt so heavy.

Her attention had narrowed to the sensation of the ring on her finger, and no matter what she tried, she couldn't pry it away.

She fidgeted with the ring through all her classes Monday morning. Turning and twisting it around her finger, trying to find some position in which it would finally vanish from her awareness. But it was always there. Binding and biting into her skin. Her hand felt cold and weighty, as though gravity had intensified on it alone and was pulling her down, making her slow and small. Even turning the pages in a textbook seemed to take more effort than usual.

She wanted to take it off, but if she did, John would notice. He'd ask if something was wrong or if she didn't like it, and she would have to give him an answer. A not-insignificant part of her wanted to do exactly that, because John wasn't just her boyfriend; he was her *friend*. Even before Mallory, they'd been friends, and right now, what she needed more than anything else was a friend she could talk to. She didn't trust anyone to help her untangle the new knots in her heart the way she trusted him.

But telling him anything meant hurting him. Taking off the

ring meant hurting him. Maybe it even meant losing him.

And that made Jaq feel trapped. Caged. Like she couldn't draw a full breath. But something had to change. She just didn't know what.

It was starting to drive her toward panic when she opened her locker after lunch and something tumbled out, landing at her feet. She picked it up to discover it was an origami dragon. The paper was bright purple, and someone had drawn a little face with black ink. On the wing, in tight boxy letters, was written PULL HERE.

Intrigued, Jaq pulled and the whole design unfurled, each crease unbending until the paper was flat and the note hidden inside was visible.

FEELS LIKE WE LEFT THINGS UNFINISHED.
MEET ME AT FRANK'S?
TONIGHT, 10PM.
−D

There were only thirteen words, but Jaq read them three times. Carefully. Her heart picking up speed as she entertained the thought of seeing Devyn again.

"Planning some sort of secret rendezvous?" John looped one arm around her waist and settled his chin in the crook of her shoulder, causing Jaq to gasp and crush the note in her palm.

"Whoa, now I know you are," he said, stepping back and giving her a playful grin. "Why so jumpy, Jaqueline?"

"I'm not," she said, doing her best to cover her reaction with a laugh. "You just surprised me."

"So, that's not someone asking you out on a date?" he asked, gaze dropping to her hand, where the note was still clutched tight.

"No, oh my gosh, no. It's just a note from a friend in AP Calc. I don't even think you know her—Grace Seltzer? Anyway, she's begging me for my notes from the last section and clearly trying to win me over with super cute origami skills."

John hesitated, and Jaq had the sudden, terrifying thought that he'd seen the note and knew she was lying. But he recovered with a quick grin.

"That makes more sense than a torrid affair," he said. "But just to be clear, I'm the only man in your life, right? You don't even notice other guys because when you see them, all you can think of is my beautiful face?"

This time, Jaq did laugh. John's natural charm and humor made it so easy to be with him. He was kind and thoughtful and good. That was all still true. She still felt all the same warmth and affection for him she always had, but it was tempered now. Subdued, as though it were a harmony playing alongside the melody inside her.

"You're such a cheese," she said, pushing lightly at his chest, the band on her finger glittering.

"My mother prefers 'ham,' but I'll take it because I find almost all food comparisons to be okay." He stepped forward, letting the humor fade. "Seriously, though, Jaq, I know that wasn't a note from Grace Seltzer. And you don't have to tell me about it, but is . . . are you okay? I keep feeling like something is going on with you, but I don't know what."

She was so far from okay. If only she could fix this—fix *herself*.

"I'm just dealing with a lot. You know, between prom and all my AP exams."

"Anything I can do to help?" he asked. "I'm not saying you should trust me with your calculus homework, but I'm very good at other things. Coffee runs, pep talks, stress breaks." He tugged her closer, ducking his chin for a kiss.

Jaq's insides rebelled even as she kept a death grip on her smile, but then the warning bell rang.

"I'm going to be late!" Jaq said, veering out of John's path to swap her books and shut her locker.

"Okay, just remember I do care about the things that stress you out." John leveled her with a firm look. "You can talk to me. You know?"

"Yeah," Jaq answered, knowing that it used to be the truth, but wasn't anymore.

————

She spent the day at war with herself. Every time she imagined meeting Devyn, her stomach flipped deliciously. And every time she imagined ghosting Devyn, her lungs deflated.

There was no denying what she wanted anymore. But the things she wanted were shrouded in a long-forgotten terror. One that was rooted in the night Mallory's parents discovered her in the closet with Mal. She'd been sure that the Hammonds would tell her parents exactly what she'd done with their daughter that night. It was so disorienting to have forgotten the taste of that fear.

She had climbed into the back of Mr. Hammond's old station wagon with a cold knot of dread making it hard to breathe. Too afraid to look at Fern sitting next to her. Too afraid, even, to feel anger at Fern's failure to warn them. All she wanted was to reach for her friend's hand for comfort. But she was sure that any contact between the two of them would ignite the rage simmering in Mr. Hammond's pale blue eyes.

That car ride had been tortuously long and quiet. But he hadn't said a word to her parents. Not to Fern's either. He'd explained that Mallory wasn't well.

"We don't want to risk Jaqueline catching what Mallory has," he'd said, giving Jaq a firm squeeze on the shoulder and ushering her through the front door.

Her parents had been grateful and unsuspecting. But Jaq had gone to bed that night beneath a blanket of doubt and worry. A sense that the Hammonds' anger was a loaded gun aimed at her back. Wishing—almost—that it had gone off already.

She had burrowed into her blankets, clutched at the friendship necklace that hung around her neck, and prayed for safety. For herself, but also for Fern and Mal.

Only a day later, that fear had vanished. Taken from her thoughts along with the reason for them, along with Mallory herself, who became nothing more than a deviant and a runaway.

And Jaq had believed it. Along with everyone else at the church, she pitied the Hammonds and marveled that they could have missed the signs of Mallory's nature when looking back. Now it seemed so clear.

She was always so opinionated.

She had that look to her.

Nothing but trouble, if you ask me.

Mallory Hammond had become a cautionary tale of almost mythic proportions. Jaq had even told it to herself on occasion, never once remembering the fear she'd experienced that night in the car with Mr. Hammond or how much she had loved Mallory in her thirteen-year-old way.

The fear was back now. And it was all she could think about as she sneaked out her bedroom window and climbed into the maple tree that stood in the side yard.

Her hands trembled as she lowered herself between the branches. Her brain screamed at her to go back, stay safe inside her bedroom, and be happy with what she had, but the rest of her reached for something else. Yearned for it. She couldn't just bury this part of herself any longer. Not even if she was afraid.

She needed to know.

Jaq hit the ground and froze, certain she'd seen someone standing on her front porch, watching her. Holding her breath, Jaq pressed in close to the trunk of the tree, squinting for a better look. The porch light was off and the little space drenched in shadows. She heard the slow creak of a floorboard, watched as the darkness shifted toward her, and for a heartbeat, she was afraid she'd been caught.

But as she studied the darkness, she found the outline of the rocking chair that had been on their porch forever. Saw it rock slightly in the breeze, whining as it moved.

"Why so jumpy, Jaqueline?" she muttered, hurrying down the dark street.

Fifteen minutes later, she was standing just inside the door of the old diner, stunned by the scene before her.

There were people. That wasn't the stunning part. There were always people in Frank's, or she assumed there were because the lot was always full. But these people were dressed in all kinds of clothes and costumes. One was in all black, the shine of pleather contrasting with their light brown skin. Another, with soft, fat curves, wore a tulle skirt in layers of pastel pinks and purples. Yet another was in a blush-red corset and jeans that made their moon-pale skin nearly translucent. They were all shapes, sizes, colors, genders. They didn't even seem to be all in the same group, but were scattered around the restaurant as though completely un-afraid to be in this very public space dressed the way they were.

Being who they were.

It was like nothing she'd ever seen. And a part of her relaxed instantly.

"In or out," a man barked, cruising past with a tray of steaming eggs and burgers.

"Out! Out! Out!" the nearest table cheered, dissolving into silly laughter.

Jaq took a step back.

"They don't mean for you to leave," Devyn said, coming up behind her. So close it made Jaq's skin tingle. "They mean they like being out better than the alternative. C'mon."

Jaq did her best to look calm as she followed Devyn to a booth on the opposite side of the restaurant from what Jaq was now call-ing "the rowdy group" in her mind.

"I wasn't sure you'd come," Devyn admitted, as they settled across from one another. Her cheeks were pastel pink, the wild snarl of her curls hidden by a braid.

"I wasn't sure either," Jaq admitted.

The waiter who had barked at her earlier arrived with menus in hand. He slapped them on the table and then stepped back, giving Jaq a full view of his outfit: a salmon-pink pullover with the words MOM MODE printed across the chest in bold black letters, and tight black jeans tucked into army boots. He was older than Jaq, but not as old as her parents. She would guess somewhere in his thirties.

"Dev," he drawled, casting a suspicious glance at Jaq. "What are we doing here?"

"She's new," Devyn answered, defensive.

"*You've* barely been here a minute," he countered, raising an eyebrow.

Jaq looked between them. Completely lost even though the conversation was clearly about her.

"Frank, give her a beat," Devyn said after a few seconds.

He nodded, backing away from the table. "You know the drill," he said, gesturing to the coffee in one corner and the soda machine in the other.

"So that's the eponymous Frank," Jaq said. "But what was that about?"

"You can't figure it out?" Devyn smiled, then nodded like she should have known better. "You really are new."

"New to what?"

Devyn's eyes narrowed thoughtfully, and Jaq swallowed hard, the answer hitting her all at once.

"I'm not—" Her voice cut out before she could say the word. As though someone had turned the volume down suddenly.

"What? Not gay? Not queer? Or not ready to say it out loud?" Devyn asked.

Jaq whipped her head around, alarmed by the sound of those words. Terrified that someone might think they applied to her.

But all around the restaurant, people were only paying attention to each other. She had the sense that even if they had heard, they wouldn't care.

"Jaq," Devyn said, pulling her attention back. "I invited you here because I didn't mean to make you uncomfortable the other week, and I can't stop thinking about it. About . . . you."

The way Devyn looked at her made it harder to breathe. Harder to think.

"I know that you have a boyfriend," Devyn continued. "And I'm not trying to break you up or anything. It's just that I know there's something between us, and I would regret it forever if I didn't say it."

"Devyn, I'm not—" Again the word vanished in her throat. Evaporated like rain on hot pavement. "I mean."

All at once, Jaq realized that she didn't want to deny it. Sitting here with Devyn, surrounded by people who weren't judging her even though a very loud voice in her head told her they should be judged. A voice that sounded a lot like her mother's.

"I'm—"

Come back.

Cold sluiced down Jaq's spine, and her lungs deflated. She reached for the cross charm at her neck and tugged, nervous tears threatening in the back of her throat.

"Hey," Devyn said with a smile that faded almost as quickly as it had landed. "Hey, what's wrong?"

Jaq had never been a crier. Not even at movies. But under the gentle pressure of Devyn's question, she was powerless. Tears flowed hot and fast down her cheeks. She didn't know what had happened, but now that she'd started crying, she couldn't stop. It was like the tears had burned through whatever thin shield had been holding them back, and now there were several years' worth racing to get out.

"I'm sorry," she said. "I don't know what I'm doing here or— Why—"

"You don't have to apologize," Devyn said, suddenly by her side, one arm wrapped around her shoulders. "You don't even have to explain."

For a long moment, all Jaq could do was lean into her. Let the tears come. And in a way, it felt nice.

Then she remembered that they were in the middle of a crowded restaurant with a very cranky owner, and she fought to regain control. Little by little, it came. And when she opened her eyes, she was surprised to find a pile of napkins on the table before her. That, and the restaurant was quiet.

When she raised her head, Frank was seated across the table from her, the rest of the customers watching her with something like reverence.

"Okay, kid, what's your name?" Frank asked with begrudging kindness.

Jaq pressed a napkin to her face before answering. "Jaq."

Frank nodded, then shifted his gaze to a point behind her. "Cole! Flip the sign!"

"On it!"

The name took Jaq by surprise. But when she looked, she found Cole Clark standing near the front door in an apron just like Frank's, having flipped the sign from OPEN to CLOSED. He caught her eye and gave her an encouraging smile, the gesture drawing attention to a faded bruise around his left eye.

"This right here," Frank said, sweeping his hands wide, "is a safe space when you need it. You come here; you're family. But keep the shit outside, understand?"

Jaq nodded, then stopped. "Actually, no."

"He means we can be messy, but in here, we support each other," Devyn said. "Even if we've only been in town for a few weeks. Even if . . . we're still figuring things out for ourselves."

"Right, and on nights like this, when someone's in the thick of it—" Frank started, rising from his seat and heading toward an old-fashioned jukebox tucked into one corner. Instead of turning it on, though, he hit the power button on a speaker perched on top. "We dance until there's nothing but glitter in our veins and hope in our hearts. Clear the floor! And, Jaq, pick a letter."

"A letter?" she asked, so confused. "Okay, how about . . ." She said the first letter that entered her mind. "D?"

Devyn coughed softly, covering her mouth with her hand.

"David Bowie it is."

The room was in constant motion as people pushed the tables and chairs aside, creating a dance floor. Then the lights dimmed, and the synthesized chords of David Bowie's "Let's Dance" flooded the room.

Apart from the obligatory school dance, Jaq wasn't really a dancer. She didn't like not knowing what her body should be doing at any given moment, and the pressure or worry that what she was doing looked silly was even worse. But something about Frank's, with the lights turned low and the floor filled with strangers who weren't strangers at all, was freeing.

Jaq slid from the booth in something like a trance, then turned to look at Devyn, who was watching her with a bemused expression.

"Are—are we not supposed to dance?" Jaq asked, suddenly self-conscious.

"We are absolutely supposed to dance." Devyn came to stand beside her. "I'm a little surprised that you want to."

In response, Jaq spun around on her heel in time with the music, the movement itself enough to make her laugh. Devyn followed her lead, and they danced. To the end of one song and into the next.

"How did you know to come here?" Jaq asked between songs.

"Have you ever seen the Pride flag out front? No business owner flies that on accident," Devyn answered with a wry grin.

"Do you come here because . . ." Jaq hesitated, not sure how to ask if Devyn's parents were as intolerant as her own, but Devyn was already shaking her head.

"My parents are cool. But sometimes it's nice to be around people who get me a little better than others. Who remind me that things like gender and sexuality are an endless garden of possibility. And we all get to bloom in our own way." She swayed as another song started to play.

"My parents believe girls all bloom in the same way," Jaq said. "A rose is a rose is a rose. So common you can buy them at the gas station."

"Sure," Devyn said, smile turning gleeful and vicious. "But even a common rose has thorns."

Jaq spent the rest of the night with tears in her throat. A bitter squeezing sensation that wasn't quite sadness, but something better and worse at the same time. She didn't know what it meant that Frank and everyone here had seen something in her that she wasn't brave enough to see herself. That they were making room for it the same way Mal had. That, like her, they were making demands of the world instead of letting it make demands of them.

As she danced, the pain in her throat eased, the feeling blossoming into something like joy, and for a few minutes she dared to think that everything would be okay because this was good. It was warm and bright and welcoming and *good*.

Just for tonight, she believed she could have something good.

Believed she was something good.

And when it was all over, Devyn drove her to the top of her

street, then waited as she climbed back through her bedroom window. When she'd silently changed out of her sweaty clothes and into pajamas, she felt good enough to do something that hurt just a little.

She slid John's promise ring from her finger and put it away.

CHAPTER
TWENTY-TWO

Fern

If there was such a thing as perfection, then it was kissing Kaitlyn Birch.

Fern lived inside the kiss for three days and three nights. She let herself sink into the memory of it, replaying the kiss, the sensation of Kaitlyn's hands at her waist, the way she had slipped through Danny into an ethereal, buoyant place within herself.

She hadn't even seen Kaitlyn on Monday because there were separate calls for the Pink Ladies and the T-Birds, but today they were running ensemble dance scenes, which meant they'd be together almost every minute.

Buzzing, Fern slicked her hair into a low ponytail at the back of her neck, then selected a plain T-shirt and jeans. The whole time, she played the drive-in scene in her mind, unconsciously reciting Danny's lines out loud along with her own as she laced up her shoes and reached for a black corduroy jacket. The ensemble wasn't quite right; she didn't seem to own much that wasn't tailored for curves or related to the pastel end of the color spectrum, but it was better than anything else in her closet. Her wardrobe was essentially a shrine to traditional femininity, which, while not terrible on its own, wasn't her. All of her. Them. Fern.

"Do you want us to try different pronouns?" Mal had asked.

She did. He did. They did.

Even just in their own mind, the words didn't feel anchored the way they once had. Fern was a girl, a boy. Neither and both. If they dug, they could find an anchor in girl or boy—a touchstone, a word, a feeling—but a gentle instinct whispered that they didn't need to. Right now, it felt good to be more fluid.

Fern was shifting. At first, after the *wake up*, the unbecoming and rebecoming of Fern's memories and self had felt disjointed and upsetting. This, though . . . this new becoming was exhilarating. Discovering something that had always been there, inside. And in a way that they would soon be able to share with someone. With Kaitlyn.

"It hasn't been *that* long since laundry day," Fern's mom announced, coming into the kitchen just as Fern was finishing breakfast. "And what is going on with your hair? With it pulled down like that, you look sick. Wait, are you sick?"

"I'm not sick, Mom. I'm fine," Fern protested, but their mother was already coming for them, brow knitted in concern.

She pressed the back of one hand to Fern's forehead. "No fever," she murmured.

"I didn't feel like dressing up today." It was a lie. This *was* dressing up. It just wasn't in a way their mother would understand. Which was evident by the way she was staring at Fern as though they'd just told her they'd committed a murder.

"Honey," she started, perching on the seat next to Fern. "I know you've been under a lot of pressure recently. Senior year is tough, and doing all of that while also being the star of a show is even harder. It's okay if you're struggling."

"I'm not—"

"Lots of girls your age struggle, and I wouldn't be surprised if being in this show is a little harder than usual," their mom continued. "It really isn't fair of Ms. Murphy to ask you to take on a role like this, playing opposite a girl. You know, a group of parents complained to the school board, and I wouldn't be surprised if she gets into trouble for this. I'm *this close* to saying something myself. It's fine if they want to do this sort of thing at the college level, but it's inappropriate in high school. I would completely understand if you're upset about it. It's truly irresponsible of her."

"Mom, I'm really fi—"

"We probably should have had this conversation a lot sooner." She gave Fern's appearance another studied glance. "I'll make you an appointment to see someone as soon as possible."

A memory of their mother walking into their bedroom one evening flashed through their mind. They were bent over a graphic novel they'd checked out from the public library with Holly. It was written by a trans author about having been a trans kid, and their mother had snatched it away. Fern would never forget the horror in their mother's face as she flipped through the pages, or the vitriol in her voice when she'd whispered, "This is *sick*."

Fern remembered trembling on the floor. The secret validation they'd felt seconds before now rotting in their chest. Withering beneath their mother's accusing stare.

"Fern, there is nothing wrong with you," she'd said, snapping the book shut and throwing it into the hallway. "You are a perfect, beautiful little girl, and we're going to get through this."

The next thing Fern knew, they'd been in a therapist's office seated next to their mother, answering questions they didn't have answers to and that made them feel uncomfortable and gross.

That made them feel unsafe.

That still made them feel that way.

"Mom, stop!" Fern's throat tightened around the words and around that old fear. The irony was that they actually did want to talk to someone, but they had learned a long time ago that they couldn't trust their mother. "I'm fine. Seriously. Wearing jeans isn't a cry for help, and I don't need therapy because I decided not to curl my hair today. I'm not sad. Actually, I feel really good about things, okay?"

Their mom considered them for a long moment, as though the idea that Fern—or anyone—could be okay in this situation was cause for alarm all on its own. A familiar spike of fear wormed its way down Fern's spine. The one that reminded them it was dangerous to speak up, to give any indication to their mother that they were anything other than their mom's idea of normal. No matter how much they wanted to.

"I'm good," Fern repeated, willing their mom to believe it.

"Hmm," their mom said, rising from her seat and walking around the island to the kitchen, where she plucked an energy drink from the fridge and cracked the top. "Well, at least go put on some lip gloss or something before you go to school. You look like a boy."

"I've got some in my bag," Fern said, unable to keep the smile from their lips as they left for school. It wasn't the win they wanted, but it was enough for now.

Fern spent the rest of the day in a dreamy state that wasn't quite happiness, but almost. Okay-ness, fine-ness, trending toward good. But the second they spotted Kaitlyn waiting for them at the theater doors, their insides effervesced, bubbles rushing toward the surface of the ocean.

"Hey," Kaitlyn said, a shy, sweet smile on her face.

"Hey," Fern answered, feeling the way their own smile mirrored Kaitlyn's.

They knew they should have something more to say. In fact, they'd spent the better part of the lunch period imagining what they might say. So much so that both Cam and Melissa had snapped their fingers in front of their face more than once to get their attention. Eventually winning a "What the fuck, Fern?" from Cam.

Fern had used the excuse of running lines in their head. Which wasn't a lie, exactly.

Now, though, everything they'd practiced was gone. Evaporated under the heat of Kaitlyn's presence.

"I've wanted to tell you all day, but I love this look on you," Kaitlyn said. "It's really different, and I like it."

Fern pulled their bottom lip between their teeth and bit down, doing their best to contain a sudden swell of emotion. "Thanks," they managed.

"Come with me," Kaitlyn said, taking Fern's hand and dragging them both down the hall, wending their way through the passages that always smelled a little like rain even when the sun was out.

Fern dared to hope that they were headed for a bathroom stall to kiss, but they zipped right past the nearest restroom. "Where are we going?" Fern asked.

"Murph's classroom," Kaitlyn answered. "I want to catch her before she leaves for the theater."

"Why? Won't we see her there?" Fern asked, genuinely confused now.

"We need privacy for this," Kaitlyn said.

Fern didn't have time to ask what Kaitlyn meant by that before they rounded the corner and caught Ms. Murphy just as she was about to lock her classroom door.

"Murph!" Kaitlyn called. "We need to talk to you."

Ms. Murphy took in Kaitlyn's urgent expression and Fern's confusion, then pushed the door open and flipped the lights back on. "Better make it quick. We only have two more rehearsals until opening, and every moment is precious."

"This won't take long," Kaitlyn promised, pulling Fern inside without releasing their hand.

Fern still had no idea what this was about, but with Kaitlyn's hand in theirs, it almost didn't matter.

"The thing is"—Kaitlyn paused to take a deep breath—"I think we should switch roles. I should be Sandy, and Fern should be Danny."

"What?" Fern and Ms. Murphy said in unison.

"Do you realize that today is Tuesday, and we open on Thursday?" Ms. Murphy asked, thin brows arched high above her cat-eye glasses. "Why on earth would you think that's a good idea?"

Kaitlyn shrugged, unbothered by Ms. Murphy's very valid concerns. "I know the part. So does Fern. And you've seen what happens when we switch roles. It's better."

"I won't argue that the energy is particularly vivid when you switch, but this is a big change so close to opening. Not only for the two of you, but for the whole cast."

"We can do it," Kaitlyn said without hesitation. "Aren't you always telling us that we have to be ready for anything in theater? That the challenge and fun of a living art form is learning how to adapt to last-minute changes?"

"Missed cues and lines and broken zippers! Not the two leads deciding they'd been assigned the wrong parts!" Ms. Murphy huffed and held up one finger to indicate that she was thinking. "Okay, I know what Kaitlyn thinks. Fern, do you also agree that this is what you want? You didn't ask to be considered for Danny, so I need to know that this is something you want to do."

Want.

Fern had never wanted anything more. They had never felt as clear about themself as when they played Danny. There was no question that it was the right role for them.

And yet, thinking of standing in front of the entire school—their friends and their *mother*—as Danny Zuko was overwhelming. It was like taking the plunge into the pool at Whisper Falls, a shock of cold.

The more they imagined it, though, the more they wanted the role and the opportunity to stand up and show their mother how brilliant they could be inside it, how happy it made them to be seen in that way. How utterly perfect and normal it was.

"I realize that this is a big decision, but we don't have the luxury of time here," Ms. Murphy said, gently cutting into Fern's thoughts. "Kaitlyn has made the offer, and I need a yes or a no. Once we've made the switch, it's full steam ahead. I will need you both to give me one hundred and twenty percent from this moment until we strike."

Fern swallowed hard and turned to Kaitlyn, searching for any indication that Kaitlyn would regret this or resent them. "You really don't have to do this for me," Fern said.

"I'm doing it for us," Kaitlyn answered easily. Then she squeezed Fern's hand and lowered her voice, whispering in Fern's ear, "We're making the change for each other, remember?"

Fern nodded. That was exactly what Kaitlyn had said about Sandy and Danny. They changed for each other, and that's what made them brave enough to tell the world.

With Kaitlyn's hand in theirs, Fern was ready to be brave. For Kaitlyn and for themself.

"Can you do this, Fern?" Ms. Murphy asked.

Come back, hissed a voice in their head, close and threatening. *Come back.*

But Fern ignored it, looked straight into Ms. Murphy's eyes, and answered, "I can."

CHAPTER TWENTY-THREE

Jaq

The trees were thick around Jaq, the pines stretching up and up, the thatch-work canopy of oak and spruce and hemlock knitting tight over a midnight sky, their craggy trunks softened by layers of fragrant moss. Her eyes had adjusted to the low light, allowing her to distinguish a path through the underbrush, but Jaq had no idea how she'd gotten here.

She didn't remember leaving her house or entering the woods. Had she walked all the way?

A hand slipped inside hers. The touch cold. Jaq startled and turned, surprised to find Mallory by her side.

She looked exactly as she had the last night of her life. Her red hair was vibrant even in the dark, her white skin tinged blue in the moonlight. Her face was rounded with the last remnant of her baby fat, features poised on the brink of a transformation that would take her from child to adult. She was trapped between the two—her blue eyes sharp with cunning, carrying more anger and wisdom than so many of her peers, yet in her wry grin there was a gap where one of her molars had yet to come in, the impish gleam of someone who still thought fart jokes were funny. A child but not. An adult but not. Her body and heart forever and always a tension of opposites.

"Hi, Jaq," Mal said, smiling with her eyes first. Always.

"Mal." Jaq was breathless with loss, her grief thunderous inside her heart.

She'd tried to avoid it. To push it back and down and away. But here and now, as she looked directly into the face of the first girl she'd ever loved, there was no ignoring it.

"What happened to you?" Jaq asked, her voice wretched with tears. "And why can't I remember?"

Mal frowned and shook her head. "He doesn't want you to."

"Who doesn't?"

At the question, Mal faded and flickered. Her expression shattered, flipping through amusement, fear, anger, delight, grief in rapid succession, like someone was changing the channels of a TV. Then she stabilized.

"You have to come back." Mal's words echoed as though coming from very far away. "It's the only way I can help you."

"Come back where?" Jaq asked, breath puffing white where Mal's had not.

Mal raised her eyebrows, incredulous and amused as only she could be. Then she tipped her head to one side, indicating that Jaq had missed what was right in front of her. Laughing because wasn't Jaq always missing what was right in front of her?

Jaq turned her head, and where there had only been forest—she would swear to that—there was now a house. Or the memory of a house.

The frame stretched up unevenly, some walls ending in sharply peaked rooftops, while others gaped at the sky above, drinking in the moon. Windows grinned like jack-o'-lanterns, their teeth jagged and sharp, and vines snaked in and out of dark crevices. The door alone remained solid and whole, a flat plane at the top of a crumbling set of stairs. Above it, the words PROMISE HOUSE had been carved into stone, now softened by time and moss.

The house stood at the edge of a cliff, beyond which the woods parted, offering a view of the valley where Port Promise lay knitted between tree and rock, tacked down by a long, glittering stretch of water.

Jaq knew this place.

She had seen it in her memories. Surrounded by mystery and wonder, confessions and laughter. It had been their place. The only place they'd ever felt safe.

Safe.

But here, now, it was anything but. The house was leering and sinister. Cavernous and carnivorous. This was a house of death, she knew it in her bones.

"Come on." Mal walked ahead, crossing the clearing toward the stone steps.

Jaq didn't want to go. She stood still. As still as the house. She considered it as much as it considered her, staring down at her through holes blacker than the night sky. From inside, an eerie crooning sound seeped into the air. Like the house itself were crying.

"There's something I have to show you." Mal was standing beside her again, though Jaq hadn't seen her turn around.

"I don't want to go inside."

"You've been inside a hundred times," Mal reminded her.

"I know, but—"

"There's something I need to show you." Mal grabbed Jaq's

hand and pulled her toward the steps, beginning to climb. The mournful song grew louder.

"Wait." Jaq pulled back, stopping inches from the bottom step. Trepidation grounded her where she stood. "I don't want to go inside," she repeated.

Mal's expression hardened. "Jaq. I can't fix anything until you *come back.*"

The words were like a lightning bolt.

Come back, the voice had called in the meditation room at her church, and then again in the dressing room, when the dress had constricted around her. Again at Frank's.

"You want to kill me," Jaq said, backing away, certain now that Mal's spirit was malicious.

"He's coming," Mal said, eyes shifting to a spot behind Jaq.

Jaq froze, unwilling and unable to move. Then, slowly, she forced herself to turn, to look into the dark of the woods. At first, she didn't see anything but the deepening dark, the gray slip of a path winding between tree trunks. But there, creeping along the trail, spidering fingers of mold, pale as starlight and crawling toward her as though searching for her.

She stumbled, but Mal caught her hand and squeezed. Then pulled. Dragging Jaq toward the house with more strength than a thirteen-year-old should possess. Jaq tried to resist, leaned back and pulled, but her shoes skidded across the dry earth.

"Mal, stop!" Jaq yanked again, but it didn't matter. Mal's grip was iron, and Jaq couldn't help but move toward the stairs, her eyes locked on the black door at the top.

"Don't be afraid," Mal insisted. "You have to listen to me!"

But there was always something to be afraid of. That truth had been drilled into Jaq's mind again and again and again. And she knew—without knowing how—that whatever was behind that door was worth being afraid of.

Jaq sucked in a deep breath, gathered her strength, and threw herself away from the house, shouting, "Mal, stop!"

She wasn't prepared for it to work, so when the tension eased suddenly, she stumbled back, struggling to stay upright, teetering perilously close to the cliff's edge.

Mal reached for her and Jaq caught her by the wrists, spinning them both away from the drop. For a fleeting second, it was a dance. The two of them twirled, skating along the very edge of the cliff, then Jaq's foot hit the ground at an angle, and she crumpled, losing her grip on Mal's wrist.

Mal tipped, and then she was gone. Plummeting to the ground below.

Jaq screamed, falling to her knees at the edge of the cliff. In the moonlight, the flat rocks at the bottom were the shocking white of a blank canvas. Against them, a spray of mahogany hair and a puddle of blistering red were now drawn in vibrant strokes. But it wasn't Mallory lying there, Jaq realized with growing horror.

It was Devyn.

Jaq jerked awake. Heart pounding and shirt soaked through with sweat. She was in her room. Not in the woods by an old house with a girl who had died long ago. Not staring down at the broken body of a girl who was still, hopefully, very much alive.

She climbed out of bed and made her way to the bathroom for a glass of water, then returned to her room and swapped sweaty clothes for fresh ones. She couldn't get the image of Devyn splashed across gray rock out of her head. The way her eyes had been pinned open, her neck twisted to the side, one arm bent unnaturally behind her body.

It had felt so real. So violently real.

She reached for her phone. It was three in the morning, but she scrolled to Devyn's contact info and almost called, but hesitated.

A dream. It had only been a dream. A nightmare. Her brain punishing her for all the fun she'd had at Frank's. The thought of it was enough to push away the lingering chill of the nightmare. She swiped Devyn's contact away and—

Jaq dropped her phone on the bed and stared. Her eyes caught on a delicate band of rose gold wrapped around her ring finger, a familiar green stone clutched in the center. John's ring.

She remembered taking it off when she got home from Frank's last night. Tucking it back into its velvet-lined box and storing it in the top drawer of her bedside table. She remembered spending all day without it. Finding creative ways to hide the fact from both her mother and John.

She didn't remember putting it back on.

But she must have. Maybe before she'd gone to sleep? Between putting on her lip balm and braiding her hair? Or maybe she'd done it *in* her sleep.

Whatever had happened, she wanted it off, but when she pulled on the ring, it wouldn't budge. She pulled hard, dragging at the band until her skin bunched.

But no matter how she tugged and twisted, the ring wouldn't move.

Panic made her frenetic.

She pulled harder and harder, digging her nails under the band until her skin was red and her knuckle bruised. She sucked on her finger and tried again, reached for lotion and tried again and again until she was panting, a fresh sweat prickling at her temples and along her spine.

But no matter what, the ring stayed put. It was stuck as stubbornly as the dress had been, forcing her to accept all that it represented. It was as if she were being steered, herded onto the road her parents had chosen for her like a disobedient sheep.

Only this wasn't her parents. Or at least, not *just* her parents.

The thought gave her enough focus to push past the panic. She ignored the ring cinched tight around her finger and took three deep breaths. Then, abandoning her phone on the bed, Jaq opened her laptop and folded herself into her desk chair. She opened a fresh browser, not sure what she was going to search for until she was typing the words *Port Promise + Promise House.*

The search came back with a short list of hits. At the top was a link to an article titled "What's the Matter with Port Promise?: The Truth About the Promise House." Jaq clicked and opened the page.

Then she read the article.

Then she read the comments.

With each page, her stomach tightened, balling around a seed of dread that had been planted five years ago. On the same night she and Fern and Mal had gone into the woods for the last time.

When she'd read every word, she raced to the bathroom and retched, emptying her meager stomach contents into the toilet.

She returned to her bedroom and picked up her phone. This time, she didn't hesitate. She opened a message to Fern and wrote: **We have to talk.**

Then she hit send.

CHAPTER
TWENTY-FOUR

Mallory
THEN

Mallory was used to being in trouble.

She was in trouble so often that her parents' punishments almost seemed like chores, one more thing to get through before bed. When they spanked her, she knew how to count the lashes and breathe through the pain. When they made her memorize Bible verses, she knew how to divorce the words from her parents' righteous interpretations. And when they made her sit quietly in a room with the lights off, she knew how to dream.

This time, though, in the pitch-black closet, she was afraid.

It would be bad enough if she'd kissed a boy. She could imagine the lecture her mother would have given about how important it was to protect her virtue and how quickly innocent kisses might lead to something less innocent.

But she had kissed a girl. And in her mother's eyes, that was plain evil. Maybe they would beat her with a wooden spoon until it broke or make her bathe outside using the garden hose. Whatever the consequences, they were bound to be bigger than any Mallory had experienced before.

Even knowing that, she didn't regret kissing Jaq. Even if she had left without looking back.

That night, Mallory slept on the floor of her closet. Nestled in the clothing on the floor while she cried angry tears until she finally fell asleep. It was daylight when her mother finally let her out.

There was no speaking. No eye contact. As Mallory slowly went to the bathroom and washed tears off her cheeks, she felt it grow. A chill that settled in slowly, building up like ice until she was nearly immobilized by it.

Neither of her parents would speak directly to her. Her mother spoke around her. Instructions for the day that were never specifically addressed to her, though the expectation that she would comply with each was loud and clear.

"It's time to leave for church," or "I think we'll have soup and bread for lunch," or "This seems like a good time for everyone to work quietly."

Her father avoided looking at her, and when he did it was with an anger so certain that it made Mallory's breath stick in her lungs. It had physical pressure. His vitriol transformed him into a stranger, one who might be willing to hurt Mallory more than a father might.

That night, as Mallory got ready for bed, her mother came into her bedroom.

"I have something to discuss with you," she said, standing in the doorway with her hands clasped before her. Her red hair and blue eyes were a more severe version of Mallory's.

"Yes, ma'am," Mallory answered, working hard to keep any irreverent notes from her tone.

"What happened last night was appalling," she began. "So appalling that I don't think I can be trusted to help you."

"Appalling?" Mallory asked, but her mother just ignored her.

"Your father and I have been in touch with a school in California in a little town called Dovepoint, and they have a spot for you," she said, not pausing at her daughter's stricken expression. "You'll be leaving in the morning, so take a minute to decide what you'll need and then I'll come help you pack your bag."

"You're sending me to a conversion camp?" Mallory asked.

"A private school," her mother corrected her. "That focuses on helping young people like you achieve their full potential."

"No." Mallory could barely contain the rage rising in her, driving her to her feet and demanding that she shout, scream, *run*. "I'm not going."

"I'll travel with you and help get you settled. You'll stay through the summer, and we can reassess at the start of the next school year."

"No," Mallory repeated.

"This isn't a negotiation."

"No! I don't want to go!" Mallory said, raising her voice. She could feel the tears already burning in her eyes, summoned by her fury.

"'No,'" her mother said, finally acknowledging Mallory, "is a word that would have served you better last night. But since you aren't capable of thinking clearly, it's up to me to do it for you. I'm doing all of this for you. Because I love you, and I want to help you." She paused. "Before it's too late."

Her mother had already decided what Mallory needed. Just like she'd already decided that what Mallory had done was *appalling*. Wrong. And, worse, something she could fix.

Rage simmered up from Mallory's toes. It skimmed through her veins like fire, heating her blood and burning off the fear that always clung to her bones. Mallory had never been so angry in her entire life. And it felt good. It felt clarifying.

Emboldened, she glared up at her mother, then she opened her mouth and said, "Bitch."

For an electric moment her mother merely stared at Mallory, her blue eyes wide and uncomprehending. Then, with liquid speed, she stepped into the room. Her hand lashed out, striking Mallory across the face.

Mallory heard the snap of it before she felt the sting. Like a light bulb popping or a single concussive clap of thunder.

The pain came a few seconds behind, sinking into Mallory's cheek like nausea. The tears brimming in her eyes spilled over, hot with fury.

Her mother stepped back, her hands clasped before her once more, her expression as placid and unmoving as the surface of a lake. Then, without another word, she turned and left, closing the door behind her.

Mallory stood in the center of her room. Alone. Angry. But not afraid. As the tears coursed down her cheeks, she didn't wish them away. She let them come. Let them tear sorrow up from the root of her until all that was left was resentment.

And a plan.

Mallory wiped her cheeks and started to create stacks of clothing on her bed as her mother requested. Later, she would pack her bags and set them by the front door.

But that was the last thing she would ever do for her mother.

Tonight, everything would change. One way or another.

CHAPTER
TWENTY-FIVE

Fern

"I'm pretty sure you're making Port Promise High history with this." Cam spoke with her eyes glued to her tablet as she updated her own notes and cues to accommodate the last-minute change while simultaneously striding down the hallway toward first period. "Mostly because no one in their right mind would ever do something like this. Or ever will again. Do you realize that it's Wednesday? We open *tomorrow*."

"I know," Fern said, tipping a smile at their friend.

For the last twenty-four hours, every single person involved with the show had set the rest of their lives aside to make this work. Fern went to sleep reciting Danny's lines, woke up with song lyrics in their head, and was ignoring absolutely everything else. Including Jaq, who had sent a text about wanting to talk. But there was just no room in the schedule. The cast and crew were living and breathing *Grease* right now, and in spite of the frenzied chaos of it all—doubled-up dance rehearsals and reblocking and Fern buying the whole crew pizza to get them to stay late—neither Cam nor Melissa had suggested that it was a bad idea. Nor had they interrogated Fern about the change in their wardrobe. They'd simply rolled with the punches, taking everything in stride and finding ways to make it all work.

Even if they complained about it. Cam more than Melissa.

"That's one rehearsal left to work out all the kinks," Cam continued. "Do all of Kaitlyn's costumes fit you?"

"Most of them. And—" Fern held up a finger at Cam's alarm. "I've already replaced the pieces that don't."

"Why are you doing this to me?" Cam muttered, making a note.

"Because you are marvelous and capable, and I knew you could handle it," Fern offered with a hopeful smile.

"And?" Cam asked, clearly waiting for more.

"You . . . love me?" Fern guessed.

Cam gave them a big thumbs-down and turned to Melissa for an assist.

"Given the circumstances," Melissa said in her deadpan way, "I invoke the Starbucks rule and declare that Fern owes both of us Starbucks for a period of two weeks after the conclusion of the show."

"That's more like it," Cam said with a firm nod.

"Does the defendant agree?" Melissa asked.

"I do," said Fern, and when Melissa banged her imaginary gavel and sealed the deal, Fern grinned and added, "But I would have given you three."

The bell rang, and Fern spent every spare moment furiously studying the script. By the end of the day, they were a ball of energy and nerves. But there was only so much time to indulge in them because as soon as they entered the theater, the entire cast and crew was in full dress-rehearsal mode. The auditorium was half-full. Members of the theater club and a good portion of the orchestra and band as well taking the opportunity to see the show for free and making this moment feel intensely real. Once the curtain went up, Fern went from nervous to Danny in the blink of an eye. After that, there was only room for the show.

And what a show.

The second Fern stepped onstage as Danny, they knew they would never be the same. The elation of that moment sang through them and made them feel expansive and bright. They hit their cues, found their light, and nailed every line so perfectly that by the end even Ms. Murphy was on her feet, cheering and clapping loudly enough to be heard above the applause of the audience.

And then everyone was cheering. Clapping and whistling. Screaming and laughing with so much relief and amazement. Kaitlyn grinned at Fern, and the entire cast rallied around them. The furious joy at having stuck the landing after so much upheaval made them giddy, and they collapsed on the ground in a heap. Even Cam abandoned her sacred tablet and hurtled herself onstage to tackle Fern in a hug.

They'd done it. The show had come together perfectly, and so had Fern.

They were so happy they could hardly breathe.

"Everyone!" Ms. Murphy called, whistling to bring the raucous energy in the room back to her. She smiled, mischievous, but also proud. "You've worked hard to get to this moment. Maybe harder than any group I've ever had the pleasure of working with. Especially in the last two days! Fern and Kaitlyn brought us a challenge and you all rose to it. And I am so pleased to say that this is it. We have taken an old show and found a new way to tell it, and you should all feel very good about what we've accomplished together. Now, I want you all to go home and get a good night's rest because tomorrow is the day!"

Everyone cheered again and broke apart slowly. They clustered around Fern and Kaitlyn, reluctant to leave the perfection of this moment. Fern didn't want to leave either; then Kaitlyn was standing at their side, bright-eyed and beaming, and Fern suddenly wanted to be alone with her.

"I have a question," Kaitlyn said. Her curls were up in a high pony, bobbing playfully around her shoulders. "Did you ever find a touchstone for Danny?"

The question took Fern by surprise. After failing to find one for Sandy, they hadn't even considered finding one for Danny, but now it seemed obvious and important. They should find a touchstone before opening night. They needed to find one.

"I completely forgot to look for one," they admitted.

"I think I have just the thing." Kaitlyn dug into her pocket and produced a smooth, gray pebble.

"I'm not sure I understand," Fern said, trying and failing to make a connection in their head.

"It's from the pool at Whisper Falls. That jump was bigger for you than for most people," Kaitlyn explained, an embarrassed smile rounding her cheeks. "You did something that scared you, and you did it with an audience. The way Danny makes a change in front of all his friends." She shrugged. "I thought it might make a good touchstone, but I can see that I was wro—"

"No!" Fern reached for the stone before Kaitlyn could put it away. "It's perfect. I'm sorry for whatever my face is doing, but it's only because I never would have thought of this and it's . . . perfect. Thank you."

"You're welcome," Kaitlyn said, gracing Fern with a smile that was as warm as the sun. "See you tomorrow."

"See you tomorrow," Fern repeated, not really hearing the sound of their own voice. Not really hearing anything except the pleasant buzzing in their head.

They hardly remembered shedding their costume and collecting their things—even the drive home passed in a blur. All they noticed was the feeling expanding inside of them. The absolute euphoria of being perceived by another person. Of being seen and respected and understood almost better than they understood themself.

They were so happy that when their mother came in from work and asked why Fern was smiling that way, they answered honestly.

"I get to play Danny tomorrow," they said.

"What?" Their mom stopped with her hand on the refrigerator door, shock written across her features. "The *boy*? I thought Kaitlyn was playing that part? Did something happen to her?"

Fern heard the judgment and panic in their mother's voice. But they were too happy in this moment to worry about it. "Nothing happened to her. We decided to switch roles."

"Decided? To switch?" Their mom paused, considering the words. "You mean you did this on purpose?"

Fern nodded, let a smile unfurl on their face. "I did. And I'm really excited for you to see the show."

For you to see me, they added silently.

CHAPTER
TWENTY-SIX

Mallory
THEN

Mallory waited until her parents had gone to bed, face hot from her mother's slap, half-packed suitcase open on the floor. Then she padded silently into the little room off the kitchen that her father used as his study. From experience, she knew that they would have locked her cell phone in the top drawer, just like she knew that the key to said drawer was hidden beneath the heavy porcelain lamp that hulked in the corner.

Careful to move as silently as the night itself, she retrieved her phone. Then she returned to her room and fired off an SOS text to Jaq and Fern.

The response from Fern was instant: Mal! Are you okay?

Mallory nodded to herself as she typed her response: Fine, but I have to get out of here. I have a plan. Can you meet?

In the space that followed, Mallory shoved her feet into her tennis shoes and tied them up, then pulled on a rain jacket. It wasn't actively raining at the moment, but that didn't mean anything in Port Promise.

Finally, Fern answered: Okay. Coast is clear. Jaq?

Jaq gave a thumbs-up and asked, Where?

Mallory wondered what had happened to her friends in the aftermath of that night. Not knowing had been chewing at her insides, tearing her apart little by little. She wanted to ask for details, but if they were both on their phones, then they were at least mostly okay.

At the usual trailhead, she sent back, then shoved the phone into her pocket and eased her window open.

A sound somewhere in the house made her pause, one leg thrown over the windowsill, her heart hammering at her chest.

Another sound. This one closer than before. Followed by something that sounded distinctly like footsteps.

Mallory froze, not sure whether it would be better to fall back into bed and pretend to be asleep or drop out of the window to the ground below and make a run for it. It didn't matter if they saw her running, only if they chased.

The steps drew nearer, pausing at her door.

A small voice in the back of her mind urged her to go, go, go!

She jumped just as she heard the click of the door behind her. She landed on her hands and knees, the shock of impact singing through her bones, but she ignored it. Jumping to her feet, she sprinted away from the house.

"Mallory!" came the hiss of her mother's voice in her wake, but she didn't look back.

She had decided that she would never look back.

She ran as hard as she could down the darkened streets, passing the same houses she'd passed nearly every day of her life, until she came to the gap between them that marked the trailhead closest to Fern's neighborhood.

"Mal!" Jaq jumped out of the shadows where she'd been hiding and hurried to Mal's side. "Are you okay?"

"In the weirdest way possible, yes," she said, once she caught her breath.

"What did they do to you? We've been texting. Well, Fern has," Jaq amended with a guilty frown. "I was worried that my name on your phone might make it worse. After—"

"Do you regret kissing me?" Mallory asked, stepping closer to Jaq.

"I—I, no, I don't, but I'm so sorry that—"

Mallory pressed her lips to Jaq's, silencing her with a swift but gentle kiss. She pulled away with a gasp. "I don't want you to be sorry about anything. Nothing you do or did made any of this happen, Jaq De Luca." Mallory spoke with her whole voice, a sudden vicious desperation driving her to make this one point as clear as the brightest star in the sky. She turned to face Fern and reached for their hand, drawing them close so that the three of them made a little circle. "And nothing you did or didn't do got us caught, Fern Jensen. They're the assholes. Right?"

"Right," Jaq and Fern answered, voices soft.

"Say it with me," Mal said, and then she waited while the two of them mustered the energy to say it with her.

"They're the assholes," they said.

"That's better," Mal said, smiling.

"Oh my god, did they hit you?" Fern asked, narrowing their eyes in the moonlight.

Mallory's hand flew to her cheek, where a little bruise was starting to form. "A parting gift," she said, shrugging off their concern. "Are you both okay? What happened to you?"

Jaq and Fern shared a nervous look.

"Um, nothing, really." Jaq said it like it was a confession.

"Your parents weren't angry?" Mal asked.

"Your parents didn't tell them," Fern explained. "They said you came down with a bug, and they took us home so we wouldn't catch it."

"Huh," Mal said, but it made sense: they didn't want anyone else to know.

"What did your parents do to you?" Jaq asked.

Mal took a steadying breath. She hadn't said it out loud yet and wasn't sure that she could manage without breaking into another round of angry tears or shouting loudly enough to wake half the neighborhood. She reached for the coldest part of her heart and imagined sidestepping it.

"They're sending me away," she said. "In the morning, my mom is taking me to a special facility in Dovepoint, California, where they will 'correct my undesirable behaviors.'"

There was some satisfaction in the looks of abject horror on Jaq's and Fern's faces.

"But I'm not going," she continued. "I'm never going back home again."

"Then a-are you running away?" Jaq asked. "For real this time?"

"Not exactly," Mal said. "I'm going to ask the Patron for my wish."

"What?!" Fern and Jaq hissed together.

"He's protected us this long, hasn't he?"

"'Find his house, make a wish, he'll do just as you please,'" Fern breathed. "You really think it will work?"

Mallory wasn't sure why she was so certain that it would work, but she was. The house had appeared to them and no one else. It had provided things for them. Shelter and privacy, when they'd needed it most. A lot more than Jesus had done. She had never trusted in anything as much as she trusted in the Patron.

Her mother had threatened to take the world from her, but the

Patron could give it back. She believed that the way she'd never believed anything in her life.

"What about the price?" Jaq asked. "'The price is small and with it all, you'll never be adrift'?"

Mal raised a hand to her throat, where her friendship necklace sat, the blue and purple gems winking in the moonlight. "That's one of the reasons I wanted you both to come with me. Maybe— maybe if we—" Mal hesitated, embarrassed to be asking for something potentially so silly.

"You want us to do it together," Jaq finished.

Mal nodded, grateful that the friends she'd known for such a short amount of time already knew her better than anyone in the world.

"I'm in," Fern said.

"Me too," added Jaq.

And feeling better than she had in days, Mal actually laughed. "Thank you. I love you both."

Then they joined hands and, together, entered the dark woods.

CHAPTER
TWENTY-SEVEN

Jaq

Jaq texted Fern three more times before she got a response and a promise to meet up after rehearsals. Which was strange, considering Fern had been the one so intent on talking about things before. But Fern looked different. Her hair was slicked back in a low pony, she wasn't wearing an ounce of makeup, and she was dressed in jeans and a T-shirt. Not that that alone was unusual, but it was unusual for Fern.

No, Jaq realized. It wasn't. It was the way Fern had always wanted to dress. The way she'd felt most comfortable in her own skin.

"You look happy," Jaq said, climbing into the passenger seat.

Fern had pulled up at the end of Jaq's street and waited while Jaq slipped out of her window for the second time this week.

"I am." Fern swiveled, glowing. "We had our dress rehearsal tonight and we nailed it, which, some people might say is a bad sign for opening night, but in this case . . . I'm playing *Danny*."

"The boy part? How— What about your mom?" Jaq stammered the question. She remembered Fern's mom. Willow Jensen hadn't seemed dangerous on the surface. She wasn't like Jaq's or Mal's parents, who weaponized their religion. She was a feminist, single mother of four children; she'd seemed like the kind of person who would have been ally.

But her feminism adhered to a rigid sense of who was considered to be a woman. It was hard to imagine that she would be even a little bit okay with Fern playing a boy onstage.

"I just told her, so I guess I'll find out later," Fern admitted with a little laugh. "You said you wanted to go to the Dormouse? It's kind of late for coffee."

"Exactly," Jaq confirmed. "We'll have the place to ourselves."

As they turned out of Jaq's neighborhood, her phone buzzed with a text from John. It was a picture of the portrait she'd given him with sample matting and a frame on one corner.

Feels a little weird to be framing my own face, but a treasure like this deserves to be on display. <3

Her breath squeezed in her throat. The ring squeezed on her finger. The band seared into her skin like a brand, its presence menacing and unnatural.

She didn't want to hurt John, but things had changed. She had changed. She knew who she was and what she wanted, and now she needed things to change even more. Plus, she would never convince anyone that she didn't want to be with him if she couldn't get the ring off. And she'd tried everything. Except a knife.

The image of a blade cutting into skin, through bone, severing her finger from her hand flashed through her mind before she could stop it. She shivered.

Everything was just so, so messed up.

"Also," Fern added, "and this is just between us for now, but you're one of the only people I can tell: my pronouns are . . ."

"They/them," Jaq supplied, memories tumbling through her mind.

"Yes! "Joy was seeping off Fern. In a way Jaq had never thought possible for any of them. But Fern was happy. Instead of dwelling on all the things they'd lost, they'd found a way to take them back. "I mean, it's still a secret, so it's mostly just for me, but one day it won't be."

"That's the way it was before, too. When it was just us," Jaq murmured. She was simultaneously glad for Fern and irritatingly jealous that while she'd been haunted by visions and nightmares and a malicious ring that wouldn't let go, Fern had been rediscovering the person they wanted to be.

Fern nodded. "It took me a minute to make my way back to the right words, but I feel like everything is finally sorting itself out. I feel like *I'm* sorting myself out. Whatever happened to us, it's over now."

Jaq let the uncertainty show on her face when she shook her head and said, "That's what I wanted to talk to you about."

"Well, that's not ominous," Fern muttered, pulling into a parking spot at the Dormouse Coffee House. "What is it?"

"Coffee first," Jaq instructed, climbing out of the car and into the salty evening air. "Do you know what you want? I'll get it. You grab a table out here on the patio." Jaq paused while Fern recited their order—a Triple Chocolate Death by Mocha—then ducked inside.

She returned moments later to find Fern seated at the table farthest from the glow of the Dormouse lights. It was an uncharacteristically clear night, and the sky was draped with stars that vanished behind the jagged profile of the mountains that loomed over Port

Promise. A cold breeze blew off the water, carrying a thick, almost rotten scent that clung to everything.

Jaq set the coffees down, then chose the spot directly in front of Fern, who sat with their knees drawn up against the chill.

"So?" Fern prompted, licking a tuft of whipped cream from the top of their drink. "What is your ominous news?"

"It's about the woods," Jaq said. "More specifically, the Patron. You remember we used to tell those stories about him? And we found his house?"

"I remember," Fern said.

Jaq popped the plastic lid off her coffee so it could cool. "I only kind of remembered it until last night. I dreamed of the woods, and it was so real, Fern, it felt like I was actually there. The house was exactly the way I remembered it, but Mal was there, too, and she wanted me to go inside. To—" She stopped herself. Shook her head. "The point is that I remembered something about the house. It had a name. Do you remember that?"

A frown creased Fern's brow as they thought. "I do," they said, tentative. "I didn't, but now that you mention it . . . There were words above the door, right?"

"Promise House," Jaq whispered. "Its name was Promise House."

Fern nodded, the frown still pinching their brows together. "Why is that important?"

"Because." Jaq licked her lips. She hadn't said any of this out loud yet. Once she did, there was no going back. It would be real. A shared realness between her and Fern. Something that happened to them. Without their consent.

"Jaq?" Fern prompted when she'd been silent for too long.

"It *was* his, but it wasn't an orphanage," Jaq blurted. "It was a house for girls. Specifically, deviant girls. Girls who needed to be reeducated and 'reintroduced to the right path.'"

Recognition lit in Fern's eyes. They drew back, expression darkening with understanding. "What are you saying?"

"I'm saying that Promise House—the house we found when we were kids and thought was so safe—was a conversion camp. And the Patron ran it. Not only that, he *built* it. He was a real man. His name was Elijah *Patron*. I found an article from just recently written by a woman who lived in that house and survived."

Jaq was shivering. It didn't matter that she'd been living with this information for nearly twenty-four hours—knowing it had left her shaken. To her core.

The same was clearly true for Fern.

They wrapped their hands around the paper cup, but Jaq could see the tremble in their fingers. It was a long moment before Fern spoke again.

"So, you think the Patron was, what? A bigot?"

"A bigot with money," Jaq answered. "Who moved here in 1917, bought up all that land, and built a house specifically so he could 'fix' people like us. He took in something like two dozen girls before the house burned down."

Fern had gone so pale, even their lips were devoid of color. "You said you knew what happened to us out there."

It seemed obvious to Jaq, but she understood Fern's reluctance. Jaq had had an entire day to get used to the idea. But Fern needed to hear the words strung together so that they were undeniable.

Below them, gentle waves lapped at the shore. Rushing in and out in an irregular rhythm as the tide pushed one way or another. Jaq tried to let the familiar sound settle her.

She said, "We went into the woods that night looking for an escape. For us and for Mal because her parents caught us ki—" Even now she couldn't say the words out loud. They got caught in her throat, sticking to the walls like mold. She tried again. "They caught us together in the closet and were going to send her to a conversion camp. We were afraid, and we wanted to live in a world where we weren't afraid of ourselves anymore." Jaq reached for her coffee and cupped its warmth close to her chest. "I think— whatever happened that night—the Patron granted our wish in the way *he* wanted to."

"What does that mean?" Tears glimmered in Fern's eyes. They knew the answer to their question already, but Jaq understood that they needed to hear it. To feel it and mourn it.

"He converted us. He 'fixed' us," she spat.

The lights in the coffee shop snapped off, plunging them into sudden darkness. A moment later, they heard the sounds of the barista locking the front door and tossing the trash in the dumpster before driving away.

Fern stared at Jaq, coffee forgotten on the table. This was when one or both of them should have argued that this was impossible. The Patron wasn't real because ghosts weren't real, but they'd seen too much to deny it outright.

Even if they wanted to.

"And you're saying that . . . we asked him to?" Fern sounded out of breath, the words forcing their way out.

Jaq gritted her teeth at the thought. "I have a hard time believing we would have asked for something like that. Well, maybe I would have if I'd been on my own, but you wouldn't, and Mal definitely wouldn't have. But it happened, didn't it? We came out of the woods that night different people."

"He took it away from us." Fern leaned over the table as though they were about to be sick. "Made us believe we were something else. Oh my god."

Jaq watched as a wave of grief or anger rolled though Fern, the reaction so visceral it made Jaq want to reach across the table and take Fern's hand. Let them know that they weren't alone, and it would all be okay. Maybe not now or even soon, but eventually.

Fern shook their head as they sat up again. "At least we have answers now."

Jaq looked at Fern as though they'd just sprouted a second head. "We don't, though. We're still in the dark. We know more about the Patron and have most of our memories back, but that night is still missing. He's still out there, and it seems like maybe Mal is, too, which means he's going to keep finding ways to torment us."

The ring on Jaq's finger pinched. Promising a future she didn't want anymore and one she had decided to fight. And that was exactly why she'd asked Fern to meet her tonight.

"I think we have to go back," Jaq started. "To the woods and the house. Whatever happened back then, there have to be answers somewhere. I have a feeling they're inside that house."

Fern sat up in alarm. "No way. I don't think we should ever go back there. *He's* out there."

"But so is Mallory," Jaq pleaded, reaching for the cross at her throat. She felt certain this was true. The dream had felt threatening, but what if it had been a plea? "What if she needs our help?"

Fern considered this for a minute. "But things are okay now. Things are actually pretty good. Maybe we don't need to know what happened that night. If we go back in, he could make us forget all over again. Or worse. We just need to move on with our lives."

"Look at this." Jaq thrust her hand out and pointed to the ring. "John gave this to me a few weeks ago, and now it won't come off. I've tried everything—lotion, oil, that ribbon trick—but it's stuck. Don't you see? It's the Patron. He's still doing it! Maybe we remember who we are, but he'll never just let us move on. If we do nothing, I'll end up married to John."

"What makes you think going into the woods will help?" Fern asked, voice rising. "Maybe what we need is to get away from the woods. As far as possible, and things will get better."

"Wait and see? Keep our heads down and hope? *Pray?*" Jaq asked in disbelief.

"What else am I supposed to do?" Fern nearly shouted.

"Something! Anything! Weren't you the one trying to get me to do something after a ghost attacked you in the costume basement?" Jaq was on her feet now, the vision of Devyn's body at the base of the cliff surging into her mind. "Mallory is *dead*, Fern. And I don't want anyone else to die because of me or because of what I am or because of what I feel or don't feel!"

It felt good to shout. Out here, with only the night sky and sea to hear them, where it was only Jaq and Fern and the pain they shared.

"And I don't want to mess things up when, for the first time in my life, I'm actually living how I want!" Fern shouted back.

Jaq thought of that night in the closet with Mal. How that honest moment had shattered against the rocks and how a question had always remained: Why hadn't Fern warned them that Mallory's parents were coming?

Any anger she might have nursed about that night had been stolen along with everything else, but it was here now, and without thinking, Jaq lashed out with it.

"You always were good at saving yourself. Especially when your friends were in danger," Jaq snapped, regretting it instantly but unable to take it back.

Fern drew back. Visibly hurt, and opened their mouth to respond. "Fu—"

A scream cut through Jaq's mind. Scraping at her thoughts, binding her tongue. It seared her from the inside, stopping her in her tracks.

Come! Back!

The words shattered through her, shrieking and screeching. A feeling of anger and helplessness in their wake.

The voice was there and gone in a flash, but the words had been unmistakable.

One look told her that Fern had heard them, too. The two of them were frozen in place. Eyes locked on each other. The only sound was the water rushing up and away, up and away.

It took Jaq a minute to realize she was crying. Thin tears sliding silently down her warm cheeks. Snot tickling in her nose.

"I can't go back to those woods, Jaq," Fern said. "No matter what. It's too dangerous. Promise me you won't go either."

Jaq studied Fern for a long minute, silence opening between them like years. Finally, she nodded. "Okay," she said.

But it was a lie and they both knew it.

CHAPTER
TWENTY-EIGHT

Fern

The next morning, Fern dragged themself out of a series of ghost-riddled dreams to the realization that it was opening night and they were about to stand up in front of everyone as Danny Zuko.

Before they could make their way to the bathroom, they found a card slipped beneath their door written in their mother's bubbly script:

> *YOU ARE THE KIND OF STAR THAT WILL*
> *ALWAYS RISE ABOVE, AND THE SHOW*
> *MUST GO ON! XXOO, MOM*

They kind of wanted to puke, but they forced themself to put on their brightest face and get ready for the day like they hadn't spent the night fighting with their once-best friend about a nasty spirit in the woods who cast some kind of conversion therapy spell on them and might or might not still be out to get them.

Like they weren't being silently shredded by an old guilt they would have rather never remembered.

Jaq wasn't right, but she wasn't wrong. The night Mal's parents came home and found the two of them kissing in the closet, Fern had been there. They'd been *right* there, and to this day, they couldn't pinpoint why they hadn't banged on the door the second they heard the knob turn on the front door.

All they remembered was freezing up. Their brain locked up as surely as their muscles, and they spent the precious seconds they could have used to warn their friends in a mindless kind of terror.

Now guilt was a ghost they would live with forever.

But as guilty as they felt, they couldn't risk going back in. Five years had been stolen from them. Five years where they weren't allowed to be themself, where every day was a performance.

And they'd had *no* idea.

In some ways, that was the most horrifying realization of all. If they hadn't gone to Karima's party, they never would have known. And if it happened again . . . would they stay that way forever?

"Nerves," Fern's mom trilled when Fern had rejected everything except a pot of stovetop ramen for breakfast. "All the best actresses get them. It's a sign that you're doing things right. You're being incredibly brave by taking this role, and I think that's admirable. You might not remember this, but Holly could never eat anything except toast and tea for the entire week before opening night. You and she have always been a lot alike. My daintiest girls."

Fern braced against the comparison. As though "dainty" was something girls should be, something that made Fern better or more worthy of attention and love.

"I'm not nervous about the show," Fern tried, but their mom wasn't hearing it.

"Of course not," she said with a conspiratorial wink. "But just in case, I'm not supposed to tell you this, but I don't want you to be caught off guard on opening night."

"What?" Fern asked, stomach clenching.

She spun around, raising her spoon so fast she flung drops of chicken broth across the kitchen. "Clover and Ivy are coming into town to see you perform! Holly wanted to make it, but since she's just booked the *Chicago* revival, she can't take the time right now. She made me promise to record it for her. But isn't that exciting?!"

Fern reached for a happy smile, sliding into the motion with more difficulty than usual, and nodded. "That's amazing!"

"They're going to be so impressed. Especially with how you're playing a boy. I mean, I know that kids these days have a lot of strange ideas about things, and at first, I'll admit, I was a little concerned about everything, but then I started thinking about it—I mean, really thinking about it—and you know what I remembered?" Fern's mom asked, pouring the steaming soup into a bowl and setting it on the kitchen counter in front of them.

The fragrant steam lodged itself in the back of Fern's throat, tempting nausea. "What?" they asked in a tight voice.

"I remembered that back in Shakespeare's day, they wouldn't let girls act at all. It was considered indecent or something. So, all the girl parts were played by boys, can you imagine?" She laughed, deeply amused at the thought. "Those people would be appalled that we ladyfolk take the stage now, and that we take boy roles, too? Well, that makes this production part of a long and revolutionary theatrical tradition. You should be proud."

"Thanks," Fern said, the smallest ember of hope stirring to life. If their mom had come this far in so little time, maybe she could come even farther. Maybe, when Fern stepped onto the stage as Danny, their mom would be okay. Or at least not upset.

"Well, eat up, but don't overdo it. And I'll get you a fresh shirt." She flapped a hand at Fern's shirt. "I know you say you like this, but it's opening night, and you should look your best."

This was how it had always been in the Jensen household. Fern's mom wasn't as overt as Jaq's or Mal's parents, but Mrs. Jensen applied pressure with every breath she took. Tying Fern's value—as a daughter and a person—to these narrow ideas of what girls were like. What they did and didn't do. How they dressed and styled their hair. How they sounded and smiled.

Fern had learned it all. First, without even meaning to. And then, because anything else would be questioned or discarded.

When their mom returned with a baby-blue eyelet shirt and a hairbrush, Fern had to say something.

"Mom." Fern held up their hands and backed away. "I'm sorry, that's—"

Too pastel.

Too femme.

Not who I am right now.

"My favorite. Thank you so much." The words weren't what Fern had intended to say. Not even close.

"I thought so." Fern's mom set the shirt on the counter and held up the brush. "Want me to do your hair? It's looking a bit rough."

I already did it. Fern drew their bottom lip between their teeth, prepared to say that they didn't need help. "Yes, please."

A cold feeling slid down Fern's spine. These weren't their words. But it was their voice. Their mouth. But not their choice.

Ten minutes later, Fern's mother had pulled their hair half back, teasing up the top so that it crowned Fern's face and twisting the rest into soft curls. She set it all in place with a quick spritz of hair spray, then thrust a rose-pink lip gloss at Fern to complete the look.

"There," she said, giving Fern an appraising smile. "You'll feel better all day now that you look good."

Fern couldn't speak around the growing lump in their throat.

"I'm heading out, but have a good day, okay? And try to eat a little something for lunch." She planted a quick kiss on Fern's cheek, then spun on her heel and left.

For a long moment, Fern remained at the kitchen counter. Their ramen had stopped steaming and sat untouched. Outside, the sky was gray and heavy with rain clouds.

Fern took a deep breath. "I'm"—*Queer. Gay. Bigender*—"straight."

They took another breath and tried again. "My pronouns are"—*They/them*—"she/her."

The lump rising in their throat stretched, straining the muscles painfully. Still, they took a third breath and tried again. "I like"—*Girls. Boys. All genders. But mostly Kaitlyn*—"boys."

Fern shook their head. They knew it was going to be hard to say, but this was ridiculous.

"What the fuck," they whispered, and that, at least, came out exactly right.

———

Fern made it to school before the bell and was just leaving their locker when they crashed into someone.

"Whoa, foul play to the queen." Cam caught Fern's shoulders with a steady grip, her brown eyes quirked in confusion. "Hey, you okay? Wait, let me rephrase because I can see that you're not. What's wrong?"

Fern started to shake her off, but Cam held on tight. "Nuh-uh. Something is going on with you. Usually, I would give you space, but tonight is opening night. You've got to process."

Fern checked one hip against the wall for support as they stared up into Cambria's beautiful brown, deeply sympathetic eyes. "I can't really talk about it," they said.

Cam's eyes narrowed suspiciously. "Okay, well, I'll tell you what I think, then. I think that you and Kaitlyn Birch discovered that you actually like each other after years of rivalry, and I think that you started getting a little too close for comfort, maybe. And I want you to know that even if we've never talked about it, I'm cool. Know what I mean?"

"No," Fern answered stubbornly. "I mean, yes. I know, I just—"

"You don't have to say anything." Cam raised a hand between them. "I wanted you to know that whenever you're ready, I'm here. Okay? This isn't end-of-the-world shit."

Fern swallowed hard, grateful for a friend like Cam, then bobbed their head once. "Okay."

"Are you going to be able to hold all of this"—Cam gestured to Fern's entire body—"together for the performance tonight?"

"Yeah," Fern managed, every muscle in their torso tightening against a swell of nausea. They reached for a smile. Ever the liar, they said, "I've got this."

CHAPTER TWENTY-NINE

Jaq

In the hours since her conversation with Fern, Jaq had made several crucial decisions. The first was that she wasn't going into the woods by herself, so she needed a different strategy.

The second was that she needed to focus on getting her life under control. If some strange, supernatural force didn't want her kissing girls, well, then she could avoid kissing girls. At least until she left Port Promise. She'd done it most of her life, after all.

She also didn't want to kiss John, which was the real problem.

Well, that and the fact that she couldn't stop thinking about Devyn.

And when she thought of Devyn, she thought of Mal. And how kissing Mal somehow got Mal dead and maybe she should keep her distance from Devyn. But when another origami note—this time in the shape of a lightning bolt—fell out of her locker with an invitation from Devyn, an electric thrill skittered through her veins.

Meet me tonight, the note said. *At the end of your street, 8 p.m. I'll have you home before curfew. x D*

Just beneath it, Devyn had drawn a picture of two stick figures riding a motorcycle beneath a crescent moon and five twinkling stars. Jaq crushed it in her hand, crushed it in her heart, and slammed her locker shut.

She stared at her hand pressed against the locker. At the ring. The skin around the band was red and raw, burst capillaries scattered around it in bright red from where she'd twisted and tugged with no success. It was like the metal had fused with her skin.

It made everything inside of her clench and resist. The ring was a constant reminder that something out there was driving her decisions, forcing her onto a path this supernatural force found acceptable, and if she didn't do what it wanted, there would be consequences.

Just like there had been consequences with Mal.

The thought sent a fresh wave of panic coursing through her. Stealing her breath. Bringing with it flashes of a broken house, a sharp cliff, a girl splashed across the rocks at the bottom.

Devyn.

Dead.

"Wanna go out tonight?" John appeared out of nowhere, and she jumped.

"John," she breathed, pressing a hand to her chest.

"Whoa, sorry. Didn't mean to scare you." He leaned against the locker next to hers. "I know it's Thursday, but I think I can convince your mom to let me take you somewhere nice. We could even go see the musical if you want. See what all the fuss is about."

Jaq did want to go to the musical. She wanted to see Fern be glorious onstage as Danny. But she was still too disappointed with them to do that tonight.

"Maybe tomorrow? I'm not feeling great. I'm worried I caught something."

John studied her for another second, disbelief and maybe even a little irritation flashing across his face. "Really?" he asked.

She'd lied without even meaning to. And she could see plainly that he knew it. They'd known each other so long and had shared so many secrets and truths between them that he knew she was hiding something from him. Something important enough to lie about. It gutted her to see the flicker of hurt in his expression, but he swallowed hard and the hurt vanished.

He said, "You know, in a way this is really a relief."

"That I'm sick?" Jaq asked.

"That you *can* get sick," John corrected. "In all the years I've known you, you've never even complained of a headache. I was starting to think you were like a goddess in disguise or something. So this is good. You're definitely human. And I am definitely taking you home."

Jaq's protests were only half-hearted because, honestly, being home by herself sounded pretty good right now. So she let John take her home and spent the rest of the day in bed with her nightmare on repeat.

Mal at the top of the cliff.

Devyn at the bottom.

Both dead because of something Jaq had done.

The hurt in John's face when she'd lied.

She had to do something about it. But what?

When her mother finally came to check on her, she was almost happy for the interruption.

"John called to check on you. Such a sweetheart," Mrs. De Luca said from Jaq's bedroom door. "Why don't you go out with him tonight?"

"I—um," she stammered, confused. "I still don't feel good."

"Jaqueline." Her mother laughed. "He clearly wants to spend time with you."

"But I—"

"That sort of thing doesn't last forever, you know. And it will fade faster if you let it." Her eyes were bright.

"But I don't feel good?" Jaq was getting angry now.

"Alice!" Mr. De Luca called up from the first floor, the patience in his tone practiced and even a little amused.

Jaq's mom straightened, her smile broadening in response to her husband's call, her entire body responding to the sound of her husband's voice in a way that was so normal Jaq had stopped seeing it years ago. But she saw it now in a new way. She saw the adoration that sparked briefly in the corners of her mother's mouth, saw the way she angled her body in his direction even though he wasn't physically present. Alice De Luca loved her husband deeply. Completely. She would do anything for him.

"Mom?" Jaq asked.

"Your father and I have to run an errand. We might be a little late, so if you do decide to go out, let's just say your curfew is midnight, okay? Have a good night, honey."

Jaq watched her mom go, stunned but not surprised.

She was saddened that her mom lived a life in which she prioritized someone else's feelings and desires over her own. That she would tell her daughter to go out on a date when she wasn't feeling well.

Saddened, also, that her mom would never have her back. Ever. A reminder of what Jaq had known since she was only twelve years old.

She listened for the sound of the garage door opening and closing again, then watched the clock until it was time to go. At least now she didn't have to worry about the curfew. Just doing what she needed to do.

Still, Jaq fired off a text to her mother: **I'm going out with John. Thanks for extending the curfew.**

Then, leaving her window unlatched, she left through the front door and hurried to the corner of her street to wait for Devyn. The ground was wet from the recent rain, and the air hung heavy with earthy scents. Dirt and the rot that seemed to follow Jaq wherever she went.

Now she actually did feel sick. Not a headache, but her stomach was thick with nausea.

"Don't throw up," she muttered, bouncing on her toes in the hopes that movement might trick her body into feeling better. "Don't throw up."

She'd never broken up with anyone before. She'd heard Susan talk about breaking up with Tommy, which she did every six months or so, but the reasons were always small or silly. One time, they broke up because he refused to stop using cherry-flavored Chap-Stick, which he loved and Susan found revolting. It had seemed like a world-ending issue, and one week later, they were back together and Tommy was using a different brand of lip balm.

Which wasn't useful to Jaq in the least, but at the time all she could think about was how waxy and weird it would be to kiss someone who only ever wore cherry-flavored ChapStick.

"Hey." Devyn's voice cut through her thoughts. She'd been so distracted that she'd missed the purr of the motorcycle as Devyn drove up.

"Hey," she managed as Devyn rolled her bike to the curb and pulled her helmet off, mahogany hair glinting beneath the street-lights.

"You look like you're having deep thoughts. Care to share?"

Jaq was relieved when Devyn leaned against her bike instead of coming closer. She languidly crossed her legs at the ankle, watching Jaq with a loose smile. An undemanding smile.

"Not really," Jaq admitted.

"That's fair. Wanna go for a ride?" Devyn gestured to the bike.

"I do, but—" Jaq held her hands up between them. "But I can't. There's something I need to say."

"Okay. What is it?" Devyn asked, something in Jaq's voice adding a note of suspicion to hers.

Jaq caught a breath. Held it. They were exposed out here. They were far from Jaq's house, but they were still in the neighborhood, and the houses on either side of the street glowed warmly with light. There were families here—people here—and any one of them might glance through their front windows and see what Jaq was up to.

Still, there were things she had to say.

"Jaq?" Devyn pushed off her bike and started to come closer.

"Wait," Jaq expelled along with her breath. "Wait, please, just . . . stay there. Saying this is hard enough as it is."

"Okay." Devyn stopped moving. "I'm waiting."

Jaq opened her mouth, but once more she hesitated. There was just no easy way to say that she knew they weren't really dating, but they had to break up.

"I—" Her throat cinched tight.

"You want to stop this," Devyn supplied, understanding Jaq's distress without any explanation. "You're afraid, and you want to tell me that you can't see me anymore. Maybe ever again," she continued, not resigned or angry or anything Jaq might have expected, but gentle. "It's for my own good. It's for your own good. And maybe it isn't even forever, but it is for now. Right?"

Jaq swallowed hard. "I'm sorry," she said, voice barely above a whisper. "But I can't do this. Not right now. Not yet."

"Because *you* don't want to? Or because someone else doesn't want you to?"

"Does it matter?" Jaq asked.

"It's the only thing that matters." Devyn's answer was swift and sharp, taking Jaq by surprise. "Are you breaking things off because you don't like me?"

"I—" Jaq started and stopped. "I just—"

Can't.

Shouldn't.

Don't want you to die.

An image of Devyn's body. The blood so bright against the pale stone. Jaq was even more certain that the dream had been a message and a threat, but she couldn't say any of that to Devyn. There was only one way to protect her. End this. And then end this strange haunting.

The thought was sobering, and Jaq found all the words she'd been missing.

"I'm sorry. I don't think I can explain everything to you right now, but I can't do this anymore. I can't see you anymore." It felt like enough, but even as she said the words, she could see an argument building in Devyn's eyes.

If she wanted to save Devyn, she was going to have to break her heart.

She took a breath and continued. "I don't want to see you anymore. All of this was just a phase for me, and now I know what I want, and it isn't you."

For a second, Devyn only stared at Jaq. Comprehending, but unmoving. Jaq wished she would turn around and go so Jaq could let the scream scraping at her throat claw its way free. Let the tears scour her cheeks and sobs wreck her lungs.

"I'm going to kiss you right now," Devyn said, shocking a small gasp from Jaq. "I'm going to take three steps and put my hands on your cheeks and kiss you. If you don't want me to, then stop me. Tell me to leave and I'll go. Forever. You'll never see me again."

Jaq's breath caught in her throat. A traitorous thrill raced up her spine, dispelling the tension in her lungs. Devyn took one step forward.

"That's one," she said, voice soft. "You have two more to decide. No matter what you choose, I'll respect it. Because I respect you."

"Devyn," Jaq whispered as Devyn took another step forward, bringing the distance between them down to mere inches.

Devyn stopped, raising an eyebrow. "You want me to go?"

There was no malice in her. She was open and honest, her question to Jaq bristling with gentle intention. Every word from her mouth was a promise. One that meant Jaq got to choose because Devyn was calling her bluff.

"No," Jaq whispered, closing her eyes. "I want you to stay."

A third step and now Devyn was only a breath away. Her nose, her lips, her hips. Jaq breathed in the heady mixture of gasoline and jasmine. The faint hints of leather and lemon. It was too much. It was just enough.

Devyn slipped her hands along Jaq's jaw, their breath mingling as chills raced from Jaq's throat to her knees. Then their lips were together, and Jaq was lost.

The kiss was warm and slow, Devyn's lips soft and so sweet. Jaq melted into her, wanting nothing more than for this moment to extend forever.

The world vanished but for a sweep of light that encased them, shearing away everything else so that it was only Devyn and—

"Jaqueline Marie De Luca!"

Jaq flinched. Jerked away from Devyn's kiss, a dense ball of dread lodging in her stomach at the sight of a familiar car on the road.

At the sight of her father's face glaring out from the open window. At the eerie reflection in the rear window: a man with pale skin and a cruel smile standing on the sidewalk next to her.

"Get in the car," Dad growled.

And in the reflection, the man's lips moved in sync with her father's. Silently echoing the command.

Cold sweat slicked down Jaq's back.

And with a quick glance at Devyn, she got inside the car and closed the door behind her.

CHAPTER
THIRTY

Fern

"Kaitlyn's looking for you," Cam said, catching Fern just as they stepped inside the greenroom.

Tonight was opening night, and every square inch of the room was in use. Costumes were strewn over every available surface, cast members were bent over mirrors while they applied their makeup, and the room hummed with nerves and excitement. It was at least twenty degrees warmer inside the classroom than in the hallway because of how many bodies were crammed in, and it was blissfully familiar to Fern. They loved everything about it.

"Do you know where she is?" Fern asked, grabbing their things.

"She's in the trailer," Cam answered, then hurried off to address a late-breaking costume crisis that would definitely not be the last of the evening.

Leaving the chaos of the greenroom behind, Fern headed down a darkened hall toward the bathroom the theater kids had dubbed "the trailer" and reserved for the leads to get ready. The tradition predated even Holly's time in the theater club.

The noise faded into the distance and the air cooled, giving them room to enjoy a sudden, almost overwhelmed swell of love—there wasn't a better word for it than that. They couldn't have asked for a better senior-musical experience, and they couldn't wait to step onto that stage tonight.

They imagined themself standing next to Kaitlyn beneath the red drape of their proscenium; they imagined the audience on their feet, overcome with what they'd just witnessed. And they imagined the moment they saw their mother again and told her who they were. It was so good to picture it all, and soon, it would be a reality.

When they came to the bathroom doors marked with big poster-board signs that each said THE TRAILER, Fern paused. They could hear Kaitlyn humming along to music piping through her phone. It was from *Into the Woods*, which was surprising and endearing all at once. She probably had some superstition about not listening to the songs she was going to perform right before a performance.

Fern couldn't wait to ask. But first, there was something they needed to say.

It was important to Fern that when they stood on that stage as Danny, someone else knew just how much it meant to them. Someone who would hold on to the joy of it with them. They wanted that person to be Kaitlyn.

Their entire body was alight as they knocked, their mind cycling through three opening lines.

You've probably guessed this already, but I'm queer.

This is something I haven't told anyone else yet, but I'm queer.

I've been hiding this for a long time, but I'm ready to come out now: I'm queer.

They all felt a little inorganic, and *queer* wasn't entirely accurate, but no word was—they were gender-fluid and bisexual or maybe nonbinary and pansexual or maybe something else. At least *queer*, as a word and an idea, felt big enough to leave room for exploration. A resting place while Fern figured out which words worked better.

Fern's stomach pitched for five separate reasons when the door opened. Kaitlyn stood there, halfway into her makeup. Her skin was covered by a thick layer of base that perfectly matched her soft brown skin. Lightly blended lines of contour were drawn along her jaw and down either side of her nose, accentuating her feminine features and somehow drawing her kaleidoscope eyes into hyperfocus. The effect was startling. It hit Fern right in the chest, and for a second, all they could do was stare.

"Um," Fern said, catching their breath. "You look amazing."

"Thanks," Kaitlyn said. Fern's eyes were pulled to Kaitlyn's lips, the memory of kissing them still near enough to make them shiver.

They wanted to do it again. Kiss Kaitlyn again. But right now, Fern just wanted—no, *needed*—Kaitlyn to know the truth.

"What's up?" Kaitlyn asked when Fern still hadn't moved. "Do you want to come in?"

"Not yet." Fern cleared their throat. Now that the moment had come and they were sitting inches from Kaitlyn, looking into her kaleidoscope eyes, Fern couldn't remember any of the lines they'd prepared. "There's something I need to tell you first."

They opened their mouth and closed it again. Once, twice. And a third time. "I'm sorry," they gasped. "I guess I'm nervous."

"You've never been one for stage fright," Kaitlyn teased, but there was no cruelty in her voice. She reached out and took one of Fern's hands in hers, the touch thrilling and electric. "Take your time. But also, if this is about the kiss, then you don't have to say anything you're not ready to. I mean, I don't think we should do it again until we do talk about it, just to make sure we're on the same page, but there's no rush."

Warmth flooded Fern's cheeks, flushing them pink, no doubt. "I understand, and this isn't about—I mean, I wasn't going to try and kiss—"

"Oh, I didn't think that you were!" Kaitlyn hopped closer, squeezing Fern's hand. "I didn't mean to suggest that. I just wanted to say it, and sometimes I say too much. I'm kind of a talker. But I just believe it's important to be super clear. Especially when it comes to things like kissing and feelings. Because the truth is that I like you, Fern. And I don't want to mess that up."

A soft ringing filled Fern's ears, their head growing light as a balloon at the notion that Kaitlyn Birch liked them. That Kaitlyn cared enough about them to be super clear.

Kaitlyn wrinkled her nose at Fern. "And honestly, I've admired you forever. You're talented and brave and prickly in a way that I like. You're classy. But also, that day at Whisper Falls, I feel like I saw a side of you I'd never seen before. A side I recognize. You were dealing with something really big up there, and you jumped anyway." Kaitlyn sat back, regarding Fern with kind and admiring eyes. "I want to know that person better. Whenever you're ready."

"Oh," Fern gasped, blinking back tears. "Oh, shit. I'm sorry. That was just . . ."

"Eggplant parmesan."

That stopped the tears entirely. "What?"

Kaitlyn laughed. "I told you, I'm a talker. And sometimes I overdo it, so my mom told me that I needed to practice using disruptive phrases, that's what she calls it, to give people a life raft, if that makes any sense."

"It does," Fern said slowly. "I don't know how, but that eggplant parmesan is holding me together right now. Which is extra weird because I'm allergic to eggplant."

"Oh, I am very allergic to eggplant," Kaitlyn deadpanned. "Literally and metaphorically."

Fern snorted and then they were both laughing too hard to talk.

When they could breathe again, Fern felt ready to say what it was they'd come to say. This time, it was Fern who reached for Kaitlyn's hand.

"The thing I wanted to tell you is that I've been figuring a lot of things out recently, and I like you, but that's not what this is about. I'm not telling you this because I expect anything of you; I just want you to know. Since we're being super clear."

Now that they'd started, the words were flowing. That had everything to do with Kaitlyn. She made this so easy.

"You know I love being super clear." Kaitlyn's smile was beaming.

"Exactly, which is why I want to tell you," Fern said, swept up in Kaitlyn's kindness. In how easy it was to be here with her. To tell her, "I'm definitely, one hundred percent, straight."

The smile vanished from Kaitlyn's face. She pulled away.

Fern blinked, and felt their whole face go hot.

"Wait! No! That's not what I meant to say, oh my god." They waved their hands as though they could erase it all. "I meant to say, I'm *not* queer."

What the *fuck*.

Kaitlyn's expression didn't change. The hallway was suddenly too cold, all the warmth of their laughter drained away.

Fern felt like they were standing in cold acid rain. They snapped their mouth shut so hard their teeth clicked.

"Oh. Kay," Kaitlyn said, stepping back. Physically distancing herself from Fern.

"No, I mean, I'm—" Fern stopped. This time they could feel the way their mouth was prepared to move of its own accord. How their body would betray them if they pushed it again.

Something was happening to them. And they weren't in control.

"I'm—" They stopped again, clapped their hands over their mouth.

"You know what?" Kaitlyn said, backing away. "Don't bother."

"Kaitlyn, wait. Please, I don't—I mean, that isn't—" Fern willed Kaitlyn to see the desperation in their eyes. Willed Kaitlyn to understand what Fern had intended to say over the horrible things they'd actually said. Hear the jewels instead of the rot and worms that fell out of their mouth every time.

But Kaitlyn's eyes were hard and unforgiving. Holding Fern at an oppressive distance.

The weight of that glare made Fern step back.

"Have you been fucking with me this whole time?" she asked, voice low. "I didn't think you were like this, Fern. I thought you were—" Kaitlyn choked on the word, and for just a second, tears glimmered in her eyes. They vanished just as quickly. Replaced by a burning anger. "Was it all a lie? Were you leading me on to get me to switch roles with you? So you could have Danny? Have you been fucking with me this entire time?"

Tears squeezed in Fern's throat.

No, they thought.

"Yes," they said.

Like someone had possessed them. A frozen hand around their neck, their ankle.

Kaitlyn nodded as though seeing Fern clearly for the first time. "What the actual fuck?"

The world was spinning beneath Fern's feet. They shook their head, but didn't dare open their mouth again. Terrified of what would come out.

Kaitlyn was staring at them. Waiting. Her expression hurt and bewildered.

Fern understood, wanted so badly to explain that none of those words had been theirs, but they could feel the specter of a hand at their throat. Squeezing their words into the wrong shapes. If they tried again, they knew it would only get worse. They'd rather bite off their own tongue.

Finally, Kaitlyn had had enough of silence.

"Anything else to add?" Kaitlyn threw a hand up between them. "You know what? You've said enough already. I don't want to hear anymore. If this is how you feel, then you should just back out of the show tonight."

"Wh-what?" Fern almost choked.

Surely Kaitlyn hadn't meant that. This was the senior musical. And while that alone made it an important moment in their life, over the past few days, it had become so much more than a single show. It had become a part of who they were. The show itself had become a touchstone for Fern. They couldn't just not perform. This was how they were going to show their mother, their sisters, and their friends who they really were.

"You're a monster. I'm not going on with you tonight. So either you back out or I will."

A faint humming started in Fern's ears. A quiet siren that blotted out the silence of the hallway.

They understood what Kaitlyn was offering them. It was a choice, except that it wasn't. Not really. Either they ignored Kaitlyn's feelings and took the stage as Danny or they demonstrated how sorry they were and stepped aside. Let someone else take their place instead.

There was only one real answer. One right thing to do.

But Fern didn't want to do it.

"So?" Kaitlyn folded her arms against her chest.

"I—" Fern swallowed hard and nodded. "Okay."

"Okay, what? Okay, you're going on? Or okay, you'll back out?"

"I'll—" Fern snapped their mouth shut, terrified that they would say the wrong thing. Make this all even worse. But Kaitlyn was waiting, and every second that passed made Fern look like even more of a dick that they already did.

"Break a leg," they managed, then they turned and hurried down the hall, not even picking a direction, just moving as fast as they could until they were sure they'd put enough distance between them and Kaitlyn.

When they stopped, they were somewhere near the gym. Far from the theater and Kaitlyn and their mom and sisters.

No one would look for them here because no one would look for anyone here, so they picked a spot and sank to the floor with their back pressed against the wall. The tears came at once. Unleashed and rushing as though someone had turned on a spigot.

It had been the right choice, but it wasn't fair. And for a long minute, Fern let themself feel the depth of that pain. They hadn't intended any of this. That it had happened anyway was a kind of violence they couldn't explain. That it might keep happening was too horrible to think about right now.

Their phone buzzed in their pocket with a message from Ms. Murphy checking in to see if they were okay. Fern started to respond, then stopped. They couldn't risk undoing what they'd already set in motion, and they didn't trust that anything they tried to say or type would come out the way they intended, and the last thing they needed right now was to tell Ms. Murphy that they were on their way. Which meant they would have to let Ms. Murphy believe not only that they'd abandoned the show, but that they weren't even brave enough to say so.

They silenced their phone and tucked their head into their knees while the tears soaked into their pants. Only when they heard the distant strains of music echoing down the hall did they raise their head again.

The show had started.

Slowly, Fern stood up and headed down the hall, back toward the theater. Avoiding the greenroom, they took the long way to the backstage door no one ever used and slipped inside.

They watched from the wings as Kaitlyn as Danny and Teagan, the Sandy understudy, sang and danced and won the hearts of the entire audience. Teagan was good, but Kaitlyn was effervescent in a way that made Fern at once so happy for her and so tremendously sad.

If anyone noticed them, they didn't say anything. And when it was time for the scene at the drive-in, Fern had to leave.

Their thoughts tangled around all they'd lost in the span of a few moments.

Except it had been more than a few moments.

This entire thing had been set in motion five years ago. When they'd all sought shelter in the woods. When they'd asked the Patron for help. And he'd taken so much more.

He was still taking things from them. Still trying to force them into the kind of shape he found palatable. And if Fern didn't do something about it, then they might spend the rest of their life a prisoner in their own body. Unable to say or express the things they most needed to. Alienating the people they cared most about.

Jaq was right. There was only one way to stop it.

As muffled applause sounded from inside the theater, Fern pulled out their phone. Cleared the five notifications from Ms. Murphy and twice as many from Cambria. Ignored the three missed calls from their mom and collection of texts from their sisters, and opened a text to Jaq:

Okay. Let's do this. Tonight.

Then they shoved their phone in their pocket set out toward the woods.

CHAPTER THIRTY-ONE

Jaq

Seated in the back of her parents' car, fear bloomed inside of Jaq. Surging up from her guts with such force she could only clench her teeth against it.

The drive home was short. Jaq held her breath the whole way, doing her best not to think of the last time she was in a car like this, bracing against whatever was going to happen next. Her mind spun through possible excuses or explanations, anything to dull the reality of the situation and convince her parents that she wasn't as rotten as they feared. She could be "good." Better. And she needed them to believe that, too.

When they stepped inside the kitchen, she opened her mouth, an apology on her tongue, but before she could speak, her mother's hand lashed out, slapping her hard across the cheek.

Jaq gasped, raising a hand to cover her cheek, eyes pricking with sudden tears. The sting wasn't nearly as shocking as the violence itself. Her mother had never hit her before.

"Mom?" Jaq's eyes flew from her mother's livid expression to her father. He stood several paces behind with his back to them, one hand braced against the kitchen counter. "Dad?"

"Don't." Her mother's hand came up again, and Jaq flinched.

"You don't speak. You have forfeited the right to say anything. I can't believe you would do something like this. To us and to *John*."

Jaq clenched her right hand, the ring glittering and bruising. She did feel guilty about that, but not for the same reasons as her mother.

"I—"

Her mom continued before Jaq could say anything. "We can fix this, but right now, you need to give us time. Go to your room and wait there while we decide what to do."

"What does that mean?" Jaq asked. She hadn't even finished the sentence when her father aggressively cleared his throat, knuckles rapping on the counter like a judge calling for order.

"Now, Jaqueline," Jaq's mom said, reaching back and covering her dad's fist with her hand. All at once, Jaq understood that her mother had struck her so that her father wouldn't. "Not another word."

Her parents were so angry and confident in that anger that they didn't want her to speak. The only way they could deal with what she'd done—with what she *was*—was to strike out at it. To punish and reject her.

They thought she was terrible and wrong. But not because it was true. It was what Devyn had said that night at Frank's.

Everyone got to bloom in their own way.

Her parents wanted a rose, but she was something else. An aster, maybe, or a morning glory, a dahlia, or sunbright daylily.

It was suddenly so clear to Jaq that what they wanted had nothing to do with her. It was about them. Their fears. Their desires.

Not her.

Jaq turned on her heel and headed up the stairs to her bedroom, where she shut the door firmly behind her. She was upset and sad, but the most surprising thing about this moment was how calm she was.

There was no panic clawing at the back of her throat. She wasn't even afraid of what they were going to do. Because it had nothing to do with her. Their shame didn't have to be hers.

It was so clarifying that she nearly laughed out loud. She wasn't afraid anymore. At least, not of them. What could they really, truly do to her anymore? Humiliation? Abandonment? Fine. She didn't need their judgment, and she had places to *go*.

Jaq tugged her phone from the back pocket of her jeans and found a message from John checking in on her and one from Devyn asking if she was okay and offering an escape. At least, that's how Jaq interpreted the string of question marks followed by a dragon. Coded in case it was Jaq's parents and not Jaq who saw the message.

Jaq fired off a response: I'm okay. And I'll tell you more later.

She swiped away from the message and started to mentally compose a message to John. There was a not-insignificant chance her parents would call his parents, and she wanted to be the one to talk to him. She might not be in love with him, but she loved him and he deserved to hear this from her. She was about to tap on his name when she noticed the text she'd sent to her mother just before leaving the house. Telling her that she was going out and thanking her for the extended curfew. But that wasn't what was written.

It said, Mom, I need you to come home. Now.

Adrenaline shot through her veins, the urge to run manifesting in the cold sweat at her temples. She hadn't even stopped to consider why they'd come home at that exact moment when her mother had said they'd be gone for several hours. She'd been too wrapped up in the panic of it to marvel at the timing. How perfectly timed it was that she was kissing Devyn at the precise second their headlights hit them.

She swallowed hard. These weren't her words. She hadn't typed them. At least, she hadn't intended to. The same way she hadn't intended to put John's ring back on her finger. These were things that had been done to her.

By the Patron.

And she knew now that until he got what he wanted, the Patron would not stop.

Her phone buzzed in her hand. The message was from Fern:
Okay. Let's do this. Tonight.

For the past five years, Jaq had been so safe. She'd had the perfect family and boyfriend, the perfect life with a perfect future mapped out before her. Most of the time, she'd been happy, but there had been moments when it felt like she was trapped behind a layer of glass, watching her life play out on the other side. Moments when she couldn't explain the sudden overwhelming sadness or discomfort she felt. When the panic cinched around her lungs like ice closing over the surface of a lake.

She'd been the person her parents wanted her to be. The person the Patron wanted her to be.

She'd been safe because she'd been living a lie. But all the things she'd been afraid of before had happened. She'd let herself fall for another girl, and her parents had caught her in the act. Exactly as she'd always feared they would.

And instead of falling to pieces, she felt like she was falling together. Becoming a whole version of herself.

She couldn't control her parents. She could mourn the relationship she would never have with them, but she couldn't force them. She could only control what she did and didn't do. She could only control her choices.

Jaq didn't hesitate before responding: I'm coming.

CHAPTER THIRTY-TWO

Fern

"That was fast." Fern rose from their spot on the bleachers and wiped their face along their sleeve. They couldn't seem to stop the tears pouring out of their eyes. It was surprising that they could produce so much when they felt this hollow inside. But as Jaq strode across the football field with a bag slung over one shoulder, they felt the constant press of tears relax just a little. "What's in there?"

Jaq dropped the bag to the ground and crouched to reveal its contents. Flashlights, a first aid kit, phone chargers, a few protein bars, and a bright red Swiss Army knife. "Just in case," she said, handing a flashlight to Fern.

Across the yard, fluorescent lights glowed around the school, drawing the redbrick towers in sharp relief against low-hanging clouds. The show had ended a while ago, but Fern knew most of the cast and crew were still inside, ensuring that everything was cleaned up and ready for the show on Friday.

They should have been with them.

"You're really up for this?" Jaq asked, testing the beam of the light, then tucking it into the back pocket of her jeans.

"It's like you said, we have to go back to the house," Fern answered. "Like Mal told us to."

"Like the Patron also told us to," Jaq reminded them. "Which is why you didn't want to go before, right?"

"Yep," Fern said without a hint of hesitation.

Fern knew that Jaq was watching them. She was waiting for some kind of explanation, but Fern couldn't give one right now. They were barely holding themself together as it was. Later, they promised themself. They would tell Jaq everything later.

If they could get the words out.

"Okay, as long as we're both clear that we're doing the thing that seems like a bad idea but also our only option." Jaq turned her eyes to the dark line of the woods. "Just like that night. Although I still don't remember anything that happened that night after we went into the woods, do you?" When Fern shook their head, Jaq added, "The only thing I know is that the Patron has been messing with us since that moment, and I'm done."

"Me, too," Fern answered, doing their best not to think of Kaitlyn. Feeling the sorrow of that intractable moment solidify inside of them. It made them feel heavy and gross, swinging back and forth between the desire to make things right or run very far away. "Also, I think you were right. I think Mal is out there, and whatever happened, I think she needs us. We have to help her."

"He's out there, too, remember," Jaq said, as she shouldered her pack and stood up. This close, Fern could see a reddened outline on her cheek. The echo of a hand against her soft skin. There was only one reason they could think of that someone would hit Jaq.

"Did your parents find out? Or John?" Fern asked as they started toward the woods.

"Not John," Jaq answered, quick to defend. "He's . . . he doesn't know. And even if he did, I don't think he'd ever hit me. This was my mom. Just like Mal's." She heaved a sigh. "I don't *think* they're going to try to send me to a conversation camp, but who knows."

"I'm sorry." Fern almost reached out to take Jaq's hand. Five years ago, they'd have done it without thinking, but even though they were friends now—again—things weren't the same. Their own mother and sisters had just sat through a show expecting to see Fern perform as a boy. Who knew what they were thinking now. The possibilities made Fern want to vomit.

Jaq shrugged, her smile coming easily. "It happened, and I'm still here. I can figure everything else out. Tomorrow. After."

"I hope so," Fern said, wishing they had any of that same certainty.

At the edge of the woods, they stopped. The path tunneled into the dark, an open throat waiting to swallow them whole. A breeze drifted out, looping around their ankles and wrists before changing direction and looping back inside the woods. Like the forest itself was exhaling. Inhaling. Like it had lungs and breath and spite.

Suddenly, Fern felt the same way they had five years ago. Standing at the edge of the woods with a tremulous mix of fear and hope. That things couldn't get any worse. That things could get *better*.

"Ready?" Fern asked, extending their hand.

Jaq took it, squeezing once as they stepped across the threshold and into the woods.

It was like stepping through a portal. On one side, the night was vibrant and alive, moonlight washing everything in silvery light, crickets and frogs adding their song to the distant sounds of traffic and wind in the trees. And on the other, nothing.

Inside the woods, the air was still and silent. Frigid and sharp with the scents of moss and pine. They paused, both waiting to see if simply crossing the barrier would unleash the remainder of their memories. But none came, and the only sound in the entire woods was the arrhythmic huffs of their breath, so quiet and yet so loud. Fern had never felt so exposed. Even the smallest shift of their feet felt like shouting, "We're here!"

For a second, it was impossible to move, then Fern gritted their teeth and flicked on their flashlight. Light bounced off the nearest trees, turning their low branches into a dense, impenetrable thatch and hiding whatever lay beyond—nocturnal animals, the ghosts of dead girls, the Patron himself.

"Let's go," they said.

They traveled in silence. The sounds of their steps on the trail thunderous in the quiet woods. With every step, Fern felt eyes on them. Greedily tracking their movements. The trees holding their breath in anticipation.

When they'd been walking for some time, Fern pointed their flashlight back in the direction they'd come, but it illuminated only a wall of trees. The woods were seamless and flat; the path they'd just traveled had vanished like footprints washed clean from the beach.

"Where did the path go?" Jaq asked, voice strained thin.

Fern didn't answer because the answer was more terrifying than the question. The path was *gone*.

"Which way?" Jaq murmured.

Just then, their flashlights burst. Plastic and glass shattered, spilling to the ground.

Jaq gasped. The night enveloped them, quickly obliterating their sense of direction. And the silence of the woods wrapped around them like fingers curling into a fist.

"Look," Fern whispered, pointing to a familiar chunk of basalt marking a nearly invisible fork in the path. It snaked off between the trees, vanishing into the shadowed distance.

The house would be at the end of this trail. They remembered that, but they still couldn't remember what had happened that night. They turned to Jaq. "Do you remember anything yet?"

"Nothing," Jaq confirmed with a shake of her head, eyes traveling along the narrow trail that climbed steeply upward. Fern watched an almost imperceptible shudder move through Jaq's shoulders before she muttered, "Here we go."

"Here we go," Fern echoed.

When they'd stumbled upon this place all those years ago, it had felt like the house had found them and not the other way around. The house had responded to their need for someplace that was theirs, far enough from their homes that no one would find them.

But as they climbed up the hill toward the little clearing at the top, Fern couldn't shake the sense that this time, they were being drawn into a trap.

And suddenly, there was the house.

It loomed up against the night sky, its walls splintered like bones, jagged points limned in a thin wash of cold moonlight. As if held together by a viciously stubborn spirit that refused to let any part of it rest. Most of the roof had burned in the fire, and what was left slouched inward, leaving the place hollowed out. Moonlight shone through the empty windows, giving the impression of eyes watching over them. Around it, the world rushed away, tumbling down the side of a cliff, tearing a hole in the forest as though even it was afraid to be too close.

Only the front door remained whole. It stood at the top stone steps that lolled on the ground like a desiccated tongue, its wood stained a rich cherry red. Its pewter knob and knocker were unblemished by age or wear. Arching over the elegant high curve of the door, the words PROMISE HOUSE were stamped into a bridge of cement, the letters softened and barely legible in places.

And standing in front of the door, in the same blue rain jacket she'd been wearing that night, was Mallory.

Fern wasn't sure if they stopped walking first or if Jaq did. They both stared at the thirteen-year-old girl they'd known and loved in their own different ways. She was faded and pale, and a gash opened across her belly, spilling blood down her front. It seemed to drip as though the cut were fresh, leaking and dripping out of her, soaking into her jeans and staining her shoes. The colors were all muted in the darkness, but they glistened wetly. She was a vision of death, and when she smiled, Fern couldn't help but shiver.

"Hurry," Mal said, holding out her hands, a look of wild uncertainty on her face. When neither of them moved, she pushed her hands out again. This time with more force. "C'mon! If I come to you, he'll know. He always knows when I leave the house."

"The Patron?" Fern asked.

"Yes, the Patron." Mal's voice was urgent.

"Why can't we remember what happened that night?" asked Jaq.

"He's furious enough that you remember as much as you do, but if you come here, I can help, and we can undo what we did."

"What did we do?" Fern took a tentative step forward.

"I can't tell you. I have to show you," Mallory explained, giving her hands another little shake. "Take my hands."

Fern caught Jaq's eye, seeing the same wary hesitation in her expression that Fern felt. But it lasted only a second. They both knew that this was why they'd come, and giving in to their fear wasn't going to get them anywhere.

Together, they climbed the steps and took Mal's hands, and everything went white.

CHAPTER
THIRTY-THREE

Mallory
THEN

They found the house much sooner than they should have. It was as if the house could sense them, shifting closer to open its doors like a mouth eager to swallow them down.

They ran for only ten minutes, then there was the black rock, the narrow path, the steep hill, and the house. Waiting for them in a spill of moonlight with the wall of mountains at its back. The purple curtain waving hello from one window. The doors sighing open as they climbed the front steps and stepped inside.

"Feels creepier at night," Jaq said, wrapping her arms around herself. "Colder, too."

"How do we do this?" Fern was almost as eager as Mal.

"We offer him a gift. A price like the song says and then we make our wish." Mallory began to unfasten her friendship necklace. "These."

"You think that's enough?" Jaq asked, as she unclasped her own necklace.

"Mine is the most important thing I own right now," Mal admitted, and she smiled at both of her friends in turn. "I think that probably matters more than anything, don't you?"

Fern's mouth tightened as they removed their necklace and held it out to Mallory.

Mal took all three, tied a little knot at one end, and then braided them together. Her fingers trembled a little, with excitement or anxiety, she wasn't sure, but Jaq noticed and reached out, covering Mal's hands with her own.

"It's going to be okay," Jaq said. "No matter what happens, you don't have to go back."

"If nothing else, you can stay here for a few days while we figure things out." Fern added their hands to the pile. "We can bring you supplies, and no one will ever find you."

Tears pricked at the back of Mal's eyes. "It's going to work," she whispered, squeezing the necklaces so tightly the metal bit into her palm. Then she started to sing.

"Come out, come out, wherever you are, the Patron's in the trees . . ."

The other two joined, their voices growing stronger and louder with each verse until it didn't feel like a song at all. It felt like a spell.

When they finished, Fern and Jaq turned to Mal, silently waiting for instructions. Mal had given this some thought. She could wish for a lot of things right now, and there was a substantial, wicked part of her that wanted to wish her parents were dead, but that wouldn't necessarily change her life for the better. She needed a wish that was as simple as it was powerful. Something that would ensure she never spent another day locked in the closet.

"I wish—" Mal started, but stopped when Jaq cut in.

"*We* wish," Jaq said.

The words warmed Mal to her bones, and she started again. "We wish we were safe."

"We wish we were safe," the other two repeated. All three jumped at the sudden crash of thunder. There was a flash of light that shattered through the walls, a shriek that seemed to drive up from the basement, and a voice that answered from somewhere beyond the door, "As you wish."

Mal's eyes were wide, frantic with hope as she leapt to her feet. "Did you hear that?" she asked. "That was him, right? That was the Patron."

Fern climbed to their feet, then offered a hand to Jaq, helping her up.

"You both heard him, right?" Mal repeated her question, breathless.

"Yeah." Jaq nodded, except where Mal was elated, Jaq was clearly terrified.

Then, before any of the three of them could say another word, the voice came again.

"Come in, come in, whoever you are," it reverberated through the front door. So much bigger than a voice should be. "Receive your Patron's gift, the price is small and with it all, you'll never be adrift."

"It's him." Mal hurried toward the front door, but Jaq was faster, blocking the way.

"Mal, I don't think we should go out there."

"Of course we should," Mal answered, anger perched close behind her words.

"Jaq, what are you doing?" Fern stood at Mal's shoulder.

"I think we should think about this for a minute."

"Think about what?" Mal snapped, tears shining in her eyes. "This is why we came, Jaq. Because I need help. *I need help!* You can stay here if you want to, but I'm going out there. Are you coming or not?"

271

Jaq swallowed hard, and when she stepped away from the door, the house screamed.

Silver lights flickered across the walls, swirling and surging toward the door and coalescing around the knob. Fern and Jaq drew back, but Mal had seen these same lights before, and she wasn't afraid. She had assumed that they were evidence of the Patron. If he was a spirit, then surely he had a form. But now she wondered if there was something else in this house, too.

Whatever it was, it didn't want her to leave, and Mal didn't have patience for that. She stepped up to the door, gripped the knob, and pulled with all her strength. The spirits screamed and resisted, but Mal was determined. Bracing one foot against the wall, she wrenched the knob harder and pulled.

The door opened. The screaming stopped. And Mal led Jaq and Fern out into the clearing.

The trees began to whimper and whine, filling the woods with their eerie calls. Then the Patron's voice returned. Booming from everywhere and nowhere.

"Who will pay me in return for such safety?"

"What do you want?" Mal asked.

But the Patron's only response was to repeat the question: "Who will pay me?"

"All of us," Mal suggested.

And the Patron answered, "Eventually," in a voice that carried a dark note of amusement. Then he added, "First."

"Okay," Mal said with a frustrated sigh. "Who's going to go first?"

Behind Mal's back, Jaq met Fern's gaze. They were both thinking the same thing. Both conflicted in the same way because while they felt in some way responsible for Mal's situation, the wish had been her idea. Her choice. She should be the one to go first and pay the price, whatever it was.

"Me," Mal announced when neither of her friends spoke up. "I'll pay the price."

"I accept," rumbled the voice.

There was a brief moment in which the girls thought everything was going to be okay. Just long enough for Mal to tip her head toward Jaq, the beginnings of a mischievous smile on her lips.

Just long enough for them to miss the way the shadows lengthened out of the woods, sliding toward her along the earth.

Then she was snatched up. Her body raised above their heads. She hung there for a second, silent in her shock.

Jaq would remember the way tears had started to brim in Mal's wide, bewildered eyes. Fern would remember the mud stain on an elbow of her blue jacket.

They would both remember the way an invisible blade opened a second, gruesome smile across her belly. The way her expression went slack. The gush of blood that fell like rain. The way the house shrieked behind them.

The way fear gouged its way from their lungs and throats as they screamed into the night.

The way they ran.

The way they ran.

The way they ran.

And then they would remember nothing at all.

Until now.

CHAPTER
THIRTY-FOUR

Jaq

Mal was still holding on to Jaq's hand. The gash in her belly ran bright with blood. Her touch was cold pressure. The grip, Jaq realized with a shock of discomfort, of a ghost, but her eyes were full of life. Of hope.

It was one thing to know that the girl Jaq had loved was dead, and another to see it happen. Or, to remember it happening. To feel the memory lodge into her sternum like a knife.

It hurt. Gouged deep into her guts and twisted.

Jaq gritted her teeth against this grief that had waited for five years. She put it away again, shoved it down. When this was all over, she would give herself permission to be furious about the prolonged violence the Patron had put Mallory through. But right now, she had to focus.

"You've been trapped here ever since?" Jaq asked, not because she didn't know the answer, but because she needed confirmation. To hear it and make it real.

"Ever since that night," Mal said, nodding once. "Not exactly like this." Mal gestured to her body. The open wound of her belly and the ghastly blood that dripped still. "I was more of a spirit, stuck inside this house."

"But if you're here now, why didn't you reach out to us?" Jaq asked.

"I wasn't exactly in my right mind after it happened. I think I spent a few years so mad that I didn't fully realize I was dead. But at some point I did, and that was when I realized that I had a choice: I could stay chained to my anger and dissolve into a mindless spirit, or I could try and do something about it."

As she spoke, the gash across her belly stopped bleeding and closed. The skin stretched across layers of muscles and intestines and knit itself together. The jacket followed suit until she looked almost as she had in the last moments of her life.

"You tried to reach us," Jaq said.

"I tried. And I was getting better at it. Sometimes, I could hear you or see a glimpse of you and what was happening in your lives, and I could almost push through, but I couldn't talk directly to you. Not until you both came into the woods that night."

"You gave us our memories back," Fern said. "Why not this one?"

Mal heaved an empty sigh. Jaq wondered if she needed to breathe or if it was something she did out of habit. The same way she blinked or scratched at her wrist.

"That was him," she said, and her wound opened again. Blood spilled out of her like rain. "He noticed what I was doing and stopped me at the very last second. And if we don't get inside soon, he's going to figure out you're both here."

"Where is he now?" Jaq asked.

Mal threw her hands up in frustration. "No clue. I'm a ghost, not a god, unfortunately. He roams. Hunts. Waits for some other poor, vulnerable kid to come asking for wishes, I guess. But he always comes back eventually, and you don't want to be out here when he does."

Still standing on the crumbling front steps, between the house and the forest, Jaq looked up at the fractured walls rising overhead. Uneven rows of jagged teeth chewing at the sky.

"But we remember now. Everything. Why do we still need to go inside?" Jaq asked.

"The wish," Fern and Mal said at the same time.

"What about it?" An image of the tangled knot of necklaces flashed in Jaq's mind.

"You think we can undo it?" Fern asked. "And things will go back to the way they were?"

"That's exactly what I think. I think that our necklaces were powerful because they were important to *us*. They bound the three of us together, and when we gave them to him, we gave him power over our bond. Our secrets. And then he fucked us over!" She shouted this into the woods as her wound continued its gruesome cycle, healing and reopening. "I think if we take our gift back, we can undo the wish itself and give him a taste of his own medicine. Then maybe you'll be safe again and I'll be free." Mal's confidence waned, and Jaq realized that even though she and Fern had spent the past five years growing up, Mal was still the same kid she'd been. Angry and brave and full of innocent hubris only kids can achieve, but a kid just the same.

And she was still trying to help them.

Having made a decision, Jaq climbed the last two stairs to the door, then turned back for Fern. They stood with their mouth pinched shut, their eyes pinned to barely legible letters bending over the front door.

"Coming?" Jaq asked.

Fern pried their eyes away from the sign, then climbed the remaining steps. Together, they pushed open the door.

A gust of stale air greeted them. Thick with the earth-sweet scents of mildew and rot. Jaq tipped her head back to look up at the broken ribs of the staircase, the long walls plagued with holes and threaded with vines. It was at once familiar and terrifyingly strange.

"Have you been alone in here?" Fern asked.

"Not exactly." Mal smiled and pressed one ghostly hand against the wall.

A silvery glow appeared beneath her fingertips, then shot up like a flame, fanning out until the entire room was consumed by the same cold fire. As the fire burned itself out, the air filled with a dozen overlapping whispers, the susurration disquieting and beautiful.

"What is that?" Jaq asked.

"I call them the Gray Whales," Mal said fondly, eyes skimming over the broken walls. "They're always together like a pod, and they sing. Or scream. I think they died here a long time ago. You remember the story about how the Patron died in a fire? They started it. And they've been protecting this house ever since."

"It was them all along," Fern said with wonder. "Protecting us in this house when we were kids. But who were they?"

"The orphans," Jaq murmured.

Mal nodded. "Except they weren't orphans. Not in the traditional sense."

"The girls he took in over the years," Jaq added, recalling the article she'd found. "They must have been the last ones who were sent here."

"Queer kids," Fern said, sounding like they might vomit.

"Angry queer kids," Mal confirmed. "Angry enough to kill the Patron."

"Their parents left them here to die. In more ways than one." Fern wrapped their arms around their stomach. "And they're still here? Can they help us?"

"They aren't coherent the way I am. Or the way he is," Mal spat the words. "I think it's because of how they died. Consumed by rage almost more than they were by fire. They don't speak, and they don't leave the house. But we're all connected."

Mal moved ahead of them, stepping lightly over weakened floorboards and pointing out holes until she came to a spot in the center of the room and crouched down. Brushing aside dead leaves and forest detritus, she revealed something Jaq would have glanced right past if she'd been the one looking.

The chains were balled up, their golden shine so tarnished they appeared to be fused together. Their friendship necklaces.

"It could take us all night to untangle these." Jaq crouched at Mal's side and gently lifted the knotted bundle, letting it roll around in the palm of her hand.

"Let me see it. This happens to theater jewelry all the time. You just have to find all the ends and work from there," Fern said.

Faster than Jaq imagined possible, Fern had the ends of three distinct chains from the mess. Once it was started, the rest went easily with the three of them working in a circle, their hands moving in concert, as seamlessly as if they'd been working together for the past five years. Then, all at once, the necklaces came apart with a loud clap. A sound like breaking.

Like the slap of a hand against a cheek.

The concussive shock of reality shifted beneath their feet.

It snapped through the broken house, startling a groan from its ancient bones, then silence rushed back in. Settling heavily around them.

"Do you think it worked?" Fern asked, sitting back on their heels.

Jaq cast a wary glance around the house. "There's only one way to find out." She looked at Mal, a flutter in her own lungs. "We have to leave the house."

It was a terrifying reality. But the only way to know if they'd changed anything was to leave the protection of the house. To step into potential danger.

Mal pursed her lips in a gesture that was so familiar to Jaq it made her heart ache. She was every bit as brilliant and angry as Jaq remembered. She wasn't just a girl. She was a force. Demanding and rebellious in a way that had always inspired Jaq to be brave. To take her natural desire to resist her parents' rules and sneak out.

There was no way to know what would have happened between the two of them had Mal lived. Maybe they would have had a sweet, secret relationship for years, going off to the same college where they could be together without worrying all the time. Or maybe they would have been explosive. Constantly pushing at each other's hearts and boundaries, reshaping each other with each fight or kiss, redefining who they were and who they wanted to be.

Or maybe they would have gone back to being friends. It was impossible to say. It didn't matter anyway. Not now. Jaq just loved her. Mal deserved to be free. They all did.

"Right," Mal said at last.

Jaq reached into her bag and found the Swiss Army knife, flipping out the blade as Fern curled their fingers into fists, and Mal drew open the front door and boldly descended the stairs.

Jaq followed more slowly now, eyes on Mal and the forest beyond. Breath held and heart thumping.

Silence unfurled between them. They watched the woods and

they waited. They were apprehensive and hopeful and a little bit sure that they'd done the right thing.

Mal took another tentative step away from the house, and when nothing happened, she turned to face Jaq and Fern, a triumphant grin on her pale face.

"We did i—"

Jaq heard Mal choke an instant before her own body was snatched up by an invisible hand. For a second, Jaq dangled in the air, then she was thrown backward. Slammed into what could only be the house. Pain like a knife through her lungs. Vision going white, then dark.

The forest falling away.

Or was she the one falling?

Sliding through the air, through the ground, under, beneath, until she was standing again.

No, she'd been standing all day. Hadn't she?

She blinked and glanced down an aisle lined with pews to the familiar sight of a polished cedar cross. The one that stood behind the pulpit in the sanctuary of her church.

"Jaq," her mother whispered. "Step back now or John will see you. Oh, Jaq, you look so lovely. You have something old, new, borrowed, and blue, right?"

Jaq glanced down. At the wedding dress she'd picked out with her mom. It was perfect. Binding layers of white satin and lace. Buttons linked in a chain from the modest neckline to the hem that hovered a mere centimeter from the floor. It was gorgeous. Yet something inside Jaq bucked at the sight.

It seemed wrong in some way she couldn't quite describe.

"Right?" her mother prompted.

"I do," Jaq confirmed, listing the items in her head. An old comb

COME OUT, COME OUT

from her grandmother, a brand-new one tucked into her hair along-side it. Her underwear was blue, and she'd borrowed her necklace from . . .

The name teased at the back of her mind. It was important, yet she couldn't remember. She *needed* to remember. Needed to find M—

"My, you do look exquisite," her mother said, stroking her cheek. "John is going to be so pleased when he sees you. You've done everything exactly right."

The comment slid over her skin like oil on water, leaving a greasy residue behind. A familiar feeling of rot.

Jaq swallowed it down. Willed the feeling to go away. Because today was good. She was good. She was just out of college with a degree in elementary education. She was marrying John Nichols. Her parents were proud of her. So proud. She had no right to be anything but deliriously happy.

"There's my beautiful girl." Her father came around the corner and stopped to appraise her. "Are you ready for the rest of your life to begin?"

Jaq frowned at the strange wording, but there was no time to respond.

Her mother gave her a quick hug, then hurried down the aisle to take her seat an instant before the music started. Before Jaq knew it, they were walking down the aisle toward John's sweet face.

The music drew her forward one step at a time. One step and then another.

Until she had reached the altar and looked up into the face of the preacher, expecting to find the familiar smile of Preach Meach. But there was a different man standing at the altar. Taller and younger than Preach Meach, lithe with amber eyes, a kind smile, and white, suntanned skin. Salt-and-pepper hair curled softly against his forehead, and he was smartly dressed in a suit that tried—and failed—to hide the strength of his long body.

With an open Bible held loosely against his chest, he seemed to resonate with the kind of peace that came with surety of faith. It put Jaq at ease. If everyone else was so sure that she should be here, there must be some truth to it.

"Jaqueline," the preacher said, voice warm and soothing, "I was starting to worry that you wouldn't join us after all."

"Sorry," Jaq answered, a blush exploding on her cheeks. "I was nervous, I guess."

"Understandable. Today is a big day. I wouldn't want— Oh, what is that?" The preacher bent his head slightly to frown down at something on Jaq's hand.

She followed his gaze to a green spot on her right hand, in the webbing between her thumb and forefinger.

"I don't—" Jaq tried to rub it away, but when she touched it, she knew exactly what it was.

Mold.

It began to spread, spidering toward her wrist, silky fronds of a sickly, pale green sinking into her skin and refusing to budge. She rubbed at it harder, shooting a panicked look up to John, who frowned, not with concern, but with disgust.

"I thought you'd taken care of that," John said, drawing away from her.

"Help," Jaq gasped, looking up at the preacher.

Who was smiling now in a sinister way. Eyes narrowed with dark delight.

"The rot inside you will never go away on its own," he said.

"You must cut it out. Cut away all the bad so that the good has room to grow."

He held out the Bible and there, cradled in the ravine of the spine, was a bright red Swiss Army knife, its thickest blade open and gleaming.

"You must find the root and dig it up, cut it off at the source."

"Cut it out, Jaq," John said, still keeping his distance.

And from behind her, in the congregation, she heard her mother echo the command: "Cut it out, Jaq."

"Cut it out, Jaq." Her father's voice.

"Cut it out." More voices now. Blurring together and building, their words getting louder with each repetition. "Cut it out. Cut it out. Cut. Cut. Cut."

Jaq's breath came quickly as she reached for the knife, a distant part of her mind screaming for her to stop. Put the knife down. Run away and—

"It will only hurt for a second," the preacher whispered, slicing through her thoughts.

And without another thought, Jaq pressed the knife to the top of her wrist, where the mold had paused before driving beneath her sleeve, and she cut.

CHAPTER
THIRTY-FIVE

Fern

Fern screamed as they were foisted into the air and slammed back against the house. They squeezed their eyes shut. A tightening sensation cinching their ribs. They expected pain would follow, but none did.

The squeezing released, and they slid down the wall, dripping down, down, down until they stood before their bathroom mirror. The sticky scent of hair spray hung in the air, and Fern could feel the heat of a curling iron at the back of her head.

"Just a few more," their mom said, releasing the hot curl and letting it fall against the bare skin of Fern's neck. So hot it burned. Fern hissed, but their mom only laughed. "Who ever said girls aren't tough? You've gotta be tough to be beautiful. And you are stunning."

Fern opened her mouth to respond. To protest; but instinct fizzled on her tongue. What was there to argue about?

In the mirror, her reflection was a picture. Her blond hair hung in perfect coils like a halo around her face. Her creamy skin was flawless, the contours of her cheekbones highlighted with the lightest touch of peach blush. Her eyes were lined in soft black, and her lips glossed a glittery pink. Even Fern had to admit she was gorgeous.

Yet, looking at her, Fern felt splintered. Like she was simultaneously looking at herself and someone else.

Another hot curl landed on her back.

"I have to go," Fern muttered, overcome with the sudden urge to go. "I have to find M—"

She stopped. A second ago, she'd known who it was she needed to find, but the name had vanished. Evaporated like steam from a curl.

"Maybe we should pull these into an updo when they're cool?" her mother said, as though Fern hadn't said a word. "You know, pin it up so you look like a real princess?"

"I don't—" Fern started, but once again, the quiet spark of resistance flickering in her mind was snuffed out. "Sure."

"Trust me, headshots can make or break a career. We want directors to be stunned by this classic feminine beauty of yours and show them exactly who you are." Her mother added another curl as she spoke, fingers positioning each one just so. "You are such a lovely girl."

"Mom. Stop." There was that spark again, struggling to life.

"Oh, let me do this for my baby girl, Fern. Don't take this moment away from me. Okay?"

Mrs. Jensen smiled over Fern's shoulder, a playful gleam in her eye. A look that said she expected Fern to agree. To relent.

But something was wrong here. Fern needed to get out. To find . . . who? The name had been on her tongue a second ago.

"Okay?" her mom repeated, fingers twisting into Fern's hair.

As Fern watched, her mother's face shifted, elongated into that of a man with amber eyes who looked at Fern like he knew the worst parts of her and delighted in hating them.

No. "O-kay," Fern's reflection spoke. Not Fern. She—no, they, that felt right—they, they, they were sure that they hadn't opened their mouth, but as they watched, their reflection had. Pink lips curving up into the perfect imitation of Fern's ingenue smile. Sweet, hopeful, yearning.

"What a pretty *girl*," the man said. Not a compliment, a threat. The final word driven forward like a sword.

Girl, girl, girl.

Fern's mind was like a deep pool that was slowly icing over.

They—no, she was trapped between the hot iron and the counter. She couldn't move away, but maybe she could still move. She raised her hand, dragged it across her mouth. Pink gloss smeared across her skin, knuckle to wrist.

It felt good to wipe it off. To see the brief flare of irritation in the man's eyes. To feel the ice receding again as the spark inside warmed again.

"Now, Fern, that was silly. Let's try again," the man said, with a light shake of his head. "Be a good *girl*."

The ice returned. Her thoughts trapped behind layers of cold. And when Fern looked, her lips were coated in the same pink gloss. The lines clean and unsmeared.

With a shove, Fern pushed away from the counter, forcing the man to step back so she could get the hell out of there. Out of the bathroom, out of the house, she kicked off her kitten heels and ran.

Two steps later, the heels were back on her feet. The soles slapping against the pavement, making Fern slip and slide over the thin layer of grit.

She paused long enough to kick the shoes off again. This time, the return was faster. In the blink of an eye, they were back on her feet, tightening around the toes and heels.

Fern tried again to kick them away, but they wouldn't budge.

This couldn't be happening. It was a dream. A nightmare. Something too strange to be real.

But the ache in her feet was real.

The shoes tightened, the line of fabric cutting in beneath their ankle until a line of blood appeared, the narrow point of the toe box crushing in until Fern heard a crack, felt pain bolt through her.

The agony brought Fern to her knees, but it also brought a glimmer of clarity. Fern was not a girl. Not only a girl. But their mind was slippery and dark. The spark they'd managed to hold on to shuttering and weak. And they had to find—

At the far end of the street stood a young girl in a blue rain jacket, red hair blowing around her shoulders.

She turned and walked away, rounding the corner of a cross street. Guiding Fern.

Fern ran after her. Ignoring the pain. Going as fast as their feet would allow. The world seemed to blur and shift in their peripheral vision, as if it wasn't really there, and when Fern rounded the corner, they found themself in front of a church.

They hesitated. The sight of a cross conjured feelings of judgment and a frantic desire to stay far, far away from the people inside, but the girl was there again. Standing at the church doors, waving a hand that was clearly meant to tell Fern to hurry up.

Fern hurried forward and pushed through the front doors of the church.

There was no one inside the entryway. The sanctuary doors were closed. Fern could hear the sounds of a preacher's voice ringing out on the other side.

This was no place they'd ever wanted to be, but they felt compelled to keep going. One deep breath and Fern pulled the door open just wide enough that they could slip inside.

At the front of the church a bride and groom stood at the altar, hands clasped between them while the preacher recited the vows they were about to take. There was no sign of the little girl, and for a second, Fern didn't know what to do.

Then the bride tilted her head. Just enough that Fern saw her profile clearly. The long slope of her nose, her dark hair, and olive skin. Blood pouring over their joined hands. Dripping onto Jaq's white dress.

"Jaq," they gasped. They drew in a breath to shout. "J—"

A hand clamped down on their mouth. Cold and firm. Strong enough to hold them in place as a voice sifted down around them like rain.

"It isn't polite to interrupt." The voice slid against Fern's cheek like a cold tongue. The Patron.

Fern struggled, tried to step out of his grasp, but to their horror, their feet sank into the floor, vanishing beneath the worn brown carpet.

"She is in the midst of creating her own happiness. She is choosing the right path forward, something I offered to you as well, but you are too stubborn." He made a tsking sound in Fern's ear. "Some girls are simply beyond help."

Fern felt bile rising in their throat. He sounded truly remorseful. Like he believed every word he said. He believed there was a single way to be. To belong. And that belief made him terrifying.

"But that's not the case for your friend. Don't you see how her heart wants it?" The Patron's voice was soft and deep. "Let her have it, Fern. All you have to do is nothing. I can trust you to do that, can't I?"

The pressure on Fern's mouth disappeared as the Patron pulled his hand away. He was so sure that they would stay quiet. Stay there and silent and cowering in his shadow.

The horrible thing was, he was right. Fern couldn't move.

"Every time you open your mouth, you hurt someone." His voice ghosted along their neck and shoulders, circling around like a rope. "Do you really want to hurt Jaq? Again?"

They didn't. They'd never wanted to hurt Jaq. Or Kaitlyn. Or Mallory.

"People like you always hurt others," he continued, his voice slicing through Fern's defenses, finding its way into their thoughts, their heart. "You can't help it. You're too selfish. You only ever think about what you want. What you need."

It was true. Fern had been so afraid that night that they'd let their friends get caught. They'd heard the front door open and close. They'd heard the sound of Mallory's parents' voices in the front room, their footsteps in the hallway. And they'd been too afraid for their own safety to say anything. Worse, neither Mal nor Jaq had ever called them on it.

Then, years later, they'd been so focused on their own selfish desire to tell Kaitlyn the truth that they'd plowed through. Trying again and again. Making things worse simply because they couldn't stand the thought of being misunderstood.

"You should bite your tongue off," the Patron urged.

And Fern agreed. They moved their tongue between their teeth. Bit down.

Drove their teeth.

Into the muscle.

Until blood.

Blood rose around their teeth and dripped down their throat.

The pain was vivid and lush. It ignited Fern's entire body, a shudder passing through them like a scream. Vibrating inside them as the Patron whispered sweet encouragements into their ear as the preacher called for the rings and Jaq raised her bloodied hand.

Fern bit down harder.

And then they screamed.

CHAPTER
THIRTY-SIX

Mallory
NOW

Mallory was inside the house again. This was the way it always happened. He was so much stronger than she'd ever been. Anytime she tried to leave, he ripped her right back. Locked her inside this house of ash and rot until enough time had passed that she could try again.

He was bigger. Stronger. Older. And he was so sure of his power.

Now he had her friends. She could see them through the broken walls. Their bodies pinned high against the wood. They weren't struggling to get free, though. They were still. Their hands and feet dangling in the air. Like they were dead.

The sight terrified Mallory. Drove a spear of grief and anger all the way through her.

"Let them go!" Mal screamed.

"This is your fault." The Patron's voice sounded as though it were inside her own head. His words. Her words. His thoughts. Her thoughts.

It was her fault, but not for the reasons he believed. It was her fault for believing in him, for placing her faith in a story instead of herself. Her friends.

"You broke the deal, Mallory. You ruined this for them. Now I have to fix it. I have to fix them."

"You can't fix them!" Mal shouted. "They don't need to be fixed!"

"You asked for my help," the Patron answered, with a sigh that came from everywhere and nowhere all at once. "It is my job, my mission, to give you what you need, even when you lose your way. Especially when you lose your way."

For years, he'd been controlling her every move. Reminding her that she'd asked for this.

In the first year after he'd killed her, she had existed in fragments. She had been the scream against the waterfall, too small and insignificant to matter. Then, one day, she'd remembered her name, and that single word had been an anchor around which more words took shape.

Mallory and
want and
candy and
Jaq and
Fern and
pain and *hate* and *wishes* and
RUN.

She'd tried to run then, but no matter which direction she ran or how fast or quietly, he would find her. Pluck her spirit up and throw it back into the house. The doors would lock themselves tight, every shattered window and broken wall sealed against any attempt at escape, and she would stay inside with the Gray Whales, who would hold her gently, singing their wordless, ethereal song until she felt strong again. But she had never once made it past the boundary of the forest. She had been running for five years. Pursued by the spirit of a man who found her vulgar, as broken as this old house. By the spirit who had murdered her.

She ran because she had to do something, but running only made her feel small and powerless.

It was hell.

In all that time, she had never felt as much fear and hope as she did in this moment.

"We were never lost," she spat at the door. She reached out and yanked on the handles, but the doors resisted her as they always had.

"You were. So lost that you didn't even know it. Recovery is difficult because it is holy. If it were easy, it wouldn't be real. You must continue to choose the right path." The Patron spoke without appearing, spewing the same revolting rhetoric he'd been spouting since Mallory died. Mal wished he would show his face so at least she had something to hate directly. "Your friends are choosing that path right now. When they wake up, they will be renewed. Better versions of themselves. You wished for safety, and that is what I will give you—I will guide you into making the decisions that are right and good and safe."

Mal opened her mouth to speak, but it was Fern who screamed. The sound was fractured and wet and full of pain.

"Not long now," said the Patron. "Patience, Mallory."

And then the screaming stopped.

CHAPTER
THIRTY-SEVEN

Jaq

Fern was screaming.

No, that didn't make sense. Jaq was looking into John's eyes. They were getting married. He was happy. Everything was perfect. But Fern was somewhere nearby, and they were screaming.

Not just screaming. Shouting.

"Jaq! Jaq! JAQ!"

Each repetition was sharper than the one before. The words breaking through the ice in Jaq's mind, making room for the terror and the confusion and the pain. Her hand throbbed. The air smelled like moss and rain and rotting wood, and she knew without a splinter of doubt that this wasn't real.

She began to pull her hand from John's, but his grip tightened, sending a wave of pain up her arm.

"Jaq, it's time for your vows. Repeat after me, and everything will be as it should." The preacher's voice was invasive, sinking into her thoughts like mold. It spread and spread, searching for the parts of her that were already rotten and consuming them.

The part of her that liked to drive fast.

The part of her that danced with a restaurant full of strangers.

The part of her that had dared to tell Devyn she wanted her to stay.

A sinister voice in her mind whispered that those were the worst parts of her. That she should carve them out and bury them deep. The preacher's voice. The Patron's voice.

But there was another voice.

Screaming her name.

Making her feel whole instead of fractured.

"Are you ready, Jaqueline?" the Patron asked.

Jaq took a deep breath and gritted her teeth against the agony as she pulled her hand from John's, feeling her flesh tear from her efforts. She didn't stop until she staggered back. Free.

Then she turned toward the aisle and shouted, "Fern!"

Fern

Fern's throat ached from screaming. Their mouth was on fire. Blood flowed from the wounds in their tongue, filling their mouth and running down their throat until they gagged on it.

But at the sound of their name screamed back at them, they raced down the aisle, pain forgotten.

Jaq was there, trembling. "What do we do?"

The two stood together in the center of the church, but where a moment ago the pews had been filled with rows and rows of smiling people, now everyone watched with empty, stoic expressions. Even John, still standing at the end of the aisle stared after them as though he were nothing more than a puppet.

And all at once, Fern understood. These were the faces of the

Patron. He was putting on a show. But Fern had been doing the same thing for the past five years. Now they were done pretending to be something they weren't. And Mal had given them exactly what they needed to break free.

Fern turned, cupped their hands around Jaq's face, and said, "It's time to wake up."

Mal

Mal was still frantically searching for a way out when her friends' eyes suddenly opened.

Their bodies tensed a split second before they fell. Crashing into the stone steps below. Fern caught themself, but Jaq stumbled, rolling her ankle and crying out in pain.

"Jaq!" Fern grabbed her elbow. Blood seeped down Fern's chin, bright crimson against the snow of their skin.

"Oh my god, Fern. Are you okay?"

Fern nodded, teeth gritted and red. "You?"

Jaq cradled her bloody hand against her chest, where a ribbon of skin hung from the space between her thumb and forefinger, as though someone had peeled her like an apple. She squeezed her eyes and nodded, tentatively stepping down on her ankle.

A cold breeze began to seep through the woods. Driving toward them. Teasing unnatural sighs and moans from the trees as though the forest was filled with dying children.

"Get inside!" Mal shouted, peering through a large crack in the wall.

She couldn't be killed again, but the same wasn't true for her friends.

"Why didn't it work?" Fern aimed their question at Mal as they helped Jaq to her feet.

"I don't know," Mal snapped back. "I thought if we took back our gift, unpaid the price, then—"

She stopped. An idea slotted into place like the last piece of a puzzle.

Breaking the necklaces apart hadn't worked. They'd been a symbol of the wish and not the wish itself. She was still bound to this place. To the Patron and to—

Jaq and Fern.

The wish had bound her to the Patron, but it hadn't been *her* wish alone. It had been *theirs.* And if she was magically linked to the Patron, and he was linked to all three of them . . .

"That's it," she muttered.

"What's it?" Jaq asked, brow pinched in pain as she gingerly put more weight on her injured ankle.

"I died!"

Fern and Jaq shared a dark look. "We know," Fern answered.

"No, I mean, we made the wish together, but that was only the first part. It didn't work until I died," she explained as the menacing breeze drew closer.

"Your death was the final price," Jaq said, catching on.

"Yes!" Mal clapped her hands. "That's why taking the necklaces apart wasn't enough."

"But—" Fern winced in pain before continuing. "We can't undo your death . . . can we?"

"No, I wish we could," Mal answered. "But we can set me free. Take me away from here and he can't hurt us anymore."

"But how?" Jaq asked. "You said you've tried to leave and you can't."

The wind blew harder, kicking up dead leaves and creating a chorus of screaming trees encircling the house. Mal watched it all with an unexpected sense of calm.

"Get inside," she ordered, and this time her friends didn't hesitate to obey.

They crossed the threshold just as the wind hit the house with enough force to slam the door behind them. Another gust followed on its heels, slamming into the walls from every direction. Shattered glass and wood rained down, taking small bites out of their jackets and jeans. The Patron laughed, and the house shook harder.

"Mal!" Fern cried as a beam of wood speared the floor by their feet, narrowly missing their head. "We need help!"

Mal didn't know what to do. She'd never been able to fight against him, and her plan to break their wish had failed. She didn't have anywhere else to turn. She was alone, as she'd always been. A child at the mercy of a ghost kept alive by malicious glee.

Except she wasn't alone. Not really.

Mallory turned and banged her fists against the wall, waking the Gray Whales and sending shivers of silver fluttering high. "Help me!" she shouted at the house. "You want to protect us? You have to fight back!"

The house shuddered. Flickered and sighed as the Gray Whales pushed their way through the walls, coming out, out, out until they appeared as six distinct figures shrouded in silver light.

"Help us," Mal pleaded as the house shook again. "We need you to buy us time."

The ghosts gazed down, unmoving at first, then a low moan began to build. Louder and louder until it rivaled the storm outside. The Gray Whales shimmered, their edges blurring as they faded into the walls once more, then the house pulsed with silver light and the wind pummeling the house grew quiet. "I don't know how long they can hold him back," Mal said, leading Fern and Jaq down the hall to a small room where the skeletal remains of a child were laid out on the ground.

The bones weren't polished or stark white but mottled creamy white and pale brown, with bits of decay still clinging to them in places. They were webbed in thread and moss, a delicate and loving tapestry of death and earth.

"This is you?" Fern asked, tears making wet tracks down their cheeks.

Mallory nodded, serene and quiet. She knelt and placed a hand against her own skull, stroking the place where her cheek once bloomed with life. Where now roots pushed through empty eye sockets and traveled along the length of a cheekbone to dive through nostrils.

"We didn't know," Jaq said, voice choked with emotion. "We didn't remember."

"I know." Mallory took Jaq's hand, then reached up and took Fern's. She squeezed them both, met their eyes, and nodded once, resolutely.

She drank in the sight of them and they of her. Each aching for what they'd lost and what they were losing still. Each grappling with the strange joy that comes from sorrow and knowing that together they were painfully, perfectly real.

"What do you need us to do?" Fern asked quietly.

The wind shrieked outside again and slammed into the house like a fist. Little bits of charred wood rained down from above, skittering around them like insects.

Mal stepped closer to her friends. Her heart twisted to be so near and so far at the same time. She wanted time. To sit with them. To talk and listen. To know what their lives had become and what they hoped they'd become in the future. But she couldn't have any of that.

"Come out, come out, wherever you are," the Patron's voice sang, echoing through the broken walls.

For so long, Mallory had believed that he was the one keeping her here. In this wretched existence. That the reason she couldn't leave the woods was because he was stronger than she was. But she'd been wrong. She'd let his righteous enmity convince her that she had no power of her own.

The Gray Whales had made this house a sanctuary, but she had made it a home. Her bones were what rooted her here.

But safe and free were two separate things.

And she needed her friends to be free.

"You have to take me away from here." Mallory pointed to the bones that made up her hand, lying in a pile that was threaded through with dark green vines. "Take one."

"What?" Fern asked in horror. "You want us to take your bones?"

A great knock sounded at the door, reverberating through the house.

"I do." Mallory pointed again, urgently. "Take one, and then you're going to have to run. As fast as you can. Until you're out of the woods."

"Why just one?" Jaq asked. "Shouldn't we take all of them?"

"One is enough," Mal answered. "If part of me is with you, all of me is with you. You just have to get me out of here. Out of the woods."

Jaq and Fern suddenly seemed five years younger, their voices frozen in their throats, their feet pinned to the ground, the fear in their hearts bright and true and terrible.

"I can fix you," the Patron's voice rumbled up from the floor-boards. "Fix your lives so that no one will ever know the rot inside you."

When they'd been little, they had believed exactly that. They had known too much fear to believe otherwise. But they had given too much to fear, lost themselves and everything important to them.

"I love you both," Mal said, smiling with tears in her eyes. "Exactly as you are."

"We love you, too," they said.

Together, Fern and Jaq crouched and each took a single bone from Mal's hand.

The house shook violently, and an oily shadow crept into the room, seeping up around their legs with a chill.

"Ready?" Mal asked.

And even though they wanted to stay with her forever, they nodded.

"Go!" Mal shouted.

CHAPTER
THIRTY-EIGHT

TONIGHT

They run.

Though only two people went into the woods tonight, three are running now.

Two are alive. One with their arms supporting the other as they crash through the dark woods. The third travels behind them. She has cast herself wide, arcing at their backs like the palest shimmer of a rainbow after a storm. Behind her, a veil of silver gray, six spirits singing and sighing as they fly. Beating back a thundercloud of a man with arms too thin and face too long. His shadow streams forward, clawing at the rainbow girl but finding no purchase.

The two running do not stop. They do not slow. They are effervescent with the desire to fly, to live, to hold on to one another. They can hear the thing at their backs, and they are afraid, but also determined and angry.

The rainbow girl tells them that it will be all right. Don't slow down. She will be with them even if they can't see her.

The edge of the woods appears before them, the school just beyond. A glittering moon hangs low in the sky.

Now they hesitate. Worried. Scared. They don't want to forget again.

"You won't," the rainbow girl assures them. "Go."

They step over the threshold. Gasping and spent.

The Gothic towers of their school ghostly behind a veil of mist.

"Fern?" Jaq asks, turning to her friend.

Fern nods. They remember. They will always remember.

When they turn back, the woods are quiet and soft. There is no one there. The rainbow girl, the Gray Whales, and the Patron have vanished, and in each of their hands, they hold a single bone.

CHAPTER
THIRTY-NINE

Jaq

Jaq fidgeted in the passenger seat of Fern's car, trying not to bleed all over everything as they pulled into Frank's parking lot. The all-night diner was a beacon in the dark. Three cars sat in the lot. Anywhere else and Jaq would have been worried about who they would find inside at such a late hour.

Before they went inside, Jaq turned to Fern. "Before we go in there, I need to say something out loud." Fern nodded, waiting, and Jaq continued. "I'm gay. A lesbian. I like girls. A lot."

Blinking back tears, Fern opened their mouth and spoke carefully. "I'm gender-fluid."

For a second they sat in silence, basking in the words that had been denied them for so long. Then they climbed out of the car and stepped inside the diner.

The instant Frank saw the two of them, he jerked a thumb at the bathroom and followed them with a first aid kit, muttering, "Jesus fucking Christ, kids."

Fern's tongue was still in one piece, but their teeth had left deep gouges through the middle. Compared to Jaq's skinned arm, it certainly looked like the worst of the two wounds, but after a quick call to a friend who was a doctor in the navy, Frank handed Fern a cup of warm salt water to gargle and turned his attention to Jaq's arm.

He carefully unwrapped the blood-soaked hoodie she had used to stop the bleeding, then turned her arm back and forth with a featherlight touch as he considered the damage.

"I can disinfect it and bandage it up, but you really should see an actual doctor. It probably goes without saying, but this is going to leave one hell of a scar." He said it all without judgment or even too much concern, and Jaq appreciated that he wasn't pressing her for information about how either of them had managed to acquire their injuries. "Unless you want to go to the hospital right now?"

"No," Jaq and Fern answered together.

Frank frowned, but it was an understanding frown. One that recognized that sometimes even hospitals aren't safe.

"Okay," he agreed. "But at the first sign of infection, this is no longer a negotiation. Deal?"

"Deal," the two of them said.

As soon as Jaq was cleaned up with a monster bandage around her forearm, Jaq asked Fern if she could borrow the car.

"Just for a few minutes," she said, barely able to stand upright.

Fern considered her, seeming to understand exactly what Jaq's plan was. "Do you want me to go with you?" they asked, words clumsy with their swollen tongue.

"I'm okay," she said, giving Fern's hand a little squeeze before stepping out of Frank's way as he returned with a cup of ice.

"Hold a piece on your tongue for as long as you can stand it," Jaq heard him saying as she left the restaurant. She slid into the driver's seat of Fern's car and headed for home.

It was after midnight. Well past curfew. And even though she was pretty sure that didn't matter anymore, she had to find out. Close the loop. Which was a weird thing to think about her own life.

The front light was on when she pulled up, but the rest of the house was dark, which only meant that her parents weren't in the front rooms. She had a strong suspicion that they were still awake. Waiting. Simmering. Preparing.

Jaq climbed the front steps. She could have gone in through her bedroom window. Shimmied up the tree and snuck into the safety of her own room, but she didn't want to be inside the house before she looked her mother in the eye once more.

Even though it was late, and she knew her parents would be upset, she pressed the doorbell. And then she waited.

A second passed before she heard footsteps, and the porch light switched on. When the door opened, it was her father standing there instead of her mother.

He glared down at her, wearing an expression Jaq realized had become so familiar to her she hardly registered the dissatisfaction in it anymore. But here, now, she saw it plainly. This wasn't the look of a father worried about his daughter.

This was judgment.

"Hi, Dad. Sorry it's so—" Jaq started, but he raised a hand to cut her off.

"Jaqueline." He said it like her name alone was a problem. "What happened this evening was upsetting. For all of us. And I hope you've had some time to reflect on that. Your mother and I certainly have."

He gestured to the darkened hallway behind him, suggesting that Jaq's mom was hidden back there somewhere. Listening.

Jaq didn't think there was any way they'd had enough time to reflect on anything other than their own surprise, but she nodded and waited. He clearly had more to say.

"We need you to know how devastated we are. Neither of us deserved that. But we recognize that in some way, this is a cry for help." He nodded as though proud of himself for saying what needed to be said. And he probably was. Mr. De Luca had never been much for words. Especially when they were about feelings or emotions. This probably felt like a breakthrough for him. "We are willing to get you the help you need, but only if you want it. Only if you are committed to getting better. You have to choose."

Jaq drew in a sharp breath. Those words. The Patron had said something similar. And it struck Jaq now, how cruel it was for parents to present the illusion of choice inside such deceptive wrapping.

"If you do, then we won't tell a soul," her father continued. "Not even John. Everything can stay the way it is as long as what happened tonight was a mistake. Understand?"

Jaq did understand. More than he meant for her to. Some of it was about her parents, but more importantly, she understood something about herself. Only a week ago, she might have made another choice. She would have prioritized their comfort over her heart. She would have forced herself to grow into the daughter they wanted. To bloom in the way that pleased them.

Right now, standing with her father blocking her way into the house where she'd grown up, she should have been on the verge of a panic attack. Her heart should have been racing, her blood singing, her breath as shallow as a single drop of rain. But she wasn't.

The fear that had lurked in the back of her mind for so long, that had crept upon her in unsuspecting moments, making her feel weak and broken, had transformed into something new. Something small but strong. Something worth nurturing.

Her father was presenting her with a world of loss and struggle, and she wasn't even sweating.

"I understand," she said, smiling. Not for him. Rebellious and proud. But not for him.

And he knew it.

A frown darkened his face. He leaned forward slightly, the whole mass of him threatening. But Jaq wasn't scared.

She wasn't sure that it was possible to be afraid of someone who was so concerned with what others thought that they didn't have any thoughts of their own.

"We don't have a gay daughter," he growled, standing so that she couldn't have pushed past him if she'd wanted to.

Jaq smiled and took a single step back. "You're right," she said. "You don't."

Then she turned on her heel and left the front porch. Climbed back into the car and started the ignition.

Her mind buzzed and her fingers trembled from the rush of adrenaline, and she clutched the wheel tight as she retraced the path she'd just taken from Frank's to her parents' house. She even parked in the same spot before reentering the restaurant.

In a daze, she aimed for one of the unoccupied booths, barely sparing a glance for the three other people scattered throughout the diner, and slid all the way along the bench so she could press her back against the wall. Her phone was in her hand, and she sent two words to Devyn, then tipped her head back and pressed her eyes shut.

Her head was spinning, and now, after all of it, she thought maybe she was going to faint. Maybe it was exhaustion. Maybe it was shock. Maybe it was the exhilaration that comes with realizing that from this moment on, she was in charge of her own life.

At the *thunk* of a plastic glass being set before her, she opened her eyes expecting to find Frank or Fern. But it wasn't either of them. Cole Clark sat across from her. His blue eyes were soft with understanding and sympathy. Not pity. She didn't know how he knew. Maybe he guessed. Maybe it was more obvious than Jaq thought. Why else would she and Fern stumble through Frank's doors after midnight like this?

Whatever it was, she was glad that she didn't have to explain anything right now.

"Where's Fern?" she asked.

"Changing into some clean clothes," Cole answered. "Frank wouldn't let them come out of the bathroom until they weren't a walking biohazard."

Jaq thought of the hoodie she'd used to bandage her arm. Frank had probably thrown it away already, which wasn't terrible, except it was literally the only hoodie Jaq owned right now. Everything else belonged to her parents. She owned exactly what she was wearing and nothing else.

The realization didn't hurt as much as she expected it to.

"Is it weird that I feel so relieved?" she asked.

Cole pushed a bright-red cup filled with dark soda toward her. "Drink. You need the sugar," he instructed. "And no, it's not weird. I mean, I don't think it is. I think that's the most important piece. You can figure the rest out."

Jaq nodded and took a sip of the soda. Surprised to find her hands were still shaking a little. "All I have is my phone," she said, the high of the moment starting to wear off.

But Cole shook his head. "You've got more than that. You've got us."

"Us?" Jaq didn't want to sound ungrateful, but it had been years since the two of them had been friends. She barely knew Frank. She couldn't ask them for anything.

"You'll see." Cole reached across the table, gave her uninjured hand a reassuring squeeze, and left to check on one of the other guests.

It slowly dawned on Jaq that after he fell out with his parents, he'd come here, too. Just like she had. And Frank had given him a job. Cole, Jaq was finally realizing, wasn't alone.

In the next minute, the little bell at the front door announced Devyn's arrival. She blew in like a summer storm, hair falling out of a braid, helmet in hand, every part of her in motion. When she spotted Jaq, she rushed across the room and crashed into the booth next to her.

"How are you?" she asked, cupping Jaq's cheek in one cool hand. "I was so worried."

Jaq smiled. Nodded, tears pricking at the corners of her eyes for the first time. There was sadness behind them, sorrow, but there was also a kind of joy she didn't know how to describe. Not yet.

"I'm good," she answered, tipping her head into the bend of Devyn's neck. "I'm okay."

And somehow, it was completely, brilliantly true.

CHAPTER
FORTY

Fern

They spent the whole night at Frank's.

No one asked them to explain or tell the story of what happened to them. Which was good because talking was increasingly difficult for Fern. They alternated between rinsing their mouth with salt water and sucking on pieces of ice to keep the swelling down. That, combined with a hefty dose of ibuprofen, kept the pain under control.

After a shower and a quick text to their mom telling her that Fern was staying at Cam's tonight, they got dressed in a pink FRANK'S ALL-NIGHT DINER T-shirt and camouflage sweatpants and found Jaq cuddled up next to a girl with a shock of red hair.

"Fern." Jaq held out her uninjured hand to Fern. "This is my—" She hesitated and her cheeks flushed pink. "Um, this is Devyn. Devyn, this is my—um, my Fern."

There was a beat of awkward silence before all three of them erupted with laughter.

"I'm sor—" Jaq started, but she cut herself off abruptly, sharing a secret smile with Devyn. "I'm so glad I finally got to introduce the two of you," she finished.

"Me, too," Devyn said, holding a hand out to Fern. "Hi, I'm Devyn. Jaq has literally never mentioned you before, but since I'm a fan of her secrets, I'm taking that as a good sign."

Fern laughed and nodded in agreement. "Nice to meet you," they said, slowly and around the piece of ice still melting on their tongue.

"Are you sure you don't want to go to the hospital?" Jaq asked, wincing in sympathy.

Fern shook their head, but it was Frank who answered.

"They can't really do much for tongues," he explained, ushering Fern into the booth next to Jaq and taking the seat opposite. "You just have to keep it clean and let the body heal itself. You can't force it."

"Sounds like a metaphor," Jaq said with a wry smile as Cole arrived with the biggest platter of fries any of them had ever seen.

"A really painful one," Fern muttered, eyeing the fries with a particularly torturous mix of hunger and skepticism.

"Just take it slow," Frank counseled.

They spent the rest of the night putting a plan into place for Jaq. She was already eighteen, which made things easier, and Frank had a spare room over the restaurant that she could use until she graduated as long as she didn't mind sharing with Cole. It was close quarters, but Jaq would be safe.

After that, they focused on the more serious stuff, like making sure her parents didn't have any control over her one and only bank account, preparing for the moment they cut her phone off, figuring out what to tell the school.

Fern and Devyn stayed on either side of Jaq as they worked out the details, made plan after plan, redesigned her future one piece at a time right down to where and how they were going to get her essentials like underwear and a toothbrush and tampons. Jaq insisted John would help when he could. She hadn't been herself for two years, but she knew enough to know him.

It felt good to have something so important to focus on. It gave the formless night a point of focus without the threat of tomorrow, but by the time the sky blushed rosy pink with dawn, there was no more avoiding what had to happen.

It was Friday, and Fern still had to go to school.

Their mother and sisters wouldn't expect to see them until after school, which gave Fern a little more time to think about what they wanted to say.

In the meantime, they owed Kaitlyn an apology. Well, they owed the entire cast, crew, and Ms. Murphy an apology, and judging by the tone of the texts they'd received from Cam and Melissa over the last eleven hours, they were going to be buying their friends coffee until they graduated from college, but Kaitlyn needed to come first.

Just before they entered the building, Fern caught Jaq's hand and held it tight.

"I need to try something," they said. And when Jaq nodded, they took a deep breath and said, "I'm gay."

Jaq's smile softened. "I know," she said. "But it's nice to hear you say it."

Fern exhaled with relief. "Oh my god, no kidding."

With a laugh, Jaq pulled Fern into a very tight hug. "It feels like everything is about to change again," Jaq murmured.

Fern knew exactly what she meant. Last night had been terrifying and strange and wonderful. And in some way, it had felt like the world had changed. Just for them.

But it hadn't, really. School was going to treat them like the old

Fern and Jaq. It was strange. The way change could also feel so ferocious even when it was good.

"I think everything *is* about to change," Fern said. "Because we are changing. Every part of our world has to be different now. And I think that's okay, even if parts of it are going to suck or hurt."

At that moment, Fern spotted Kaitlyn Birch hurrying toward the entrance, and their stomach dropped.

"A lot," they added.

"You sure you don't want me to run interference?"

On their car ride to Frank's, Fern had whispered the truth of what had happened between them and Kaitlyn. Partly because Jaq had asked Fern to talk about anything and partly because Fern desperately needed to share it with someone who understood. Who would understand that it hadn't been their fault and also that they had no choice but to accept the responsibility for it.

"I'm sure," Fern answered, keeping one eye on Kaitlyn. "I'll text you later, okay?"

"Okay." Jaq's answer floated behind them as they hurried after Kaitlyn.

They caught up to them two steps from the theater doors, the sign for GREASE: THE MUSICAL posted in bold colors.

"Kaitlyn!" Fern called.

She turned at the sound of her name, then tensed. Regret unfurled across her face, and she crossed her arms against her chest.

"Can I talk to you? Just for a minute," Fern promised. "I only need a minute."

Kaitlyn narrowed her eyes but nodded, then she took a sharp turn and pushed through the theater doors. Which was a relief. Fern didn't exactly want an audience for this part either.

"If you're going to ask to play Danny in the show tonight, then—"

"I'm not," Fern jumped in. "I promise. The thought hadn't even occurred to me."

They could see by Kaitlyn's expression that she didn't believe it. Her opinion of Fern had fallen so far it was somewhere lower down than the costume basement.

Fern swallowed the urge to defend themself. It wasn't fair. Fern hadn't intended to say any of the things that they'd said. But that didn't change the fact that they'd been the one to say them. Trying to convince Kaitlyn that they were blameless was only going to make them look worse. Would only amplify the betrayal and hurt Kaitlyn again.

So even though it would feel unbelievably good to tell Kaitlyn the truth, to explain the wild, seemingly impossible reasons behind all that had happened, to come out, there was something even more important for Fern to say.

"I want to apologize," Fern started, unable to ignore the sudden spike of fear that the Patron's power was still there. Lurking somewhere inside them. Ready and waiting to twist their words back on themselves.

"For what, exactly?" Kaitlyn asked. Genuinely curious.

Every time you open your mouth, you hurt someone.

Fern opened their mouth. Forced the next words up, up, up their throat and out. "For saying those terrible things to you last night. For toying with you. It was cruel and deeply homophobic, and I'm sorry."

It took physical effort to restrain themself from adding that they hadn't meant to say any of it. Even if it was true, defusing the blame like that also defused the apology itself. Fern wanted it to be so real Kaitlyn could fold it up like a piece of paper, tuck it away in her pocket. Or throw it in the trash.

"Why did you?" Kaitlyn's arms unfolded. She didn't step forward, but it felt like some of the distance between them melted.

Fern shook their head. "I don't think I can explain why. I've been working through some things, unpacking my own shit, and it's been . . . weird. Awful. But none of that excuses what I did. All the time we spent together was really important to me, and I'm sorry that I hurt you."

A few seconds passed in silence before Kaitlyn sucked in a deep breath and nodded. "Okay. Thank you for saying that. I'm not saying I forgive you because I'm going to need a minute with this, but for now, thank you."

Fern smiled softly. A new smile, they thought. One that felt connected to their heart by a tremulous chord of relief and sadness. "Okay," they said, swallowing hard as Kaitlyn stepped past.

Every part of them screamed silently for Kaitlyn to understand the depth of their regret. To see the truth in their eyes and let things go back to the way they were.

Their heart thudded to a stop when Kaitlyn paused, her hand on the door handle, and turned back.

"You're messy, Fern, but I'm glad you're figuring yourself out." She smiled and it lit Fern up inside.

"Thanks," they answered, feeling the thump of their heart in their tongue. Pain and promise, mixed together.

The rest of the day passed in a bleary haze. Cam and Melissa were as concerned as they were furious, but they accepted Fern's plea to explain another day. Exhaustion kicked in right after lunch, and Fern spent the rest of the day tricking themself into staying awake.

When the final bell rang, they were suddenly very awake, and very aware of what they had to do next.

COME OUT, COME OUT

They'd spent some time trying to prepare the right words, then stopped. This wasn't a performance, and they didn't want it to feel like they were reciting lines. But now that it was time, they were doubting that decision. A script would have made this a lot easier.

There were more cars parked outside their house than usual. It took Fern a second to remember that two of their sisters had come home to see the musical. They'd been there to witness the grand moment when Fern didn't take the stage. And they were going to be here to witness whatever happened next.

Maybe it was better that way.

Inside, the house was vibrant and warm. Their sisters were talking and laughing in the kitchen, the air sweet with the scent of chocolate chip cookies. Fern could hear their mother asking if they wanted to try her low-fat cookie recipe next and Clover asking why on earth they'd want to do something like that.

Fern steadied themself just inside the front door, the long wall of photographs stretching out ahead of them. For so many years, it had felt like an expectation. That Fern follow in their sisters' footsteps, that they fit into the bouquet of them like a perfect little flower.

But maybe it wasn't that at all. Maybe it was just one version of Fern captured here. Maybe they would all be okay with another.

There was only one way to find out.

Taking a bolstering breath, they walked down the hallway and into the kitchen. Their sisters erupted with little shrieks, rushing over to wrap Fern in warm hugs while their mother hung back.

"Fern," their mother said when Clover and Ivy had released them. Her voice was thick with concern and disappointment. "Fern, sweet girl, what happened? Is everything okay?"

With a nod, Fern said, "Everything is okay. And I need to tell you something."

Fern paused to take a breath, looking from their mother's eyes to those of Clover and Ivy. They were waiting patiently, with compassion and curiosity, and Fern had to believe that that was enough. But they were still nervous.

"I am not a girl," they said. "Not always. And right now, the pronouns that feel best to me are they/them."

Confusion flickered across their mother's expression, and silence filled the room.

"You're . . ." their mom started and stopped. "Of course you're a—"

"Mom," Ivy warned, rolling her eyes and popping an entire cookie into her mouth.

"What? Am I not allowed to be confused?" their mother asked with a flutter of her hands, looking away from Fern as though uncomfortable.

The fear Fern had held inside for so many years flared to life, and a voice in their mind whispered that they'd been wrong to be so honest.

Then Clover stepped forward, wrapped an arm around Fern's shoulders, and pulled them into a tight hug.

"Welcome to the club, little sib," she said. "Mom, you're about to learn some new vocabulary."

"Wait, what?" Fern asked, surprise stealing every thought from their mind as they blinked up at Clover. "You're—?"

"Pan," Clover supplied, releasing Fern from her hold. "And cisgender."

"I still don't think I know what that means," their mom said softly. She offered Fern a timid smile and added, "But I'm willing to learn."

"On most days," Ivy added in her dry way.

"Be fair, this isn't easy for me," their mom protested. "Okay, so, where do we start?"

Fern couldn't answer right away. They were still stunned. The fear inside them taking new shape, reorienting itself away from the way things used to be to the way they were now, but it was slipping. Melting away little by little.

Leaving room for something else to grow.

CHAPTER
FORTY-ONE

Jaq

The sky was painfully blue, the wind crisp and biting, as the boat cut through the waters of the Puget Sound. In the distance and all around the Cascades and Olympic Mountains were snow-dusted shadows against the horizon. Every so often, the captain's voice filtered out over a loudspeaker to let people know what mountain had appeared to their right or where a clutch of bald eagles was nesting to the left.

"Here," Fern said, coming to stand next to her at the rail and shoving a thermos of hot coffee at her. "There's a ton of sugar in it," they said with a grin.

"Gross," Jaq teased, but she poured herself a small cup and drank it down, grateful for the caffeine and calories.

First thing this morning, Fern had picked Jaq up at Frank's, and they'd driven all the way to Port Townsend, where they'd booked tickets on the first whale-watching trip of the season. The ticket had cost a small fortune by Jaq's new standards, but it was worth it. Even if they didn't see a single whale.

A month had passed since her parents had shut the door on having a daughter, and all the bad things she'd been expecting had happened. Her parents had cut off all contact and removed her

phone from their account. She'd been notified that due to unfore-
seen circumstances, her financial aid package for Baylor had been
rescinded, which meant there was no way she could attend in the
fall, and Susan Meachem was giving her a shoulder so cold it was
glacial. It had all gone pretty much like she'd thought it would,
with the single exception of John.

One day about two weeks ago, he'd walked into Frank's looking
for her. Instead of telling her how disgusting she was or how hurt
he was, he gave her a long hug, a handful of gift cards he'd been
saving since Christmas, and a fresh package of pastels.

"I was mad at first," he'd admitted. "But I just want you to be
okay." He hesitated, awkward and unsure in a way that was so unlike him. Then he shook his head, letting some of that anger show
in the pinch of his brow. "I thought we were friends, Jaq."

"We were—"

"Then why didn't you tell me?"

Jaq had swallowed hard and offered as much of the truth as she
could. "I didn't have the words."

"Do you have them now?" he asked, a spark of hope in those
moss-green eyes.

"I don't. Not yet. But we were friends. You were my best friend,
John, and if you ever think you can, I want that still." She had
reached into her jeans pocket then and pulled out the ring he'd
given her. It had taken her days to realize that it was no longer
welded to her finger, and ever since, she'd kept it close. Now she
offered it to him. "This is yours. It wouldn't be right for me to
keep it."

John stared at the delicate band, but he didn't reach for it. Instead, he smiled and shook his head. "I didn't come here to take
things from you, Jaq. Sell it. Use it to help get you on your feet."

With that, he'd left her there at Frank's with a collection of precious gifts and the hope that maybe they would be friends again.

Regardless, she'd promised herself that one day she would repay his kindness with a better explanation.

"Have you decided what you'll do after graduation?" Fern asked, taking the thermos and pouring a fresh cup, tossing it back like a shot.

They looked incredible today. Sleek in dark colors that made their star-pale skin ethereal. Their blond locks were braided back from their temples and pulled into a low ponytail that was tucked into the slouched hood of their hoodie. And the wind pressed the front of the hoodie flat against their chest.

Their coming out had gone much better than Jaq's, but they were still struggling. Mrs. Jensen was firmly entrenched in the binary and got things wrong more often than she got them right. But with the help of Fern's sisters, she was coming around. One pronoun at a time.

Jaq shook her head. "Not really. Devyn and I might go hike around the Olympics for a while. I might get a job, save some money while I figure out what to do about college. Maybe I'll join a commune or something."

Fern laughed. "Please tell me you're joking about that last part."

"I'm joking, but only a little. I like not having a plan for once." After everything else, that was the part that made Jaq realize how unhappy she'd been before.

Every part of her life, from graduation to marriage, had been mapped out for her. Not necessarily by her, though she'd let it all happen. And it had been eating away at her. Slowly wearing down the parts of her that had anything resembling ambition independent of her parents' desires for her. Much longer and she would have been just like her mother. A reflection of the world around her. Parroting and enforcing the needs and wants of the men in her life.

Jaq might not know exactly where her next meal was coming from, but she preferred it this way. For now. And she wasn't completely on her own.

She was still living in Frank's extra room. Fern was supplying her with a steady stream of clothing as they redesigned their wardrobe in favor of their new look. And every time Jaq worked a shift at the diner, someone slipped her a massive tip.

It wouldn't last forever, but it didn't have to. This way, she had room to figure it out.

Jaq leaned into the wind, letting it strip her eyes of tears as the captain pulled the boat out of speed and they began to coast.

"All right, folks, we've spotted a few whales on sonar, so we're going to hang out here for a minute and see if we get lucky." The captain's voice sounded practiced. He'd said these exact words to countless whale watchers over the years, and it showed. "Whales tend to surface more when they're on the move, like during migration, but if they're eating or resting, they can stay submerged for long periods of time."

"Ready?" Jaq asked.

Fern cocked an eyebrow. "You don't want to wait until one of them comes up for air?"

Jaq thought about it for a minute, whether or not they needed to see the whales to know they were there. Whether or not something needed to be spoken or visible in order for them to be considered *real*.

"No," she said. "Now's good."

Fern bobbed their head, reaching into their pocket and pulling out a small bone. Jaq did the same, unwrapping her bone from one of the plain paper napkins they used at Frank's.

Last week, they'd gone back into the woods, searching for the house and the rest of Mallory's bones, thinking that they should gather them all up if they could. Not so they could contact Mallory's family—Mallory wouldn't have wanted that—but so they could keep them all together. Bury them.

But no matter how long they searched, the trail that led to the house never appeared. It was gone. And so was Mallory Hammond.

They weren't so sure about the Patron and the Gray Whales. Maybe they were gone and maybe they were still there. There was no way to know.

"Should we say something?" Jaq asked, heart lodging in her throat.

Fern was quiet for a moment, then they smiled. "Farewell, sweet prince. May pods of gay whales sing thee to thy rest."

Jaq laughed, then together, they tipped their hands and let the bones fall into the sea.

RESOURCES

Fern, Jaq, and Mal had each other, but they still needed support. There are many excellent resources available today, including:

National Suicide Prevention Hotline
SuicidePreventionLifeline.org
Crisis hotline: 800-273-TALK (8255)

Crisis Text Line
CrisisTextline.org
Text: 741741

The Trevor Project
TheTrevorProject.org
Crisis hotline: 866-488-7386 (for those ages 13-24)

National Sexual Assault Hotline
RAINN.org
Crisis hotline: 800-656-HOPE (4673)

Trans Lifeline
TransLifeline.org
Hotline: 1-877-565-8860

National Center for Transgender Equality
TransEquality.org

Gay, Lesbian & Straight Education Network
GLSEN.org

Love Is Respect
LoveIsRespect.org
Text "LOVEIS" to 22522
Hotline: 1-800-331-9474

Planned Parenthood Chatline
PlannedParenthood.org/teens

ACKNOWLEDGMENTS

As is always the case with acknowledgments, the real horror is forgetting to thank someone, but here we go.

So many people supported me in the process of writing my first true horror novel. I have to start by thanking my wife, Tessa, who held my hand both in kindness and to the fire as I excavated the metaphor at the heart of this story.

I am also grateful to my friends, colleagues, and early readers who contributed everything from a sympathetic ear to a constructive note. Most especially, thank you, Sarah Henning, for reading at a crucial moment.

I'm grateful and lucky to have a steadfast agent in Lara Perkins and a dedicated editor and brainstorming buddy in Lanie Davis. I have also had the great fortune to work with a second editor on this project and will always be grateful to Rūta Rimas for her very sharp instincts and compassionate notes and to Simone Roberts-Payne, who has done so much for this project. Working with the four of you is a true pleasure.

To all of the immensely talented and clever folk at Putnam—copyeditors Krista Ahlberg and Rebecca Blevins; proofreaders Rachel Norfleet, Sola Akinlana, and Marinda Valenti; design genius Jessica Jenkins; publicist Lathea Mondesir; the ever-incredible publicity and marketing team including but not limited to James Akinaka, Shannon Spann, and Felicity Vallence; the epic PYR sales force; and our fearless publisher, Jen Klonsky—thank you!

A very special thank-you to David Seidman for the unnerving artwork that graces the cover. I hope it haunts many dreams!

To you, whether this is the first of my books you've picked up or the eleventh, thank you for reading.

And finally, to Casey McIntyre, who I was honored to know and who left her mark on this story, all my thanks.